MURDER OF A WINCHESTER GOOSE

A HARLOWE & FITCH HISTORICAL MYSTERY

ELIZABETH ROSE

A Note to My Readers:

Dear Readers,

This book wraps up the main murder mystery of Lady Vivienne's life. It is important to read the other books in the series first, or a lot of surprises will be ruined.

The *Harlowe & Fitch Historical Mystery Series* is ongoing with a main thread that continues to develop throughout the entire series. Mixed in with each story is a new murder mystery that is solved before the book is finished. While every installment can be read as a stand-alone, it is advised, and also ideal, to start from the beginning with *Murder at Mablethorpe Castle*, Book 1, and to read them in order. If not, there will be surprises ruined along the way.

While these are murder mysteries and not romances, there is still a romantic thread woven in as well.

See more notes at the end of this book, but for now, welcome to the world of Harlowe & Fitch, where investigations into murders in Mablethorpe and the surrounding areas are underway. A headstrong noblewoman searching for justice, and a stealthy sheriff trying to secure the safety of his town, team up to uncover that which is hidden but needs to be brought to the surface.

Elizabeth Rose

Chapter One

Mablethorpe, England, Late 1300s

Sheriff Zachariah Fitch looked up from eating his morning porridge as thunderous knocking resounded from the other side of his front door. "Sheriff! Sheriff Fitch!" came a woman's voice from outside, followed by even more urgent knocking.

"Can't a man get any rest around here?" he grumbled, pushing up from the table, his eyes on the door. It was bad enough that Nairnie, his daughter's nursemaid, had woken him up before the sun even rose to eat a meal with his daughter, who couldn't sleep. He wouldn't have even stirred from bed if his brother, Isaac, who now lived with them and shared a room with him, hadn't been snoring so loudly that he'd been awake most of the night anyway. Zachariah hurried across the room and quickly yanked open the door. "What is it?" he asked, feeling agitated and edgy.

"Sheriff, come quickly!" Constable Dorson's wife, Agatha, stood there with a look of horror on her face. She was a simple woman with a rounded body. The woman held her crying baby perched on one curvy hip. Her other young children, Archibald and Anabel, were at her side, yawning and looking half asleep as if they'd just gotten out of bed.

"What is it, Agatha?" he asked in concern, realizing she seemed distraught. Her husband was out of town as a personal request for a few days, looking into another matter. "Is something wrong? Is the baby ill?" He had promised his constable and good friend, Emery, that he'd look after the man's family while he was away. He hoped nothing bad had happened.

"There is quite a commotion down on Rotten Row." She relayed the information.

"That is nothing new," he told her, stifling a yawn with his hand. "Just stay away and you'll be safe, I promise."

"Nay. You don't understand. I heard the gossip from some passersby. Someone has been murdered, I tell you!"

"Murdered?" Zachariah groaned. This was the last thing he wanted to hear this morning. "Please don't tell me that. The sun is barely up and I've yet to recover from just being on a pirate ship and solving a murder. I don't want to hear of another killing so soon."

"But it's true, Sheriff."

"Let me only be dreaming," he muttered to himself. "Can't I at least get in a day's rest or a little sleep before another murder occurs?" Lately, it seemed as if there was one murder after another, either at the castle, in town, or in the surrounding area. He'd never seen anything like it.

"It really is a murder," said Archibald, the woman's ten-year-old son. "I ran down to Rotten Row to see for myself. There is a big crowd there and a dead woman in the horse trough. Her neck is twisted at an odd angle, and I think it's broken. They are saying she fell from a second story window."

"You went to Rotten Row, Archibald?" Zachariah's attention traveled over to the boy's mother next, always having known the woman didn't watch her children well, and this was proof of it. That is why he'd stopped asking Agatha to watch his daughter, Starah, and instead hired Nairnie as a nursemaid.

"I assure you, my son went there against my will, Sheriff," Agatha replied, trying to calm her fussing baby. "Archibald doesn't listen to me much lately. If his father were home more, mayhap that would help to keep him in line."

"I don't need to listen to you, Mother. I'm in charge when Father's gone," snapped the boy, standing a bit straighter. "He told me so himself. I was just looking out for my family, Sheriff, that's all. Just like the man of the house is supposed to do."

"Archibald," said Zachariah, putting his hand on the boy's shoulder. "I appreciate you caring for and looking after your mother and siblings, really I do. However, you need to understand that what you did was very dangerous and not a good idea. I promised your father I'd look out for your family, and you shouldn't be going anywhere near Rotten Row."

"I had to know what was happening, Sheriff," said the boy.

"Then you needed to come directly to me instead of going to look for yourself."

"That's right, son," said his mother.

"Oh, all right." Archibald released a deep sigh and kicked at the ground. "Aye, sir." A frown crossed his face, his self-importance suddenly deflated.

"You must also always obey your mother and respect her. Do you hear me?" Zachariah tried to instill good morals and behavior in the young boy without sounding overly harsh. After all, he was just a child.

"Yes, Sheriff, I hear you," said the boy, still staring at the ground. "Sorry, Mother."

"That's better," said Zachariah. "Now, I want you all to stay here at my home where I know you will be safe. I will check into this matter personally."

"Did you want me to go in your stead?" asked Zachariah's brother, Isaac, standing on the stairs to the second floor, stretching and yawning. He seemed to have overheard the entire conversation. "After all, I am your deputy now and can take on more responsibility than you have been giving me."

"Isaac, how many times do I need to tell you that you're not my deputy and are still in training?" asked Zachariah. "Besides, Constable Dorson fills that role right now. You are naught but my assistant for now."

"I'm scared," whined little five-year-old Anabel, running into the house and right over to her friend, the sheriff's daughter. Starah picked up her black cat, Midnight, from the floor and cuddled her on her lap.

"Pet Midnight, Anabel. It will make you feel better." Starah did her best to calm her friend. "After all, it's nothing to be frightened about. It's only another dead body. Dead people can't hurt you." That certainly took Zachariah by surprise to hear his daughter speaking in such a casual manner about a person who had supposedly been murdered. Nairnie gasped. A small chuckle came from Isaac.

"Starah, dinna say that! It's no' proper," scolded Nairnie, waddling over to the table with her ladle in her hand. Zachariah wasn't sure Nairnie wasn't going to wallop his daughter with it the way she had used it against her husband's crew on the ship during their recent trip to Whitstable. He realized he needed to intervene quickly.

"Nairnie has a point, sweetheart," he spoke up. "It's wrong to talk like that around anyone, especially your friends," he told his daughter.

"Well, I suppose my father is right," Starah told Anabel with a slight shrug. "I mean, I'm sure dead people *can* hurt you if they're a ghost." Her words only managed to make Anabel even more frightened. This time she screamed and hid her eyes by putting her head down on the table, cradled in her arms.

"Starah, you need to realize that Anabel hasn't been around any...dead bodies the way you have. Or ghosts," Zachariah said softly, specifically thinking about their time in Maltby le Marsh and Whitstable. "Not that I ever wanted you to experience any of that, of course," he added under his breath, wondering what his life was coming to, now that his young daughter had been present for more than one of the murder investigations.

"Your father is right. You're only scaring poor Anabel," agreed Isaac with a big yawn.

"Isaac, we'd better get down to Rotten Row before the vagrants start stripping the corpse, claiming whatever they can steal as their own," said Zachariah, trying not to let the children hear.

"They'll want the woman's cloak, that's for sure," said Archibald, overhearing him anyway. "After all, it's the cloak of a noble and worth some good coin, I'd imagine. I know if I were a thief, I'd take it."

"Archibald, stop that and come sit down," said his mother. The boy hesitantly followed his mother across the room and to the table.

"What did you say about a noble's cloak, Archibald?" Zachariah turned his head so quickly, he crooked his neck. "No noble would be in town, let alone on Rotten Row. Especially not so early in the morning."

"Well, I recognized the cloak," said Archibald with wide eyes. "I'm not lying."

"You recognized it? Then tell me. Who does the cloak belong to? Who is the murdered woman? Do you know her?" He didn't really believe the child, but wanted to find out more about what might have happened.

"Yes, do tell. Is the murdered woman anyone we know?" asked Isaac with interest, reaching out for a slice of bread on the table, getting hit with Nairnie's flying ladle. He quickly pulled back his hand and rubbed it, scowling at her.

"Isaac, have some manners," scoffed Nairnie. "We have

guests now and need to have enough food for the children without ye eatin' it all."

"I just wanted a slice of bread," complained Isaac, his eyes still fastened on the food.

"Agatha, will ye and yer children please join us for a meal?" Nairnie asked the newcomers.

"Thank you, Nairnie. I'd like that, since we haven't eaten yet today," said Agatha, still holding her baby and taking a seat across the table from the girls. "I'm pretty shaken by what's transpired. Especially since my husband is still out of town." Archibald quietly slid onto the bench next to her.

"Who is the dead woman, Archibald?" asked Isaac once again, trying to get answers, even though his eyes never left the platter of fresh bread.

"I...I can't be sure." Archibald looked down to the floor and kicked at the rushes under the table.

"Archibald? If you know something, you need to tell me." Zachariah watched the child from the corner of his eye. "It could help me out a lot, and I'd be very thankful." He could always tell by one's actions when they were lying or perhaps trying to keep something from him, just like the boy was doing right now. The sheriff headed toward his cloak and sword, both hanging from a hook on the wall.

"Well, I couldn't tell for sure, Sheriff. I mean, she landed facedown in the horse trough so I didn't actually see her face. But I did recognize the cloak," he said under his breath.

"Well then, whose cloak is it?" he asked, slowly buckling his weapon belt around his waist, getting a bad feeling about this.

"It—it's Lady Vivienne's cloak," the boy quickly spat out the information and looked up to the sheriff with wide eyes, waiting for his reaction.

"Lady Vivienne?" asked Isaac. His gaze flashed over to Zachariah.

Zachariah froze. "Nay," he said, barely able to speak after hearing the woman's name mentioned. "It's not Lady Vivienne. It can't be." He felt suddenly choked. A churning sensation burned in his belly. "Lady Vivienne wouldn't be on Rotten Row. She went back to the castle last night. You are mistaken."

"Nay, Sheriff, I'm not," protested the boy. "I'd know that cloak anywhere."

"I'm sure all cloaks of nobles look similar," said Isaac, walking to the door, trying to help out the situation. "Perhaps the sheriff is right in saying you are mistaken."

"Nay, her cloak is different. It's her forest-green cloak with the gold trim and little hearts embroidered onto the edges of her sleeves," said the boy, describing Vivienne's cloak perfectly. "I saw her wearing it late last night when she went inside the inn with those two women that everyone calls ducks."

"What?" Zachariah's jaw dropped and he slowly narrowed his eyes. This sounded so preposterous. "Why would Lady Vivienne go into an inn on Rotten Row?"

"And with ducks," said Isaac, with a chuckle. "Zachariah, she doesn't have any pet ducks, does she?"

"Nay. Not that I'm aware of," answered the sheriff.

"Ye simpkins, he's no' talkin' about ducks," spat Nairnie. "The boy means the Winchester Geese."

"Oh, it could have been gooses. You're right. I think it was," said Archibald with a shrug.

"It's geese, not gooses," his mother softly corrected him.

"I'm sure he's wrong," Isaac told Zachariah. "Lady Vivienne wouldn't have stayed in town overnight...would she?"

Now Zachariah's fury rose. "I wouldn't put anything past her. Especially since she wasn't happy with me when I told Cassandra and her friend that they couldn't stay here."

Isaac and Zachariah's youngest sister, Cassandra, was a Winchester Goose, or legalized prostitute who resided in a brothel in Southwark, a borough of London. She and her friend and fellow working-girl, Fanny, had showed up on the docks just yesterday, announcing that they were here for a week's visit and that they wanted to stay with him. Since Zachariah had never forgiven his sister for turning to prostitution, even if it was legalized in Southwark, he decided he didn't want whores bedding down in his home when he had a young, impressionable daughter to protect and raise. It was already bad enough that his ex-mercenary brother was living with them for the time being.

"I think we'd better get down to Rotten Row quickly and see for ourselves," suggested Isaac.

"Yes," Zachariah agreed, swallowing the lump in his throat and nodding to Nairnie and the others. "Stay here for now where you'll all be safe. Until we know what is going on, I don't want anyone to leave this house."

"Thank you, Sheriff," said Agatha, still trying to calm her baby, but sounding relieved to hear the offer. "I feel safer here than at home alone with the children."

Zachariah followed Isaac out of the house and closed the door behind them.

"Do you really think it's Lady Vivienne who died?" asked Isaac, pulling a piece of bread out from under his cloak and taking a bite. He'd learned from Nairnie's husband, Bear, how to be sneaky and fast when it came to snitching food away from Nairnie. Zachariah hadn't even seen him take it.

"God's eyes, I pray it isn't Vivienne," he ground out, releasing a deep breath of fear mixed with frustration. "But I swear, if I find out she is still alive and stayed the night in town with whores...I might just kill her myself."

They mounted their horses and rode down to Rotten Row as the first rays of the rising sun slowly started to appear on the horizon. Zachariah could see a small crowd gathered outside the inn, just like Archibald had told them. This was the second time in a short while that a murder had been committed right here on Rotten Row. That is, if it truly was a murder, which he hoped it was not.

"I see a body in the horse trough just like Archibald told us. It seems he wasn't lying." Isaac stretched his neck to see over the heads of the crowd of the people gathering there. There was a lot of commotion and talking going on between shop owners, peasants, fishermen, and even some whores. No one seemed to want to get too near the body.

"Let us pass. Move aside," Zachariah shouted, riding through the crowd, trying to get closer to the corpse, needing to see for himself if it truly was Vivienne. The nearer he got, the sicker he felt. He didn't want to think Vivienne could really be dead. But with the things she did and the decisions she made, every damned day of her life was nothing but an invitation for danger. Not to mention, death seemed to follow her wherever she went. God's eyes, this couldn't really be happening!

The crowd parted to let Zachariah and Isaac through. They rode directly to a spot right in front of the Hogg's Head Inn. The talking now lowered to naught but mere whispers. Zachariah heard someone mention Lady Vivienne's name. The innkeeper, Orvyn, stood above the body with a flaming torch in his hand. The fire lit up the inky darkness all around them.

It didn't take the sheriff any time at all to recognize Lady Vivienne's cloak in the firelight, just like the boy had said. He slid off his steed, making his way to the prone body of the woman who was facedown in the horse trough. Her head was jarred at an odd angle, suggesting her neck was truly broken as the rumors stated. Long, loose blonde hair, the same color as Vivienne's flaxen locks, floated up to the surface of the water. The bloody water. Suddenly, he couldn't breathe and wasn't even able to take a step closer.

"Orvyn. What's going on here?" he asked in a gruff voice.

"I'm not sure, Sheriff," replied the man. "I noticed curtains blowing out the window of one of the upstairs rooms when I came out to sweep the porch this morning. Then I saw a body in the trough. I went back in and lit a torch and returned to find out more. Damn, this is going to be bad for business."

"Why hasn't anyone tried to help the poor woman?" he growled.

"No one wants to touch her. Me neither," said the innkeeper, looking at the broken, twisted neck of the floating corpse.

"I've got this, Brother," Isaac told him, dismounting and hurrying over to the trough to take a closer look. He took hold of the woman under her arms and yanked her up and placed her on the ground, but still facedown. The crowd moved in closer behind them, curious to see who she was and trying to hear what was being said.

"I'll flip her over so we can see if anyone knows her," offered Isaac.

"Nay. Wait." Zachariah released a deep breath and walked over and hunkered down next to the body. "I feel as if I'm the one who should do this." He reached out, his hand wavering above the woman. He was so upset that he wasn't sure he wasn't going to retch. A million thoughts swarmed his head, and each was laden with regret that he'd never told Vivienne how he really felt about her. Damn, why had he waited so long to relay his romantic feelings toward her? Why hadn't he taken things from friendship to something more like he'd really wanted to do, instead of pretending he didn't truly have these feelings for her at all? Why hadn't he been honest with her? He was the sheriff and should have been able to protect her. He would never forgive himself for not being more transparent with his emotions or keeping a closer eye on her. If she truly was dead...it was his fault.

Guilt ate away at him like a voracious beast. He never should have said Cassandra and her friend couldn't stay with him. Vivienne probably felt she couldn't take the whores back to the castle because her uncle would have forbidden it. After all, she was already bringing home so many orphans lately, not to mention stray animals, too. Lord Mablethorpe didn't like that at all. Of course, she'd want to help the women. Vivienne always put her life on the line for those that she felt were in dire need. He always knew her kind heart would someday be her undoing.

This was all his fault! That thought just wouldn't leave his mind. Why had he been so stubborn and hot-headed? It was a trait of his, and he realized it might have just killed someone he really cared about. Vivienne probably stayed with the girls in the tavern last night out of friendship, and now because of it...because of his stubbornness...now she was dead. God, if this was so, he'd never forgive himself for as long as he lived.

"Zachariah, move aside. I can do it," Isaac said in a soft voice so the others wouldn't be aware of Zachariah's hesitance to turn over the woman's contorted body.

"So can I," Zachariah answered through gritted teeth, pushing his emotions aside to find the strength he needed right now as town sheriff to do his job. In his profession, he had learned through the years not to become emotionally attached in any situation or to anyone at all. Today could be no exception.

With one quick movement, he flipped the girl over and onto her back. Long blonde hair tangled over her face, managing to continue to block her identity. "Give me that torch and move back," he commanded, taking the torch from Orvyn, bringing the firelight closer to the corpse. He gently reached out with his free hand and swept the woman's hair aside, expecting the worst. He had no doubt he'd be looking at the face of the woman he cared about more than he'd ever wanted to admit, even to himself. But instead of seeing a button nose, pale lips, and the delicate curves of Lady Vivienne's cheeks, he saw a face that had a slightly hooked nose, painted lips, and lots of rouge that was already half-washed away. Thankfully, this woman wasn't his Vivienne!

All tension was released and he was suddenly able to breathe again. He thankfully hadn't really lost her after all.

"It's Feathered Fanny," he announced, reaching out to close the woman's brown eyes that were so unlike the bright blue eyes of his angel, Vivienne.

"The Goose?" asked his brother, peering over his shoulder.

"Aye, that's right. The Winchester Goose from South-wark." Zachariah reached out and picked up one of the goose feathers still tied into the woman's hair, remembering how the whore had wanted to show them where else she wore feath-ers. He handed the torch back to Orvyn and then quickly checked for signs of life on the woman, but there was no need to even do so. Her body was cold and stiff and her skin was already turning blue. Her neck was cocked at such an odd angle that it was more than obvious that she was stone-cold dead.

"I see blood on her gown," Isaac pointed out. "Mayhap her throat has been slit."

Zachariah checked and shook his head. "Nay. But it looks as if mayhap she's been stabbed in the gut. We'll have to take the body to the coroner's office in better light to inspect her. One thing is for sure, her neck is broken." From his position, hunkered down next to the body, he looked up at the open window of the second story of the inn. Torn, dirty curtains flut-tered out in the breeze. "Her death was most likely sealed from the high fall." He leaned in closer to try to smell if the whore had been intoxicated, but couldn't really tell.

"Perhaps she was stabbed to death first and then pushed out

the window afterward," muttered Isaac under his breath, his gaze roving up to the open window too.

"Fanny! Nay, tell me it isn't true!" came the shout of a woman.

When Zachariah looked up, he saw a dog leading two women through the crowd. He recognized Lady Vivienne's bloodhound, Grunt, immediately. Right behind the hound was Lady Vivienne carrying a lit lantern as dawn was slowly turning into the start of a new day. At her side was his younger sister, Cassandra.

"Fanny!" screamed Cassandra, rushing past Vivienne and dropping to her knees next to Zachariah, shaking her head and crying as her gaze fixated on her good friend. Her long dark hair was loose around her shoulders and she wore only a thin night-shift under her cloak.

"Oh, no! Sheriff, what happened?" asked Vivienne, holding out her lantern to get a better look. Vivienne was fully dressed and wore no cloak at all.

"It seems she fell from up there and broke her neck," said Zachariah with a nod to the open window. The sun was starting to light up the sky now, and though it was still dark on Rotten Row from all the tall buildings looming over them, it was getting easier to see without a torch or lantern for aid.

"Cassandra, she probably leaned out for some air and slipped and fell." Isaac tried his best to console his crying sister. "These old buildings are falling apart and not very sturdy at all."

"Nay! Fanny didn't like heights. She never even went near a window," announced Cassandra, still wailing. "And what's that blood on her gown?" Cassandra reached out to touch it, but Zachariah grabbed her hand and stopped her.

"Don't touch anything, Cassandra. This could very well be a crime scene."

"Crime scene?" Cassandra looked up at him with a

distraught look in her eyes, and blinked away a few tears. "Are you saying she was...murdered?"

"I can't answer that yet." Zachariah didn't want to talk about it right now. Not to her or to anyone anymore, especially not in front of half the town. "Isaac, fetch the physician and coroner, quickly." He got to his feet. "Everyone, move back," he commanded with his arms outstretched. "I need to know if anyone heard or saw what happened."

"Nay. I already asked them," said Orvyn. "No one saw or heard a thing."

"Or at least they won't admit it," mumbled Zachariah, knowing that when crime happened on Rotten Row, people usually just looked the other way rather than to get involved. Fear ran rampant here, and no one wanted a thief or murderer coming after them next, so they never willingly offered information.

"Sheriff, how could this have happened?" Vivienne stared down at the whore's body, shaking her head. Zachariah noticed that Vivienne wasn't wearing her cloak. She was dressed in a forest-green gown made of taffeta with ornate gold trim on the sleeves and swirls and fancy designs down the back. A gown that matched the cloak worn by the dead whore.

"Mayhap you could tell me," he ground out. "After all, you're here in town when you are supposed to be back at the castle. Lady Vivienne, Feathered Fanny is dead...and in case you haven't noticed, she is wearing *your* cloak!"

Chapter Two

Vivienne stared down at Feathered Fanny, her heart aching for the poor woman even though she'd just met her and didn't know her well. Her heart cried out for Cassandra, too, because of her loss. Fanny had been Cassandra's best friend. To make matters even worse, Zachariah was acting cold and insensitive and at such a crucial moment. It didn't make sense at all. Vivienne didn't like it. Nay, she didn't approve of the sheriff's aloofness since he should be consoling his sister, but he wasn't. Instead, he almost seemed...angry. Not at Cassandra, but with *her*!

"Lower your voice, Sheriff," she warned him under her breath. "A woman is dead, and I'd think you'd have a little more compassion at a time like this."

"Compassion?" His brows arched. "Is that what you're really concerned with right now?"

"Of course it is. Compassion for your sister is important since she has just lost her best friend. After all, they did make the journey all the way from Southwark to come to Mablethorpe to see *you*."

"I never asked them to come here and neither did I ever

want them here in the first place," he ground out. "If they would have stayed home, Feathered Fanny would still be alive. I knew their arrival would mean nothing but trouble for me, and this is proof that Winchester Geese have no right to be in my town."

"*Your* town?" she asked, not liking the way he sounded as if he thought he owned it. "If I must remind you, you answer to the crown."

"I know that, Vivienne. But they should have stayed in their stew in Southwark where they belong."

"It's *Lady* Vivienne," she retorted in a hoarse whisper, reminding him to use her title. "And it is not admirable for a man in your position to be thinking only about yourself at a time like this. You need to be here for your sister right now."

Grunt moaned and lay down between Vivienne and Zachariah, almost looking as if he wanted to cover his ears rather than to listen to their squabbling.

Fire blazed in Zachariah's eyes now. "I am sheriff and have a job to do. I have no time or need for emotion. Especially if this wasn't an accident, but another murder, as I highly suspect it was. My lady, the last thing I need to be doing right now is consoling whores."

Shocked and appalled that he just said that about his sister, she found it unbelievable that he could be so heartless and cruel. And in front of the entire town! She involuntarily reacted by raising her hand to slap him, but stopped short. What was she doing? She could never hurt Zachariah. He was her best friend since childhood. And even if he didn't know it, she'd lost her heart to the man long ago. She couldn't...*wouldn't* do anything to hurt him or embarrass him in front of the entire town. Even as angry as she was at him right now, she didn't want to hurt him.

His gaze slowly traveled to her hand and pure disappointment filled his eyes. His stark features almost seemed to become shadowed. He gritted his teeth and shook his head slowly.

"Really, Vivienne?" he asked softly. "Has it come to that now between us?" He turned away from her before she could answer, talking to the crowd, trying to get them to move away from the body.

"Move aside. Get out of the way," came Nairnie's voice from the back of the crowd. "Let the coroner through, ye blasted fools!"

"Oh, nay," groaned Zachariah.

The crowd parted and Nairnie walked up and stopped next to Vivienne, screwing up her face as she looked down at the dead body. "I kent those Winchester Geese were goin' to be nothin' but trouble."

"Sheriff, I'm here, and heard there was another murder," called out Gandalf, the coroner, breaking through the crowd. "We were on our way here when we were intercepted by Isaac." Gandalf hunkered down next to the corpse. Isaac followed. The physician and the coroner's scribe, Torsten, were right behind, carrying a canvas stretched over wooden poles, made to transport a body. Zachariah joined them and they conversed softly.

"I can't believe Fanny is dead," Vivienne said to Nairnie. "I just saw her last night and she was happy and fine."

"Better her than ye, missy." Nairnie was a boisterous, hardened old woman who had lived through a lot, never letting anything get the best of her. Although she was tough, she had a kind heart, but made no secret that she disapproved of the Winchester Geese.

"Nairnie, please! What do you even mean by that?" asked Vivienne, thinking the old woman was being just as insensitive as Zachariah.

"When the sheriff heard there was a dead woman and she was dressed in yer cloak, he feared it was ye," explained Nairnie.

"He did?" Vivienne blinked twice. "Oh, I see now what you mean."

"It was a foolish thing ye did, my lady. Ye dinna belong down on Rotten Row. It is a dangerous, dirty place only suited for whores, thieves, and paupers. Ye are a noble and should be back at the castle where ye belong!"

Vivienne suddenly realized why Zachariah had been acting so odd and seeming angry at her. He must have thought she'd died, and he was thoroughly shaken. That told her that he truly cared about her. Vivienne surmised that Fanny must have taken her cloak during the night and left the room while she and Cassandra were sleeping. Vivienne had no idea the woman had even left the room until she woke up to find her gone and Grunt pawing at the closed door this morning.

Looking at it that way, Vivienne felt horrible for the way she'd spoken to Zachariah. "I realize now that I was wrong, Nairnie. But when the sheriff wouldn't give lodging to his own sister, I felt that I should step up and help her. Therefore, I paid for a room at the inn for Cassandra and Fanny so they'd have shelter for the night."

"Why didna ye leave them there and go back to the castle where ye belonged instead of sleepin' there?"

"I don't know." Vivienne shrugged. "I suppose it was because I was enjoying the visit with Cassandra. We hadn't seen each other in years. The time got away from us. Before I knew it, nightfall had set in. Cassandra told me I should stay with them since it wouldn't be safe to travel back all alone and in the dark."

"Why didna ye have an escort?"

"My guard wasn't with me because I sent him back to the castle earlier when we were by the sheriff's house. I told him that Sheriff Fitch was going to escort me home. Of course, that was before I knew he was going to object to his own sister staying with him."

"Ye should have summoned the sheriff to escort ye home, my lady."

"I had initially planned to do that after I got Cassandra and Fanny settled. But before I knew it, it was late and I didn't think it was a good idea to bother him. Besides, the sheriff believed I went back to the castle with my guard, Richard. I guess I didn't want him to know I stayed to visit with his sister when he'd told me to keep away from her."

The last thing she had wanted was for Zachariah to be privy to the fact that she went to Rotten Row when he had warned her time and again to stay away. Especially since she was with his estranged sister. And not one, but two Winchester Geese, to make matters worse. She had hoped he'd never find out about that, but her plan didn't work out the way she'd wanted. "I figured we would be safer if we stayed at the inn together through the night. Plus, we were locked in our room and had Grunt with us for protection, so I didn't think there was any chance of real danger."

"Hrmph!" Nairnie's hands went to her hips. "Most of the time ye are a smart lassie, but sometimes, ye act so daft that even Starah, who is a mere child, has more sense than ye."

"What does that mean?"

"It means ye are stupid, missy. And that dog of yers will look the other way for a good bone so he is no real protection at all." Nairnie was a crusty old woman who wasn't afraid of speaking her mind to anyone, even if they were a noble.

"Nay. That's not true, Nairnie. Grunt has helped us in every murder investigation so far and has done a good job of it, too."

"Ye are always helpin' the rag pickers and orphans and outcasts and it gets ye in trouble, my lady. Canna ye see that?"

"I can't help it, Nairnie. I have a soft spot in my heart for those types of people. Since I was once in a similar position regarding my family, I like to reach out and help those in need if I can."

"Ye are no' in that position anymore, if I must remind ye," Nairnie pointed out. "Ye have a son and brother to care for now, in case ye've forgotten. What would happen to them if ye'd been murdered? Ye should have been with them last night instead of potentially riskin' yer life in the worst part of town with two whores. Ye probably have yer entire family worried and up in arms lookin' for ye."

"Nay, I saw to that. I sent a messenger back to the castle last night to let my aunt and uncle know my plans."

"Ye did? A messenger ye say? Ye found one here in town?" Nairnie gave her that look that said she knew better and that Vivienne would never tell her uncle she was on Rotten Row. He would never allow it either.

"All right, that's not exactly accurate."

"Go on," said Nairnie, one of her eyes already closing as she crossed her arms over her ample bosom.

"I paid a boy from town to go to the castle and tell my aunt and uncle that I was safe and staying at the sheriff's house for the night with all the others."

"Hrmph. That boy ye call a messenger was most likely a thief who took the coin and ran."

"Now that you mention it, I suppose it was odd that my uncle didn't send a guard back to collect me, even if I was safe with the sheriff. He would have worried about gossip."

"Well, no one came lookin' for ye at the sheriff's home, I can tell ye that since I was there."

"I suppose I shouldn't have stayed there, after all."

"And ye didna think of this until now?"

"I guess I was so caught up visiting with Cassandra, and then so tired, that I never even gave it another thought."

"What kind of example are ye settin' for the young ones like Martin and Starah? Not a very good one, I fear."

The men headed in their direction, the coroner and his scribe carrying Fanny's dead body on a stretcher. Isaac was with them. The physician stayed back talking with Zachariah and the innkeeper. Cassandra sat by herself on the ground, crying, and with her hands covering her face.

"All right, everyone go back to your homes. There is nothing more to see here," called out Isaac with his hand in the air as they stopped right in front of Vivienne. Fanny's arm fell out from under the blanket that covered her. When it did, Vivienne noticed something grasped in the dead woman's fist. Vivienne quickly looked around and when she realized no one was watching, she put her lantern on the ground and reached out and pried open the woman's stiff fingers, quickly taking the item from her, keeping the object hidden.

Grunt jumped up and barked, causing Nairnie to turn around.

"Lady Vivienne?" The old woman scowled, her gaze going to Vivienne's closed hand. "What are ye doin'?" she asked suspiciously.

"I was just putting Fanny's arm back under the blanket." Vivienne quickly lifted the end of the blanket and pushed the dead woman's arm back underneath.

"Ye took somethin' from her, didna ye? What is it?" Nairnie slowly moved closer, all the while giving Vivienne the evil eye. It was the old woman's infamous fierce look that made even a rugged pirate spill his deepest secrets. Vivienne quickly looked in the opposite direction, knowing if she didn't leave now, Nairnie was going to get her to confess.

"If you'll excuse me, Nairnie, Cassandra needs comforting and no one here seems capable of rendering aid. I suppose I will have to do it myself." Vivienne picked up her lantern, still hiding what she took from Fanny.

Nairnie's hand shot out and she grabbed Vivienne by the arm. Vivienne highly expected the old woman to pry open her fingers to look for herself, but she didn't. Instead, she stared Vivienne right in the eye. "The sheriff was really worried, my lady. I've never seen him so upset as he was today."

"Really." She let out a deep sigh and shrugged as she let her gaze travel over to Zachariah. "He doesn't seem too worried to me. He has yet to show his own sister a little compassion when that is exactly what Cassandra needs at a time like this."

"I'm no' talkin' about his sister, lassie. I mean *ye*, and I think ye ken it. Ye need to speak with him. The two of ye canna keep goin' on actin' as if ye mean nothin' to each other. It's just no' right."

Vivienne glanced down at Nairnie's hand on her arm, knowing she was right by what she said, but also not wanting to admit it. She was still too angry with Zachariah for rejecting Cassandra, even if the girl had made a poor choice in her profession years ago.

"I could say the same about you and Bear, Nairnie. You need to contact your husband and make amends. I know how much the two of you care about each other. Don't let things between you end this way." Bear had recently left to go on another sea mission for the King. Nairnie, who was upset that she never got time to spend with her husband, told Bear she didn't want him to return and that she didn't want anything to do with him ever again.

Vivienne's words got Nairnie to stop pestering her. The old woman quickly released Vivienne's arm and stepped back.

"Nay. No amends. I have nothin' to say to that old buzzard. Now if ye'll excuse me, I need to get back to Starah. The constable's wife is with the children, but I dinna think the sheriff trusts that she can handle watchin' over his daughter along with her own three." She turned and left before Vivienne could respond.

"I'll stop by the coroner's office if you'd like," the physician said to Zachariah as they strolled past. "But as I've told you, Sheriff, the whore is dead. My quick examination shows that she probably died sometime during the night. She's been stabbed, but her neck is also broken from the fall, sealing her fate."

"No need to stop by," said Zachariah. "The coroner will examine her too. I'll be sure to send for you if I have any questions. Thank you." Zachariah turned to face Vivienne, his hand reaching out to pet Grunt on the head. The dog licked his arm. "Can I escort you back to the castle where you belong, my lady? Because I sure as hell am not going to let you stay here on Rotten Row any longer without a proper escort."

"I..." Her attention was on Cassandra who was still sitting in the middle of the street crying. People were starting to surround her. Vivienne feared that they'd begin throwing rocks at the poor girl next or possibly spitting on her. Or they might even do something to hurt her, since she was a Winchester Goose and wasn't wanted here. The town whores were watching Cassandra closely with daggered looks, seeming like they wanted to kill her. "Yes, that would be nice," she told him, looking up and flashing him a quick smile. "I just need to quickly collect something first and then we'll be on our way."

"Collect something? If you mean your cloak that the Goose is wearing, nay. That will remain as evidence until we have time to investigate the whore's death more closely."

"That's not what I mean, Sheriff. I won't be wanting that

cloak back." She ran over to Cassandra and helped her to her feet. Grunt stayed at her side, protecting her as always.

"Vivienne? What are you doing?" Zachariah followed her through the crowd. Cassandra cried and clung to Vivienne's arm.

"I will not leave Cassandra all alone in a strange town by herself. Not when she is so upset after just witnessing her best friend lying dead."

"Strange town?" Zachariah shook his head. "My sister grew up here in Mablethorpe, in case you are forgetting. She knows the town as well as everyone in it."

"Mayhap you're forgetting, she no longer has a single friend in Mablethorpe since she took up her current profession."

Zachariah snorted. "Do you really blame the town's people? After what she did?"

"That is not for me or you to judge. Now, since you won't let me stay here, I am going to take her back to the castle with me and I will provide lodging for her there."

"Oh, really?" He actually laughed at hearing that. "If you think for one minute that your uncle is going to let a whore stay at his castle, let alone in your room with you, then you'd better think again."

"Oh, my lady, I'm afraid Zachariah is right," said Cassandra, sniffling and wiping her eyes with a dainty cloth she pulled out from between her trussed-up breasts. "You are a noble. You can't take me in. It wouldn't be right. It might hurt your reputation."

"Fine. Then I'll stay here in town with you again tonight. I hope the innkeeper will let me pay him for a room again and not hold this murder against us."

"Nay, you won't be staying here," protested Zachariah. "I will not let you do that, Lady Vivienne. It is not safe and you know it. Plus, Lord Mablethorpe is already going to be angrier than a wet hornet when he finds out where you spent the night. I'll most likely be blamed for it somehow."

"If I can't take Cassandra back to the castle, and you refuse to let me stay here on Rotten Row, then the only other choice is for you to take her home and let her stay with you for now. Until she returns home to Southwark."

"What? Nay," said Zachariah with a startled jolt. "My house is already full."

"It will just be temporary. Until the investigation is over," said Vivienne, rubbing Cassandra's arm. "After all, we're going to want to question everyone. Your sister, too, I'm sure."

Vivienne realized that everyone on Rotten Row was watching her and whispering about her behind her back, but her thoughts were not for herself right now. All she cared about at the moment was getting proper accommodations and a safe place for Cassandra to stay where she could mourn the death of her good friend Fanny.

"Oh, please, don't turn me away, Brother," begged Cassandra. Tears dripped down her cheeks. "I know you are still angry with me, but I need you right now. Please, let me stay with you and Isaac. I promise I won't be any trouble at all. You won't even know I'm there. I am your sister. We are family."

Vivienne could see Zachariah's jaw tighten and his gaze drop to the ground. He needed just a little more convincing, and she hoped that she could be the one to make him change his mind.

"We have a possible murder on our hands," Vivienne reminded him. "Cassandra could very well be the next target. Until we know what is going on, don't you think it would be better to be able to keep a close eye on her? To protect her? You are the sheriff, not to mention her own brother. It is your responsibility."

There was a long pause, and then Zachariah finally let out a deep sigh. "Since I know that if I refuse, you'll be doing something stupid again, Lady Vivienne, I suppose I have no choice but to bring her home with me. For now. Cassandra, we'll escort you there on our way to the coroner's office."

"Oh, thank you, Zachariah!" exclaimed Cassandra, her arms opening as if she meant to hug him. "It will be so good to be home again with my siblings."

Instead of hugging her, Zachariah held up his hand and took a step backward. "It is only temporary," he told her. "Until the investigation is over. Then you'll go back to Southwark and not return to Mablethorpe again."

"I understand," she answered with a sad nod.

"Also, you will sleep in the same room as Nairnie, but not my daughter. Starah will be in my room with me. Isaac will sleep downstairs. I will not allow you to taint Starah's thoughts or actions by anything you might say or do. She is very impressionable at this age."

Cassandra frowned. "I don't know what kind of a woman you think I am, Zachariah, but I would never do anything to hurt Starah. She's only a child. And my niece, if I must remind you. Family sticks together and helps each other out in times of need. That is so important."

Vivienne smiled when Cassandra said this because she could see how the woman's words were making Zachariah squirm. Good, she thought. He needed to hear this from someone besides her.

"What will you tell Starah when she asks what you do for a living?" asked Zachariah.

"I...well I haven't thought about that yet. I suppose I'll just be vague."

"We'll make that decision later," said Vivienne, interrupting their conversation. "Together. Sheriff, right now, we have a corpse to inspect and a possible murder to investigate. There very well might be a killer on the loose, and if so, we need to find him or her before they strike again." She looked down at her closed fist, hiding whatever it was that Fanny had been holding. Something told her to look at it in private, because she had the feeling that whatever it was would only make Zachariah end up blaming her that this happened at all.

Chapter Three

Once they all returned to the sheriff's home, the others went inside but Vivienne stayed on the doorstep, wanting to inspect the object she'd taken from the hand of the corpse. Looking down at her closed fist, she realized that her bloodhound, Grunt, sat next to her, staring up at her with sad eyes.

"I know you want to go inside and beg for food," said Vivienne, running her free hand over the dog's head. "But I just need a minute to see something first."

Slowly, she unclasped her fingers. There in her palm was a folded-up piece of paper. Since it had been in Fanny's hand and the woman's arm had been sticking out of the trough, it thankfully had not become wet at all.

"Interesting," she said, slowly starting to unfold the paper, wondering just what it could be.

"What have ye got there, lassie?" Nairnie stood at the partially open door of the house, craning her neck, trying to see what Vivienne held.

"Nothing." Vivienne quickly snapped her fist closed again.

"Really," said Nairnie, starting to give her the evil eye. "Let me see your hand."

Vivienne raised up her empty hand.

"The other one, missy."

"Nairnie, don't ask so many questions. This doesn't concern you." Vivienne quickly slipped the paper into her side pouch that hung from her waist belt.

"If that is what ye took from the dead Goose, then ye'd better tell the sheriff about it. It might be a clue."

"My, I'm hungry," said Vivienne trying to change the subject. "Would you perhaps have a little something for me to eat?"

"Why? Didna they feed ye at that cesspool inn where ye stayed last night? Not that I'd expect anything of the kind."

"Nay, I didn't get any food at the Hogg's Head Inn," she answered. "Not that they wouldn't have offered, but with all the commotion and leaving so fast this morning, I didn't have a chance to find even a bite of bread."

Grunt whimpered at her side when he heard her mention bread, since it was one of his favorite things to mooch. His tail wagged back and forth from his sitting position, sweeping away the dead leaves that covered the sheriff's porch.

"I suppose that mutt of yers will be wantin' somethin' too." Nairnie pursed her lips, staring down at the dog.

"Yes, if you don't mind." Vivienne gave Nairnie a big smile. "Grunt's already saved you the trouble of having to sweep the porch."

"Mmmph," snorted the old woman. "Well, come on in and join the others," she said with jerk of her head. "After all, if I have to house and feed a Winchester Goose now, doing the same for a noblewoman will be a nice change of pace."

"Lady Vivienne?" Zachariah pulled the door open wide as Nairnie continued into the house. "Isaac and I are going to the coroner's office." He held a slice of bread in one hand and a hunk of cheese in the other. "Since you've decided to stay here for now, have something to eat with the others. We'll let you know what we discover."

"I'm ready, Brother," said Isaac, joining them at the doorstep, his mouth filled with food as he chewed and talked at the same time. He seemed to be concealing something under his cloak and Grunt rushed over to sniff him.

"Nay, I'll not stay here. I've decided I need to go with you. To find out what happened to Fanny," she told him.

Zachariah looked over his shoulder at Nairnie who had waddled over to the table and was glaring at Cassandra since the woman had seated herself on the bench right next to little Starah. The constable's wife was still there with her children, but she was preparing to leave, obviously not wanting to stay in his house now that a prostitute had joined them.

"I'm not sure I want to leave Nairnie alone with Cassandra since she already seems to despise her. "I was hoping you could stay here for now until Nairnie gets more used to the idea that Cassandra will be our houseguest for a short time."

"Nay," said Vivienne, shaking her head. "I'm sorry, but I feel partially responsible for Fanny's death since I was the one to bring her to the inn last night. I'm going with you, so don't even try to talk me out of it."

"Yes, I agree you are partially responsible since it most likely never would have happened if you wouldn't have gotten involved in the first place."

"You don't know that," she answered. Damn, she didn't mean to say it was her fault! She just put the idea into the sheriff's head that she was responsible, and that was exactly what she was trying to avoid doing. Her thoughts were so occupied with wanting to know what was written on the scrap of paper that she couldn't even think straight. "Let me quickly get some food and we'll be on our way," she told the men.

"Don't bother. Isaac has enough for all of us, including Grunt." Zachariah's hand shot out. "Hand it over, Brother."

"Hand over what?" asked Isaac. Grunt sat at Isaac's feet, his tail wagging, looking up at him with interest.

"Don't think I don't know you pilfered not only bread and cheese from the table when Nairnie went to the door, but a few apples as well. You are not as discreet as you think you are."

"Where did that big loaf of bread go?" complained Nairnie from inside the house as her hands went to her hips. "Isaac? Did you take it?" She looked over toward the door.

"Here you go," said Isaac, pulling the loaf of brown bread out from under his cloak and shoving it into Zachariah's hands. Grunt instantly repositioned himself to sit at the sheriff's feet now. "Nay, Nairnie, I don't have it," Isaac shouted over his shoulder before bolting out the door.

Vivienne chuckled. "Did you want to turn around and show Nairnie that you have the bread?" she asked Zachariah.

"Do I look like I'm addled? Let's get the hell out of here before she starts chasing me with that blasted ladle." Zachariah took off toward the street with Grunt right on his heels.

"I'll be back later, Cassandra," Vivienne called into the room. "Just make yourself at home. I'm sure Nairnie will help you feel comfortable." Saying that brought about a disgusted hiss from Nairnie.

"I'll do no such thing for a blasted, tarnished Winchester Goose!" Nairnie's head snapped up and her face turned red.

"Why are you calling Aunt Cassandra a goose?" asked Starah innocently, running a hand over her cat, Midnight, who had just jumped up on the table.

"Get that blasted animal off the table," scolded Nairnie,

swiping her hand at Midnight. The cat hissed in a similar manner as Nairnie had just done, and then arched her back.

"Don't hurt her," cried Starah, grabbing her cat.

"That cat is a filthy nuisance and should be out catching rats, not sitting on the table," complained Nairnie.

"Oh, what a nice cat," said Cassandra, moving closer to the little girl and reaching out to pet Midnight. That made Starah smile. Thankfully, the little girl's question regarding the goose was forgotten for now.

"Goodbye, Starah," Vivienne called back, hurriedly closing the door, not wanting to be around to hear when they were forced to explain to Starah about Winchester Geese. She ran to catch up to the men and Grunt. As much as she wanted to stay back at the house with Cassandra to console her and make her feel wanted, she would have to leave that up to Nairnie for now. There was a death to investigate and that took priority. Vivienne's head was already swarming with questions since the paper that Fanny clutched in her hand had something written on it. Sadly, Vivienne had yet to find a private moment to read it. Her stomach also churned, and that was never a good sign. Usually it meant that something bad was about to happen. This told her she wasn't going to like what was written on the paper, even though it might end up being a good clue as to what possibly happened. She continued to walk, her hand on her stomach. Nay, this wasn't going to be a good thing at all, she was sure.

ZACHARIAH SPLIT up the bread amongst them and they ate as they walked down the street toward the coroner's office. Grunt padded along at Zachariah's side, the dog's tongue hanging out, waiting for more food since Zachariah kept feeding him.

"Why do you suppose anyone would want to kill such a *beautiful* woman as Fanny?" asked Isaac, stressing the word beautiful.

"Because Feathered Fanny was also a Winchester Goose, perhaps?" Zachariah looked over at his brother and shook his head, thinking that Isaac had always overlooked a woman's faults as long as she was fetching.

"Well, if that's the case, then it wasn't a man who killed her," stated Isaac, rubbing an apple on his sleeve to shine it and then taking a big bite, making a loud crunching noise.

"Why would you come to that conclusion so quickly?" asked Vivienne, walking next to the sheriff.

"Because her death is a true waste to any and every man with a pulse, that's why." Isaac cocked a crooked smile as he continued to chew, his tongue darting out to lick up a dribble of apple juice from the corner of his mouth. "I only wish I would have had time to get to know her better. Much, much better."

"Stop being such a cur, Isaac! The woman is dead, so please have a little respect." Vivienne's brows dipped, making a crease in her forehead. Then she clenched her jaw and shook her head, throwing her nose in the air, her reaction to Isaac's comments almost laughable.

"It could have been one of the whores from Rotten Row who did her in," suggested Zachariah. He took an apple from Isaac and handed it to Vivienne, but she shook her head, so he took a bite instead. "After all, jealousy is a common motive, and the whores of Rotten Row are envious of any good-looking female who wanders into their territory. It is a motive strong enough to possibly make one or more of them want to push Fanny out a window, I believe."

"Aye, that's probably who it was," agreed Isaac with a nod. "We'd better interview the whores right away. I'll do it," he said smugly, almost sounding as if he enjoyed the idea.

"Nay. I know the girls personally, so I'll question them," stated Zachariah, swallowing his bite of apple. "After all, they might open up to me easier than to you."

"Oh, but I'd really like them to open up to me. All of them." Isaac waggled his brows.

"Stop it, both of you," snapped Vivienne.

"Stop what? We're just talking about the case," said Zachariah.

"Sheriff, how well do you really know the whores on Rotten Row?" asked Vivienne, sounding more than curious to him. If he wasn't mistaken, she almost sounded jealous. "Mayhap I should question them instead of either of you two."

"What? Nay, I didn't mean...like that," he tried to tell her. "Not in an intimate way at all."

"Then, in what way did you mean?" They stopped in front of the coroner's office and Vivienne blinked more than usual as she waited for his answer with a stoic expression on her face.

"You know very well what I mean, Vivienne. Don't play these games with me because I don't like them and neither do I have the patience or time for them right now." Zachariah opened the door and waited for her to enter.

"You meant to say *Lady* Vivienne, I'm sure." She was always angry with him when she pointed out to him to be sure to use her title.

Zachariah didn't like that game either, but she *was* a noble and he was required to use her title, so he would.

"*Lady* Vivienne, would you care to enter, or would you prefer to stand out here on the street all day?" He nodded at the open door and held out his arm.

"God's eyes," said Isaac, tossing his apple core to the ground. Grunt quickly inspected it, but decided it wasn't worth eating. "I'm not going to wait for you two to stop making eyes at each other. I'm going inside." Isaac pushed past them and entered the building first. Grunt lost interest in the core and ran inside after Isaac, probably hoping to get something better.

"Making eyes at each other? What did he mean by that?" asked Vivienne reminding him of a doe in the torchlight, sounding and looking so stunned and confused right now that it was downright laughable. Her innocence, whether it was real or not, only made him want to hug her. Damn, she seemed to have power over his emotions even if she didn't know it.

Even though Zachariah was still upset that Vivienne had sneakily stayed on Rotten Row last night without him knowing about it, he was more than happy and relieved that she hadn't been the one to die. His heart ached to tell her how he felt about her. Mayhap since they were alone right now, this would be the perfect opportunity to do so. He opened his mouth to speak, but before he could even mention it, two approaching people interrupted.

"My lady, my lady!" Lady Vivienne's handmaid, Maleine, waved to them and ran up to join them with Wymond, the rat catcher's former assistant, at her side. "Are you all right?"

Vivienne looked up in surprise. "Maleine? What are you doing here? And of course I am all right—why wouldn't I be?" She turned to face the newcomers.

"Your aunt is so worried about you that she sent me to find you," her handmaid continued.

"Aunt Ellen knows I spent the night in town," said Vivienne. "Or at least I think she does. I sent a boy to give her and Uncle Gilbert the message that I'd be at the sheriff's house with the others."

"I know," said Maleine. "He showed up. But you shouldn't have done that, my lady. You belong at the castle. I begged your uncle to send a guard for you last night, but he refused to do so."

"Really?" Vivienne asked in confusion, having highly

expected her uncle to do just that since he had never been understanding about the things she did.

"Nay. He said you were safe with the sheriff and that there was no need to worry and to let you be."

"So, he didn't know where I really was then?"

"If you mean on Rotten Row, nay, I guess not," said Maleine. "However, Wymond heard from that messenger boy this morning that you were really staying on Rotten Row."

"We let the boy sleep in the stable last night since it was late when he arrived," explained Wymond. "He was very appreciative, and also talkative this morning. I thought I even heard him talking with Castor last night, and Castor never really talks to anyone."

"Oh no. Did my uncle hear him?" she asked.

"I don't know, but I guess not, since Lord Mablethorpe didn't come after you," said Wymond. "He left the stable just after sunup to go for his morning ride like he usually does a few times a week. Lately, he's even been going out more often."

"Well, did he seem upset at all?" asked Vivienne.

"Nay," answered Wymond with a shrug. "Not especially."

"Good. Then he doesn't know the truth." Vivienne smiled in relief.

"I'm sorry, my lady, but when I heard what Wymond said about you being on Rotten Row, I thought we should inform your aunt this morning," explained Maleine. "Therefore, she does know the truth."

"Oh," said Vivienne, her smile turning into a frown. "What did Aunt Ellen say when she found out?"

"She wasn't happy," said Maleine. "Since your uncle had already left on his morning ride, she asked if Wymond and I would come to fetch you. She was going to send a guard at first, but figured the guard would squeal to your uncle and that we could keep a secret better."

"Yes, that's true," agreed Vivienne, glad that her aunt seemed to be willing to protect her from her uncle's wrath.

"I really don't think she wanted her husband to know where you spent the night," said Wymond.

"Nay, and neither do I. It would be better if we all kept that information to ourselves." Vivienne highly suspected her uncle had a mistress, since he went riding in the mornings and always insisted he go alone. Her aunt said he used to sleep late and never liked to go riding much at all, but that was before Vivienne came to live with them. Vivienne didn't want to alarm her aunt so she never told the woman her suspicions that Uncle Gilbert was probably meeting another woman in secret for a tryst.

"You are a noble, my lady," Maleine reminded her. "Staying in town all night isn't safe, even if you are with the sheriff."

"Sorry, Sheriff," Wymond interjected. "Maleine didn't mean any offense by saying that."

"No offense taken." Zachariah waved his hand through the air. "Especially since I agree with you. Lady Vivienne never should have stayed on Rotten Row with a couple of Winchester Geese. I don't know what she was thinking."

"Oh! My lady," said Maleine with a hand to her mouth. Her face reddened as if she were embarrassed to hear him say Winchester Geese aloud, even though she most likely knew the details from the boy from town who gossiped to the stable hands.

"Once again, I'd like everyone to keep this between us and not point out the fact to my uncle, please," instructed Vivienne.

"Aye, my lady," both Maleine and Wymond said, looking at the ground.

"Sheriff?" Vivienne waited for him to agree as well.

"I'm sorry, Lady Vivienne, but I cannot make a promise to withhold such information. It goes against my nature to do so since I am the town sheriff and more is expected of me. If Lord Mablethorpe approaches and asks me directly, thinking you were at my home when you were not, I'm afraid I'll have to tell him the truth."

"The sheriff is right, my lady," Maleine bravely spoke up. "The first thing you ever taught me about helping you with murder investigations is that we never withhold any information because it could end up being a very valuable clue."

"Yes, Maleine, that is true," she told the girl. "However, this is different and has nothing to do with the murder at all."

"We hope," mumbled the sheriff, looking off into the distance.

Vivienne's gaze lowered and she covered her pouch with her hand. She *was* withholding information and knew it was wrong. But she hadn't had a chance to look at the paper yet. Mayhap it was nothing of interest at all. She would just wait until she had a moment alone to investigate it further.

Zachariah cleared his throat. "Well, if you'd like to stay out here with your handmaid, my lady, feel free to do so, but I have work to do inside." He entered the building, and she hurried in right behind him.

"Go to the sheriff's house for something to eat," Vivienne instructed Maleine and Wymond over her shoulder. "I will meet you there shortly."

"Aye, my lady," said Maleine as Vivienne walked away, following the sheriff up the stairs to the coroner's office on the second floor.

"Well, Gandalf, have you discovered anything about the body that is of any interest?" asked Zachariah approaching the table where the naked corpse was laid out, partially covered by a sheet. The coroner leaned over the dead woman, inspecting her while his scribe, Torsten, took notes. Torsten was a shorter man with a balding head and strands of hair pushed over the top to try to hide his shining pate. He stayed quiet most of the time, but was always watching and listening and recording everything they found.

"Sheriff, like the physician said, the woman broke her neck and it seems also her arm. Most likely from a high fall," announced the coroner. Gandalf was a tall, old man with long white hair and a long beard. He was training Torsten to take over as coroner someday, since he had already lived longer than most men did.

"Then she did fall out of the second story window, like the gossip said," Isaac remarked with a slight nod.

"Yes. It seems so," Gandalf assured him.

"Is there any evidence of a struggle?" asked the sheriff.

"Nay. Not really." Gandalf stood upright. "There are a few bruises on her body, but I know how whores can get rough with their coupling since I've experienced it myself."

Vivienne was surprised to hear the old man say that. He had to have been talking about his experience with whores from his younger days, since she couldn't picture someone as old as him bedding any woman.

"I'd imagine such bruising is nothing more than just from a wild night with a client and not really meant to harm her since the bruises don't seem to be fresh," continued the coroner.

"What about the wound in her gut? Was it from a knife?" asked the sheriff.

"Yes. It seems so. And since there was no evidence of a struggle, I'd say she was taken by surprise and it all happened very quickly."

"Or mayhap she knew the killer. Perhaps she even trusted him," said Vivienne, stepping up to inspect Fanny's body, too.

Vivienne wasn't really a squeamish type of person. Blood, bruises, and wounds didn't disturb her much. However, standing in a room filled with men who were all staring down at the naked body of such a voluptuous dead whore did make her feel a little uneasy or perhaps embarrassed. She reached out and pulled the sheet up higher to cover Fanny's breasts.

"I have no evidence that points in that direction," answered Gandalf. "However, I suppose it could be true that mayhap she knew her attacker."

"We haven't found anything yet to tell us if the murderer was a man or a woman," Torsten pointed out, looking up from his book as he recorded something else on the page.

"True, it could be either I suppose," said Vivienne.

Zachariah noticed Vivienne glancing down once again at her pouch. Her focus was not on Fanny at all, but rather on something else. She reached out, almost in a protective manner, resting her fingers against the side of the pouch hanging from her belt.

"We should go back to the trough. Now that it's light, we can take a better look around," suggested Isaac. "Mayhap we can find some footprints or a clue that we've missed."

"I agree." Zachariah nodded. "I also want to visit the room from where she fell. Mayhap we'll find the murder weapon hidden there."

Zachariah noticed that Vivienne had walked over to a side table and was looking through the whore's clothes now. Almost as if she were searching for something.

"Gandalf, did you find a dagger on Fanny by any chance?" Vivienne asked the coroner. "I know she carried a knife tied to her leg under her skirts just in case she ever needed it to protect herself. Of course, she most likely removed it when we prepared to go to sleep."

"Yes, there was a dagger fastened to her leg, just like you said." Torsten answered, hurrying over to join her. He reached over to a shelf and picked up a blade by the handle, turning it backward to safely hand it to Vivienne.

"There was no blood on it, so that can't be the murder weapon," said Gandalf. "That's why I didn't even mention it."

"Unless the blood washed off in the water from the trough." Zachariah walked over to inspect the weapon, thinking this was such a blatant thing and not being able to believe the coroner overlooked it.

"Mayhap the killer wiped it clean," added Isaac, following him across the room.

"Very good. That is a thought," Zachariah complimented his brother. "You're getting better at your job quite quickly. Good work."

"Thank you, Sheriff. I'm glad I can be of assistance." Isaac stood a bit taller and puffed out his chest.

"Since the dagger was still strapped to her leg, I find it interesting that Fanny never even drew her weapon." Vivienne turned the dagger over and over in her hands, inspecting it, trying to find something that might be a clue. "She must not have felt threatened or in danger."

"Or she didn't have time to draw her blade if the attack happened quickly," Isaac gave them his opinion.

"We need to figure out what she was doing in that room, and why she even went there in the first place." Zachariah looked over at Vivienne, having to ask her some things that he was sure wouldn't please her in the least. "My lady, didn't you hear Fanny leave the room last night?"

"Nay, I didn't," answered Vivienne. "If so, Sheriff, I would have told you so by now, you know that."

"I understand, but still I had to ask."

"I don't think Cassandra heard her leave either, or she would have said something about it to me. Then again, we were all quite tired and in a deep sleep," continued Vivienne.

Grunt barked, looking at them intently. It was almost as if the dog was trying to tell them something.

"Mayhap Grunt saw the murderer," suggested Isaac. "I wish he could talk. It certainly would help."

"I don't think anyone actually abducted Fanny from her room," Zachariah told them. "She most likely left the room of her own accord. After all, she took the time to not only strap her blade to her leg but to also don Lady Vivienne's cloak, don't forget. It seems to me as if she planned on going somewhere."

"Or meeting someone," said Vivienne softly, her hand once more going to her pouch.

"So she must have planned on going outside all along. I mean, since she donned the cloak," said Gandalf, stating the obvious.

"I don't understand why she didn't wear her own cloak," said Isaac. "I know she had one since I saw her wearing it at the docks."

"Yes, it was hanging on the hook this morning and is still there," said Vivienne. "When I found mine was missing, I couldn't bring myself to wear hers."

"Thank goodness for that decision," commented Zachariah in a sarcastic tone.

"Fanny never mentioned anything about planning to leave the room," Vivienne told them. "We were all chatting and became tired and went to sleep at the same time. I don't think it was a premeditated action at all."

"Unless she wanted to make some money while she was here." Isaac didn't need to explain what he meant by that. Fanny was a working girl and also inside an inn with lots of drinking men downstairs. It had to be tempting.

"Were the three of you drinking at all?" asked Zachariah, waiting for Vivienne's reaction which he knew wouldn't be favorable in the least.

Vivienne gave him a disgruntled look just like he knew she would. "We might have had a few glasses of wine, sure, but we certainly were not well in our cups, if that is what you are insinuating, Sheriff. We were all in complete control of our actions at all times."

"Just not in control of making good decisions," mumbled Zachariah under his breath, still wondering what had possessed Vivienne to do such a dangerous, not to mention *stupid*, thing as to stay with whores on Rotten Row.

"I can go back and check in the water of the trough in case we missed something," offered Isaac.

"Yes, and I'll join you," Zachariah answered, heading for the door. He stopped and turned back when he realized Vivienne wasn't following. "My lady? Aren't you coming, too?"

"Nay. I think I'll go back and wait for you at your house, Sheriff. I should really check on Cassandra since she was so shaken by all of this."

Zachariah frowned, wondering what Vivienne was really up to since she always insisted on being there for an investigation and never turned down an offer to go to Rotten Row. Even if it was the very last place a noblewoman should be. This certainly wasn't like her at all. "Then I'll escort you back to my home."

"Nay." She held up her hand. "It's just down the street, I'll be fine. I can make it there safely on my own. Besides, Grunt will be with me." She reached down and scratched behind her dog's ears. "You two should hurry and get back to the scene of the crime before anyone removes evidence."

"All right then," he said, almost able to see the gears turning in the woman's head. She was trying her best to send them off without her for some reason. "Then we'll see you soon, I suppose."

Zachariah followed his brother out the door and down the stairs to the street. When they stepped from the building, he pulled his brother to the side. "Go on ahead, Isaac. I'll meet you at the Hogg's Head Inn soon."

"You're not coming to question the bystanders? Why not?" Isaac seemed confused. "I thought it was important to secure the murder site as quickly as possible after the crime."

"I'll be there, just not yet." He looked back at the building.

"Why not? I don't understand. Where are you going to be?"

"I've got another chore to do first. One that I hope will end up answering some questions and suspicions filling my head right now."

Chapter Four

Vivienne waited a few minutes and then left the coroner's office, stopping downstairs in the doorway, looking up and down the street to make sure Zachariah had really left.

"The coast is clear, Grunt," she told her bloodhound, and walked out to the street with Grunt leading the way. Since she was sure that Zachariah and Isaac had gone, she strolled down the street, pulling the piece of paper out of her pouch and carefully clutching it as she walked. Her heart pounded heavily in her chest. This paper was important to Fanny or she wouldn't have held on to it even after she was attacked and thrown out the window. Whatever was written on this scrap of paper must be of vital importance. Mayhap Fanny, even though she was now dead, would be able to help shed some light on this dire situation.

Stepping off to the side of the road, Vivienne quickly opened the paper and silently read the words on it as Grunt saw a rat and chased it down a dark passageway. Vivienne let him go, knowing he was easily distracted and would come back on his own.

"My lady, meet me in Room 6 anon. Important," she read aloud.

Suddenly, she thought she saw someone from the corner of her eye. They seemed to be following her. Her head snapped up but when she looked back, the figure had darted into the shadows. She quickly turned around, shoving the paper back into her pouch.

"Grunt! Come here, boy. Where are you, Grunt?" She didn't see the dog anywhere but could hear him barking nearby and knew that he would follow. Her hound knew the way to the sheriff's home and was sure to meet her there. She walked fast, eager to get to safety.

When she turned the corner, she looked back once again. This time she saw the figure dart down a narrow passageway to hide between two buildings. He was obviously trying not to be seen. Vivienne picked up her pace, her heart racing like mad in her chest now. Part of her already regretted turning down the sheriff's offer to escort her to his home. But she had wanted a minute alone to read the note. Besides, it was broad daylight and she was no longer on Rotten Row, so she thought she'd be safe. God's teeth, where was Grunt? Now, because of her impulsive decision, she might end up dead just like poor, dear Fanny.

My lady, those words stuck in her head like a sharp thorn in the sole of her shoe. No one called anyone a lady unless they were a noble! And certainly no one would ever refer to a whore as such. Vivienne got a sinking sensation in her gut, suddenly realizing that if the note had been slipped under their door last night...it might have been meant for her!

"Oh no," she said aloud, thinking of how Fanny had been wearing *her* cloak at the time of her death. If the hood had been covering the whore's head, Fanny could have easily been mistaken for Vivienne. That would mean that Vivienne was the target all along, not Fanny. The note must have been meant for her, a ploy to get her to meet the killer in Room 6 last night. Her breathing became labored. She picked up her pace and now walked at a near run, noticing that the man following her did the same and was never far behind her. Matter of fact, he seemed to be gaining on her, if she wasn't mistaken.

"She was wearing my cloak!" Vivienne wailed aloud, not able to get the image out of her head of poor, dead Fanny with her broken neck and bloodied gown. That could have been her! "Bid the devil, this is not good." Tears formed in Vivienne's eyes as she realized that, because of her, Fanny died when she most likely was never intended to be the victim. It seemed the woman's demise truly was Vivienne's fault.

The sound of the man's footsteps behind her got louder and louder as he gained on her, approaching quickly. She didn't even want to take the time to look back at him, and instead she picked up her skirts and started running. The sheriff's house wasn't far up ahead, but the road was bumpy and uneven and she wasn't wearing her walking shoes. Before she knew it, Vivienne twisted her ankle in one of the deep ruts. "Oh!" she cried out, her arms flailing around in the air as she lost her balance and tried not to fall.

That's when she felt the hold of the man who was stalking her. He had grabbed her from behind, around her waist.

"Nay. Leave me alone! Don't touch me!" She fought against him, trying to get free but to no avail. Then she turned and started pounding her fists against the man's chest, wanting to claw out his eyes. Unfortunately, her hair had become loose and now spilled down in a tangled mess around her face, blocking her from seeing her attacker or anything at all.

"Dammit, Vivienne, stop making a scene," shouted Zachariah, having had to run to catch up to her in time to reach her and keep her from falling when she wrenched her ankle in a rut on the road. Thankfully, he had been able to do so before she landed in the mud. But the wench was acting as if she were afraid of him. Or, more like she wanted to hurt him, since she flailed her arms, trying to punch him, clawing at his face. "Stop hitting me! What is the matter with you?"

"Zachariah?" She stopped hitting him and in a second she was hugging him instead, right there in the middle of the road during broad daylight. "Oh, I'm so glad it's you," she said, making him wonder if she was going to start kissing him next since she seemed so relieved and thankful that it was him. "I thought you were a murderer trying to kill me."

Zachariah heard a dog bark and saw Grunt running down the street toward them.

"Why would you ever think that, my lady?" He brushed the hair out of her bright blue eyes, seeing fear as well as relief in her glassy orbs. Their faces were near each other. So close that it would be easy to lean forward and kiss her dainty lips right now. Vivienne had her arms wrapped around his neck, pulling herself even tighter up against him. God's breath, he could feel her swells pushed up against his hardening body. It only managed to make him desire her even more than he already did. Not wanting anyone to say he was wooing a noblewoman in public, and not allowing himself to be tempted to kiss her, he quickly released her and stepped back. At the same time, he stayed just close enough to catch her again should she possibly start to fall.

"There's no reason to think that anyone is after me. I'm just being silly." She sniffled and wiped away a tear from her cheek with the back of her hand. "I suppose Fanny's death just has me a little spooked, that's all."

Grunt ran over to her and jumped up, putting his front feet on her, probably trying to make sure she wasn't hurt.

"Get down, Grunt," said the sheriff.

"I'm all right, boy, but I wish you would have stayed with me instead of chasing that rat," Vivienne told her hound.

"You should have let me escort you as is proper." Zachariah couldn't tell her this enough.

"Yes, mayhap that would have been a wise idea, you're right." Surprisingly, she agreed instead of saying she didn't need him.

"From now on, I'm not letting you go anywhere alone, Vivienne."

"All right, then. I agree." She flashed him a smile. "Shall we head back over to Rotten Row and start the investigation then? Together?"

Zachariah could do nothing but stand there and stare at her. Something wasn't right with Vivienne. She couldn't seem to make up her mind if she wanted him there or not. One minute she was commanding he leave, and the next she was clinging to him like she never wanted to let him go. Lady Vivienne Harlowe was a complicated woman to even begin to understand. For as long as he'd known her, he sometimes still had trouble figuring out what was going through that pretty little head of hers.

He cleared his throat. "I thought you wanted to go back to my house to wait for me. To check on Cassandra." He could tell she was hiding something from him, and he wasn't about to go anywhere until he discovered just what that was.

"I'm sure Cassandra is fine." She waved her hand dismissingly through the air. "The most important thing right now is to stick together and look for clues to try to discover Fanny's killer." She made a big deal of straightening out her gown and brushing away invisible lint. "I'm sure you agree."

"I see." He looked down at her pouch. "How is your ankle? I saw you twist it. Are you able to walk?"

"It doesn't hurt. I think it'll be just fine." She quickly bent over to pet her dog and then held up her skirts a little and raised her foot in the air, turning it back and forth to show him. "See? My ankle is not swollen, Sheriff. Of course, these shoes might have seen better days," she added with a giggle, showing him the mud caked on them.

"Vivienne, what is written on that scrap of paper?" he asked her outright.

"What paper?" She dropped the hem of her skirt and turned to go. But before she did, she had the audacity to flash him a fake smile, pretending she didn't know to what he referred.

"The paper you don't want me to see. The one hidden in your pouch." That stopped her in her tracks, and she slowly turned to face him.

"Surely I don't know what you mean." When she turned once again to walk away without him, he quickly reached out from behind her, sliding his hand into the top of her open pouch and pulling out the paper that he gripped between two fingers.

When she realized what he'd done, she spun on her heel with her eyes opened wide. "Nay. Give that back to me!" She reached out for it, but he pulled his hand away so she couldn't take it.

"Let's find out what you are hiding from me, shall we?"

"Sheriff, you are acting improperly." She grabbed for it again, but he quickly held it out of her reach a second time.

"*I'm* acting improperly? Hah!" he said, quickly unfolding the paper as he turned away from her to read it.

"You have no right to go into a lady's pouch. What is in there is private and personal."

"I have every right to demand you hand over concealed evidence," he said, reading the words on the paper that said, *My lady, meet me in Room 6 anon. Important.* "Vivienne, where did you get this?" He had the feeling he already knew, but wanted to hear the answer come from her mouth.

"Oh, all right, I'll tell you. I took it from Fanny's hand. She was clutching it like a lifeline, even though she was dead."

Zachariah turned the paper over to see something else written there. "*I have your answer,*" he read aloud.

"What did you say?" Her eyes narrowed and she turned her head slightly.

"It says that here, on the paper." He held it out for her to see.

"It does not say that! I read it earlier, so I know."

"See for yourself if you don't believe me. "*I have your answer,*" he read, pointing at the words as he spoke. "If you had taken the time to read both sides, you would have seen that it indeed does say that."

"Let me take a look." She plucked the note from him, her hands shaking as she read the words, her face turning white like a ghost. "Oh, Zachariah!" Her worried gaze lifted to meet his. "Someone was trying to lure me to Room 6 last night. They have the answer to who it was who wanted my parents killed, don't you see? They must have slipped this note under the door, knowing I was inside and that I'd find it."

"But instead of you, Fanny picked it up, thinking she could have a little fun pretending to be a noblewoman," said Zachariah. "So that's why she donned your cloak and went to Room 6, now we know." He took the paper back from her.

"And then...then she was murdered," said Vivienne with trembling hands. Her eyes rolled back in her head and her knees buckled. Her body swayed and then she swooned.

"Vivienne!" cried Zachariah, catching her in his arms once again. He couldn't help but notice all his neighbors watching him. Watching *them.* Still, he had no choice. She had passed out and now he had to carry her to his home since she couldn't walk. Thankfully, he didn't need to go far to get there.

He made it to his house in a few minutes, carrying Vivienne's limp body in his arms. Her head fell back and her long, loose blonde hair swished back and forth with every step he took.

"Wake up, sweetheart," he said softly, but her body remained still and her eyes stayed closed. At least he could tell by the rise and fall of her chest that she was still breathing. Grunt stayed close at his side, sensing something was wrong with Vivienne.

Walking up the front steps to his home, Zachariah kicked open the door. The force of his action sent the door banging as it smashed against the wall.

"Who's there?" screamed Nairnie, picking up a cleaver and jumping in front of Starah to protect her.

"Put the damned knife down and get out of my way, Nairnie," he growled, bringing Vivienne into the house.

"Is that Lady Vivienne?" came his daughter's voice, peeking around Nairnie's ample hips. "Is she dead now too?"

"Nay, she's not dead, Starah," he told his daughter. "Lady Vivienne just fainted." With Vivienne still in his embrace, he took the stairs two at a time, bringing her up to his own chamber, and gently laying her down atop his bed. Cassandra and Starah bounded up the stairs after him, following him into the room. Grunt was on their heels.

"What's wrong with her?" asked Zachariah's sister, staring down at Vivienne with tears in her eyes.

"I told you, she fainted," he explained, walking over to open the window, hoping the fresh air would awaken her.

"Did Lady Vivienne see another dead body?" asked Starah in fascination. "Is that why she fainted?"

"Nay. That's not it at all," he told his daughter. "Now please go downstairs, Starah."

"Starah, come down here and close the front door and put yer cat away before Grunt chases Midnight through town again," called Nairnie from the bottom of the stairs. Zachariah was glad because he wanted to talk to Cassandra without his daughter being there.

"You heard Nairnie. Go on, now. Watch over Midnight," he told the little girl.

"I'd better help her." Cassandra started toward the door of the bedchamber, but Zachariah stopped her.

"Nay. Wait, Cassandra." He still had the paper in his hand, and held it out to his sister after Starah had left the room. "Lady Vivienne found this clutched in Fanny's hand. You'd better take a look at it."

"What is it?" She curiously came closer and took the paper from him. She read both sides and looked so pale that he wasn't sure she wasn't going to swoon as well. "Oh, my! This is terrible," she cried.

"What's terrible?" asked Nairnie, walking into the room holding a bowl of fresh herbs. There was a pungent scent and he noticed cut onions and garlic in the bowl as well.

"Nothing," he said, quickly taking the paper from Cassandra and shoving it into the pouch at his side. He caught his sister's eye and slightly shook his head, hoping she'd understand to keep this information to herself. The last thing he wanted was for Nairnie or Starah or anyone else to find out that Lady Vivienne's life was in danger. He needed to think things through, and figure out exactly what to do and say. The less people who knew about this right now, the better.

"Nairnie, what is that for?" Cassandra nodded at the heaping bowl of herbs and vegetables.

"The strong scent of the mint and rosemary as well as the

stink from the garlic and cut onions will wake her, I'm sure of it." Nairnie pushed past Cassandra and Zachariah, sitting down on the bed with the bowl in her lap. Grunt jumped up on the other side of Vivienne and laid his chin on her chest. "Wake up, my lady. Wake up, I say." Nairnie used her flattened-out hand to waft the scent of the things in the bowl toward Vivienne. When it didn't work, she moved closer to try it again, shooing away the dog to set the entire bowl atop Vivienne's chest.

"That's not going to work, Nairnie," Zachariah told her.

"Why no'? It's worked in the past," the old woman told him. "I dinna understand it at all."

"I have something that might bring her back." Cassandra reached into her cleavage and pulled out a small glass vial.

Zachariah scowled. "Cassandra, I'd appreciate if you covered up while staying here. Especially around my daughter. And whatever that is, we don't want it, so put it away."

"It's not for you, silly. It's for Vivienne." Cassandra opened the vial and the very strong scent of roses mixed with lavender filled the air. "This is some of my lavender/rose water that I use on myself to drive men crazy."

"Now I know that I really don't want that near her," grumbled Zachariah, not desiring to see anything a whore used being even remotely close to such an angel like Vivienne.

"Just a little goes a long way." Cassandra dipped her finger in the vial and moved closer to Vivienne. She rubbed the liquid under Vivienne's chin, atop her neck and chest, and then a little more right under her nose.

Grunt sniffed it and sneezed.

"What stinks?" asked Starah, walking into the room carrying her cat in her arms. The girl was small and the cat was fat and too big for Starah to be holding without dropping her.

"That stench is no' from my herbs and vegetables." Nairnie fanned at the air and made a face.

"Nay, it's even a worse stench than the onions and garlic," mumbled Zachariah.

"It is not!" retorted Cassandra. "This is very expensive scented water that I had to save up for, and it took a long time to be able to afford it."

"Well, I don't like it." Zachariah wrinkled his nose.

"Me neither," said Nairnie, looking as if she had smelled something rancid and rotten.

"It's not working. That's odd," said Cassandra with a deep sigh, looking down to the open vial in her hand. "I wonder why."

"It probably put her into a deeper sleep," commented Nairnie.

"Enough! Put that away, Cassandra," commanded Zachariah. "Vivienne is a lady and doesn't need to be stinking like a whore."

"That was rude and uncalled for, Zachariah." His sister glared at him now.

"A whore? What's that?" asked Starah, making Zachariah's gut twist. He hadn't meant to say that in front of his young daughter. "Is that like a bastard?" she asked, innocently. "Martin said being a bastard is a good thing, like the Legendary Bastards of the Crown." She spoke about Vivienne's newfound half-brothers. "So, is being a whore a good thing too?"

"Nay, it isn't!" shouted Zachariah. "Now enough talk about whores and bastards. I don't want you to mention either of them again."

"I don't understand," said Starah with a pout, snuggling her nose into her cat's fur.

"Starah, a whore isn't like a bastard, but it is like...a Winchester Goose," said Cassandra, making Zachariah angry that she'd say this to his young daughter. He was about to reprimand his sister when the cat hissed, the dog barked, and all hell broke loose. As usual.

Midnight jumped out of Starah's arms, causing Grunt to dart right over the top of Vivienne to chase the cat. When that happened, the dog knocked into Nairnie and the bowl of herbs and onions dumped all over the top of Vivienne.

"Oh, hell no," shouted Zachariah.

When Nairnie jumped off the bed trying to get away from the dog, she knocked into Cassandra. Cassandra dropped the open vial atop Vivienne, spilling the strong lavender/rose water, soaking the front of Vivienne's gown. The room filled with noise and strong obnoxious odors.

"Everyone out!" yelled Zachariah, pointing his finger at the door. "And take your things and animals with you."

"Zachariah?" came a soft voice from the bed. "What are you yelling about?"

Zachariah spun around to see Vivienne's eyes flickering open.

"Well, the strong smells didna do a thing, but all yer bellowin' seems to have woken her," snorted Nairnie, on her way out the door with the empty bowl under her arm.

"Cassandra, you too," he continued. Starah and the animals had already bounded down the stairs.

"Oh, you're awake, Vivienne," said Cassandra with a smile. His sister corked up the empty vial. "See, Zachariah? I told you my lavender/rose water would do the trick." She slipped the vial back in between her breasts and headed out the door.

"What is all this?" Vivienne pushed up on her elbows, looking down at her wet bodice with the herbs and onions spilled across her chest. "And what is that strong stench?" She sniffed the air and made a face.

"What you're smelling is a combination of the attempted

remedies of an old crone and a silly whore as they tried to wake you after you swooned."

"I fainted?" She blinked a few times and then pushed up to a sitting position in the bed. "I'm sorry."

"You fainted on the street. I had to carry you here. I can't imagine what kind of gossip is going to be spread by that!"

"Oh, Zachariah, I don't care about gossip. Someone is trying to kill me, and for the first time in my life...I am scared." She dangled her legs over the side of the bed, meaning to stand.

"Nay, lie back down," he told her.

"I can't. I need to get back to the castle. To my son and brother."

"My lady, are you all right?" Maleine ran into the room, followed by Wymond.

"We just went out for a walk and heard that the sheriff carried a noblewoman back here and that she was dead." Maleine seemed visibly upset.

"She is not dead," grunted Zachariah, seeing how the gossip was already starting to spread. "Lady Vivienne just fainted."

"You did?" ask Maleine. "Why?"

"Are you ill?" asked Wymond in concern.

"She was frightened because someone meant to kill her last night, instead of my good friend, Fanny." Cassandra stood at the open door with her arms crossed over her chest. She looked angry, irritated and sad all at the same time. She let out a deep breath and quickly wiped away a tear from her cheek.

"All right, that's it!" Zachariah had had enough of this, walking over and helping Vivienne to stand.

"Maleine, tell my aunt and uncle I'll be here investigating Fanny's death," Vivienne told her handmaid. "Be sure to keep Adrian and Martin at the castle since their lives might be in danger too. We don't know yet."

"Oh, my lady, I'm frightened."

"Don't be. I'm here to protect you, Maleine." Wymond wrapped his arms around the girl.

"I am escorting you all back to the castle where you will stay until I have a free moment to investigate this death," instructed Zachariah.

"Nay. I have to go with you," said Vivienne, wrapping her arms around herself. "I feel responsible for Fanny's death and it is the least I can do. To find her killer."

"And put yourself in the killer's path while doing it? I don't think so," said Zachariah, taking her by the arm and heading to the door. "You are going back to Mablethorpe Castle where I know you will be safe under the protection of your uncle."

"You can't make me do that," Vivienne protested.

"I can and I will," he answered. "Even if I have to throw you over my shoulder and walk all the way back to Mablethorpe Castle with you kicking and screaming. I will not let you risk your life, my lady. Not when I know you were the intended target of the murderer all along."

Chapter Five

Vivienne watched the sheriff ride out of the gates of Mablethorpe Castle later, and already she was devising a plan to follow him back to Rotten Row. Wymond had headed back to the stables to work, and Vivienne had sent Maleine along with Grunt to check on Martin and Adrian, just needing to know they were safe.

"What in heaven's name were you thinking by staying the night on Rotten Row?" asked her aunt, who stood with her on the stoop leading into the keep. Creases around her aunt's eyes and worry lines on her forehead seemed to be getting deeper and more pronounced over the years. Lady Mablethorpe was once a happy lady, but didn't seem to smile often anymore. Vivienne wondered if the cause of this was her actions, or mayhap it had something to do with the woman's husband. Or perhaps it was just because of all the bad things they'd had to endure since the murders of Vivienne's parents.

"I was thinking I was doing the sheriff's sister and her friend a favor," Vivienne softly replied. "Zachariah wouldn't take them into his home to give them lodging, and they had nowhere else to go."

"You mean those Winchester Geese who came to the docks on a ship, right? I wouldn't imagine the good sheriff would want to taint his reputation by taking them in, so I cannot blame him. Your uncle was very upset when he saw them. He didn't like you talking with them at all."

"Yes, Aunt Ellen, I am talking about the Winchester Geese. And don't say it in that tone. After all, you know Cassandra well since she is Zachariah's sister. I grew up playing with her and being friends with Zachariah and all his siblings. Mother and Father were friends with their parents too. These people are our allies, so please do not turn your nose up at them."

Aunt Ellen let out a deep, long sigh. "I suppose we can't account for the decisions of others and what they choose to do in their lives."

"I am a perfect example of that." Vivienne smiled, knowing she gave her aunt and uncle their share of worries over the years regarding her own decisions.

"Oh no," said Aunt Ellen looking up and across the court-yard. "Here comes Gilbert now. He is not going to be happy to find out where you've been, not to mention what has happened." Vivienne and the sheriff had mentioned to Aunt Ellen that she really spent the night at an inn on Rotten Row and also that Fanny had been murdered. But besides that, they said nothing more. She didn't want to lie to her uncle, but then again, she was hesitant to tell him where she'd been and whom she was with last night, since he wouldn't take it well. Hadn't her aunt already said he was upset when he noticed the Winchester Geese on the docks and saw her talking to them?

"Uncle Gilbert is just now getting back from his ride?" Vivienne asked in surprise, looking across the courtyard to see her uncle dismount his steed. He took up a conversation with one of the stablehands named Castor. That was something he rarely ever did. Actually, Castor never talked much to anyone and mainly just did his job and kept to himself. He'd always been like that as far back as she could remember since Castor had worked there from the time she was a child. The stablehand was an odd man but a good worker, and she supposed that was all that mattered. Vivienne had tried to befriend him once she started living at the castle permanently, but he didn't seem interested in talking with her and couldn't even look her in the eye.

"Yes, Vivienne, my husband is finally back," said her aunt, sounding sad. "For years now Gilbert's been leaving by himself, and he says he is out riding and thinking, but I can't say I really believe him."

"What do you mean?" she asked, wondering if her aunt also thought he was being unfaithful to her.

"I think he has a mistress," Lady Mablethorpe admitted. "I pretend not to know, and I just look the other way and don't ask questions, but I'm sure it's true."

"Have you confronted Uncle Gilbert about this?"

"Nay. He wouldn't answer my questions even if I did, so why bother? He's become so private and distant over the past seven years that I barely seem to know him anymore."

"It could be something other than a mistress, I'm sure," she said, just trying to console her aunt.

"Nay. It's not. Besides, what else could it be?"

"Oh, I'm sorry, Aunt Ellen, but I have to tell you my thoughts as well." Vivienne could no longer hold back her suspicions. "I think you're right, and I have thought so for a long time now that Uncle Gilbert has taken a mistress. But at least he doesn't bring the mistress here to the castle," she added, trying to find some good in this dire situation.

"Nay, he doesn't do that. Thankfully," her aunt answered.

"Aren't things going well between you and Uncle Gilbert?" Vivienne wanted to console her aunt and felt as if she needed someone to talk to, so she was giving her the chance now.

"Nay. Not really." Her aunt lowered her head and slowly shook it. "Gilbert hasn't been the same ever since my sister's murder." She spoke of her sister Flanie, who was also Vivienne's late mother.

"What do you mean?"

"He's always so angry now. And too rough in bed," explained her aunt, with a blush rising to her cheeks to have divulged such personal information. "Gilbert used to be kind and gentle, but I don't see that side of him anymore. Most of the time he even seems to have forgotten anything that pertains to this family that is important. Or perhaps he just no longer cares," she added sadly, looking down at the ground and shaking her head.

"Mayhap it has something to do with the fact that he thinks he should have been able to protect my parents. He could feel as if he's let you down, as well as me. Just like Zachariah once told me."

Vivienne had noticed the change in her uncle too, but had chosen not to say anything about it for the sake of her aunt. The last thing she wanted was to upset things more at the castle. However, this is something that needed to be discussed, she supposed. "It could be that he no longer cares," she answered with a shrug. "Or, I'm afraid to even say it aloud, but I think he might be starting to...go mad."

"Mad?" Aunt Ellen's head snapped up and her eyes opened wide. "How so, Vivienne?"

"Oh, I'm sure it's nothing. Forget I even said anything." Vivienne waved a hand through the air, seeing that she was only putting more worry in her aunt's head. Already, she regretted mentioning this.

"Nay, you could be right, my dear. Think about it. His mind no longer seems as strong as it used to be. He cannot seem to remember simple things, like the answer to one of his most beloved riddles."

"Aye, I've noticed that as well," said Vivienne, thinking how disappointed her long-lost brother Adrian had been when her uncle didn't remember the riddle games they used to play when Adrian was younger. Then again, it had been seven long, hard years. She supposed stress could muddle anyone's mind. After all, she still had nightmares about the evening her parents were murdered on the road. She wasn't sure that the nightmares were ever going to subside.

Her uncle finally got done talking to the stablehand and started across the courtyard in their direction. Castor slinked away back into the stables. He was a man about her uncle's age or perhaps a little younger. It was hard to tell since the man always wore a hat and kept himself covered as much as possible with the clothes he wore. Vivienne didn't know Castor well because he always kept to himself and didn't have any family as far as she was aware of. She had tried to get to know him over the years but he didn't seem comfortable enough around her to chat. Instead, he always excused himself and left before she could find out more about him.

"Here he comes," said her aunt, speaking of Gilbert. "Now, just let me do the talking and don't say anything to make him upset, dear. We don't want him getting angry again."

"Of course not," said Vivienne, her stomach already clenching, as she expected nothing less than a small explosion of anger about to emerge from her uncle where she was concerned.

"Hello, Gilbert," Vivienne's aunt called out, waving her arm above her head and forcing a fake smile that didn't meet her eyes.

Gilbert didn't pay her much attention, but did give a small

nod in her direction. He then tarried to talk to several of his knights and then the castle steward. Finally, he started up the stairs to the keep. He looked up and stopped in his tracks when he noticed Vivienne standing there.

"Vivienne? What are you doing here?" He almost seemed perplexed by her presence.

"Gilbert, what kind of a thing is that to say?" scolded Lady Mablethorpe. "After all, Vivienne lives here."

"Hello, Uncle," said Vivienne, following her aunt's cue of faking a smile.

"Castor tells me there's been a murder on Rotten Row," growled her uncle in a deep and raspy voice."

"Yes, that's right," said Vivienne, not offering any more information.

"Well, why are you here? I figured you'd be there investigating with the sheriff like always."

"Oh, yes. W-well, I was," stuttered Vivienne. "But I came back to the castle. However, I will be joining the sheriff for the investigation soon."

"What happened? Who exactly was killed and how?" Her uncle demanded to know.

"It's unfortunate, but a Winchester Goose named Fanny was pushed out a window and died from the fall, having a broken neck." Vivienne was surprised that Castor hadn't told her uncle the details. Or mayhap with her uncle's failing mind, he'd been told by the stablehand but on the way to the keep, had already forgotten.

"Egads, what is that awful stench?" Her uncle moved closer to Vivienne, sniffing the air with a screwed up look on his face. "You smell like a whore, Vivienne. Please, don't tell me you were touching the dead body of that dead Goose."

"Gilbert! That is not nice to say our niece stinks," scolded her Aunt Ellen. "Vivienne just must have...spilled something on her gown."

"Can't you smell the stench on her, Ellen?" asked Gilbert. "She smells like she belongs in a brothel."

"Well...yes, you do have a strong odor about you, Vivienne, now that he's mentioned it. I didn't want to say anything because I didn't want to offend you."

"You didn't want to offend her? Hah!" spat Gilbert. "She's the one offending us, walking around stinking like that."

"All right, I'll tell you. If you must know, I fainted when I twisted my ankle on the street in town," Vivienne spoke up, knowing she was going to have to explain sooner or later. "The sheriff carried me to his home and Nairnie tried to wake me with herbs and onions which spilled on my gown." Vivienne figured she'd come right out and tell them rather than to let them hear it from one of the servants, especially since gossip would probably change the entire story around. "Then Cassandra's lavender/rose water spilled on my bodice when Grunt started chasing Midnight."

"Vivienne, please," whispered her aunt, looking as if she didn't want Vivienne to tell her uncle anything more. By the way her uncle's brows were furrowing, there was no doubt he was getting angry.

"What kind of improper things go on at that sheriff's home?" spat her uncle. "We'll never hear the end of the man carrying you through the streets of town! And by the way, how does someone faint from getting a twisted ankle?"

"I suppose I swooned because I was so tired after having been up most the night visiting with Cassandra and Fanny," Vivienne answered.

"You were with the Winchester Geese?" Her uncle's face reddened.

"Yes, Uncle, I was."

"You are a lady, Vivienne, and need to start acting like one. I forbid you to spend time with whores! Had I known they were with you, I would have sent a guard to collect you at once. I knew I never should have let you stay in town, but your aunt said we needed to let you make decisions on your own. Not that you would have listened anyway."

"She's fine and that is all that matters, Gilbert," said her aunt, trying to tamp down her husband's anger.

Zachariah hadn't mentioned to Vivienne's aunt about the note they'd found, because Vivienne wanted to be the one to tell her aunt and uncle that her life was in danger. Then again, she wasn't sure she wanted to tell them now at all. If so, they'd never let her out the castle gates again. Mayhap she'd wait just a little longer. Or at least until after she could help to find Fanny's killer.

"Vivienne, we were looking for you." Vivienne's brother, Adrian, ran up to greet them with Martin and Maleine right behind him. Grunt was with them, and the dog's tongue was hanging out, as if Martin had been throwing a ball for him.

"Mother," said Martin, throwing himself into Vivienne's arms for a hug and then quickly backing away. "Ugh, what's that smell and why is your gown all wet?"

Grunt sneezed from the scent of roses and lavender. Or mayhap it was the garlic and onions, she wasn't sure which, since they were both very smelly.

"It's nothing that a little soap and water can't fix," she told her son with a smile, reaching out to ruffle his blond hair.

"We missed you, Sister," said Adrian. "Especially when we couldn't find you last night."

"Where were you, Mother?" asked Martin.

Vivienne's gaze shot up to her aunt and uncle and then back down to her son. "We'll talk about it later."

"Oh, Adrian," said Gilbert, holding a finger up in the air.

"You said you knew the answer to the riddle I asked you so many years ago."

"What riddle?" asked Martin, petting the dog.

"The one that Uncle Gilbert asked me seven years ago. Before I disappeared," explained Adrian. "It goes like this: What walks on four legs in the morning, two in the afternoon, and three at night."

"That's right," said Gilbert. "And the answer is a monkey."

"What?" Martin looked confused. "A monkey? I don't understand."

"Nay, that's not the answer," said Adrian, with a dissatisfied scowl.

"Sure it is," said Gilbert. "The monkey can walk on all four or on two legs and when he holds a banana, it's like an extra leg. So three. There you go." He held out his hands and shrugged.

"Uncle, that's silly," said Vivienne, starting to wonder if her uncle truly was starting to lose his mind. After all, she knew the right answer since he'd told it to her when she was young, and the answer certainly was not a monkey!

"Nay, a monkey is the correct answer," Gilbert insisted. "I should know, since it was my riddle."

"No, it's not," said Adrian. "The answer is a man. As a baby he crawls on all fours, as a grown man he walks on two legs, and when he is old he uses a cane, so that's three."

"That's right," said Vivienne. "Good job figuring it out, Adrian."

"Thanks, and it only took me seven years to do it," said Adrian, laughing at himself.

"Riddles are stupid and make no sense at all." Gilbert walked away and entered the keep, leaving them all standing there staring at each other in question.

"Maleine can you have the servants bring a hot bath up to my chamber right away?" asked Vivienne, wanting to change the subject quickly. "I think I'd like to get cleaned up before I go out again."

"Yes, my lady, of course. Right away," she answered with a curtsy. Her handmaid took off at a run to carry out her orders.

"You're going out again? I don't like that," complained Martin. "You just got back to the castle. I want you to stay here. Where are you going?"

"She's probably going to town," Adrian answered for her. "Maleine and Wymond said that there was a murder there last night."

"Vivienne, you promised the sheriff you'd stay here at the castle," her aunt subtly reminded her.

"Nay. *You* promised him that, not me," said Vivienne, leaving for a bath and a change of clothes. If she was lucky she could get back to town in enough time to help Zachariah question people about Fanny's murder. She also wanted to check to make sure that Nairnie and Cassandra weren't killing each other.

"Vivienne, I'm coming to town with you." Adrian ran after her as she headed to her chamber.

"No, you're not, Adrian. You stay here and watch over Martin for me."

"He won't have to, since I'm coming too, Mother," said Martin, running after them both. Grunt followed, happily wagging his tail.

"Nay. This is police business." Vivienne stopped and turned to face them both, being higher up on one step. "It's not a game, boys. There is a killer on the loose and I need to help the sheriff find him or her before they strike again."

"Mother, I don't want to lose you after I just found you." Martin hugged her legs from his position on the steps, almost causing her to fall.

"I just found you again too, Sister," said Adrian. "And since I am the man of the family now, it is my job to protect you."

"Nay, it's not."

"Yes, it is," Adrian told her. "Unless I need to remind you, I've saved your life once already and I want to be there to do it again should I ever need to."

"Me too," said Martin, thumping his wooden sword at his side.

Vivienne let out a sigh. "Who said I'll need my life saved?"

"No one told us that," admitted Adrian. "But tell me the truth, Sister. Is your life in danger? Because something gives me the feeling that it might be."

Adrian was growing up so fast. His powers of observation and reading people were very impressive. He had saved her life, that was true. Using their father's sword. Vivienne had no doubt he could do so again if such aid was needed. Adrian was a man now, and no longer the child who had disappeared with the horses and cart on that awful night so long ago. Mayhap she'd be better off to keep Adrian and Martin both in her sight. It actually wouldn't be a bad thing to have someone besides the sheriff watching her back.

"Sheriff Fitch will not like it if I bring you two to town," she told them.

"I'm your escort. He can't say no," remarked her brother.

"And I'm going with you to check on Starah and keep her safe," said Martin, having befriended the sheriff's young daughter, who was the same age as he was.

Grunt sat down on the bottom step and whined, looking up at them with sad eyes.

"I think stubbornness runs in the blood of our entire family," she told them, cocking a half-smile.

"What does that mean?" asked Martin, glancing at her in question.

A huge smile spread over Adrian's face. "It means, she's taking us with her," he told the boy. "Because she knows if she doesn't, we'll only follow her on our own."

"Yes, you two are certainly from the same blood as me," she said, loving how they wanted to protect her. The last thing she wanted was to push them away. Now she just had to figure out what she was going to tell Zachariah when he discovered that she had not followed his orders once again.

Chapter Six

Zachariah set up a table in one of the upstairs rooms at the inn, where he and Isaac would be questioning people about the murder. He was told that this was the same room where Vivienne had spent the night with Cassandra and Fanny. Now he was just waiting for his brother to return.

The door opened and Isaac stood there. Zachariah could see a swarm of people in the corridor behind him. "I've rounded up all I could find. Shall I start bringing them in for questioning?" asked his brother.

"Nay, not yet. Come in first and be sure to close the door."

"It'll be just a minute," Isaac told the crowd.

"But I need to get back to work," complained Orvyn, the proprietor of the Hogg's Head Inn.

"And we need our sleep so we can be fresh for customers tonight," complained one of the whores.

"We'll get to you momentarily, I promise," said Isaac, slamming the door and resting his back upon it. "It's going to get ugly if we don't start questioning them soon, Zachariah. The crowd is already restless."

"We will, but I wanted to take a better look around the room

73

first. That is, before we bring in people to question." Zachariah started poking around in the corners and running his hand over the pallets where the girls had slept. "I can't believe Vivienne stayed here." He clenched his jaw and shook his head in disgust at seeing the used, lumpy pallet covered by old, worn-out blankets.

"I can't believe you're actually touching that pallet, since there is no telling what kind of vermin is lodged in there." Isaac faked a shudder.

"Just hurry up and look around, will you? We need to find clues."

"What exactly are we looking for?" Isaac walked over to inspect the cloak hanging on a hook on the wall.

"Look for anything that seems suspicious or that might give us an idea as to why Fanny went to Room 6 disguised as a noble. Or why someone would want to kill her."

"Like her cloak?" Isaac used two fingers to pick up the whore's cloak that was still hanging there, trying to keep it far away from him. It had a blue-and-gray striped hood, which was the required dress to identify and shame a whore. "I remember seeing Fanny wearing this the day I first saw her on the docks."

"Let me see that." Zachariah walked over and took the cloak from him, checking it for any possible hidden pockets. Sure enough, he found one concealed in the lining. He ripped it open and pulled out a handful of coins.

"Looks like Fanny kept a little money hidden away for emergencies," said Isaac. "Must be from her clients at the stew."

"Her very wealthy clients," said Zachariah opening up his hand to show his brother the several gold coins that were mixed in between the others.

"Are those...gold?" Isaac moved closer and his eyes bugged out at seeing this. Silver was usually what coins were made from, and only the rich had access to gold ones.

"There are quite a few gold florins here," said Zachariah, clinking the coins together in his hand.

"Those must be worth at least, what? Two shillings each?" Isaac leaned in to inspect them.

"Three shillings, or seventy-two pence each, to be precise," came a female voice from behind them.

The men spun around to see the sheriff's sister Cassandra standing in the open doorway.

"Cassandra, what the hell are you doing here?" growled Zachariah.

"I came back to collect Fanny's cloak. And the coins that were in it," said his sister, holding out her open palm.

"You were supposed to stay at my home with Nairnie." Zachariah spoke through gritted teeth.

"That old woman and I don't get along, so I don't want to be there," said his sister with a sniff, still holding out her hand for the coins and the cloak. "Now please give me Fanny's personal things. I know she'd have wanted me to have them."

"Nay. This is evidence," said Zachariah snapping closed his fingers just as Isaac was reaching out to take a coin. "And mayhap you can tell me where the hell a whore would get so many gold florins."

"I'll tell you nothing of the kind." Cassandra looked around the room. "Where is Vivienne? I want to speak with her." She walked over and picked up Fanny's bag of clothes.

"Her name is *Lady* Vivienne," snorted Zachariah, stressing the word *lady*. "You need to use her title since she's a noble. And she is not here. I have her safely tucked away at Mablethorpe Castle where she'll stay until I tell her it is safe to leave. Now put down the bag until I can inspect it."

"This only contains her clothes and jewelry." Cassandra handed it over and Zachariah quickly dug through it. "You won't find anything of interest in there. Fanny was one of the highest paid Winchester Geese, but she was also very frugal. She didn't like to spend money on anything. Except her feathers, her lavender/rose water, and whisky."

"Mayhap so, but I still need to take a look." When all he found were a few pieces of the whore's clothing, a bunch of feathers, and a pair of shoes, he was satisfied they meant nothing, closed up the bag, and handed it back to his sister. "Here. Just please don't wear her things around Starah. Actually, while you are here, I am going to ask Lady Vivienne to bring you some more respectable clothes."

"I can't wear the clothes of nobles and you know it."

"I don't expect you to. But even if she can bring you a tunic and some breeches, it would be better than that!" He nodded at her tight gown with her breasts hiked up and spilling out.

"Oh, Zachariah, I am not going to dress like a man. Don't be silly!"

Zachariah heard the barking of a dog from in the corridor as the crowd rustled and spoke softly amongst themselves.

"Get out of the way. Nobles coming through," he heard a male voice that he recognized as Adrian's.

"Oh hell, no," he groaned.

"Move aside before I hit you with my sword," came the voice of Lady Vivienne's young son Martin. Then, before he could even react, the door swung open completely, and sure enough, Vivienne stood there with a smug look on her face.

"I hope I'm not late for the questioning," said Vivienne. "Oh, hello, Cassandra. I didn't know you'd be here too. So nice to see you again."

"I'm glad someone is happy to see me," said Cassandra, giving Zachariah a dirty look.

"Cassandra is just leaving, and so are you, Lady Vivienne," snapped Zachariah, walking over and taking her by the arm to turn her around.

That's when Grunt ran into the room, almost knocking him over. Adrian followed, holding his sword outright in two hands. Martin ducked under the sheriff's arm and ran into the room followed by another young boy.

"What's going on here?" asked Isaac. "Oh, it's Mouse. How are you, Mouse?" Isaac bent over to talk to the young boy whom they'd found on their last journey. Mouse had been a street rat, thieving with other orphans. With the loss of his older brother, he had no family, and of course, Vivienne saw to bringing him home to Mablethorpe to live with her.

"I'm going to help solve the murder of the dead duck," said the young boy with the dark hair. Mouse and Martin were inseparable lately.

"Hen. Not duck. She was an English Hen," Martin corrected his friend.

"It's actually Winchester Goose," said Adrian with a roll of his eyes. "Get it right."

"Lady Vivienne, these children cannot be here," ground out Zachariah. "What would possess you to bring them to a murder investigation on Rotten Row? And why have you left the castle when you know your life is now in danger?"

"What?" asked Adrian and Martin at the same time.

"Zachariah, is this true?" Isaac wanted to know. "If so, why didn't you say anything about it to me?"

"I meant to, but haven't yet had the chance," he answered.

"Mother, I'll protect you," shouted Martin, pulling his wooden sword from his belt. "Please, don't die."

"I'll protect her, not you," said Adrian, holding up his sword. It was the sword that used to be his and Vivienne's father's weapon, and it now belonged to him. Vivienne decided to take a sword from the armory as hers and give their father's sword to Adrian, now that he was the man of their family. Adrian looked over to Zachariah. "Who is trying to kill my sister?"

"No one said anyone is trying to kill me," Vivienne interrupted, scowling at Zachariah for mentioning this aloud. He now regretted speaking so freely and carelessly. Especially around the children.

"The sheriff just said so," came the small voice of Mouse as he played with Grunt. Grunt barked and jumped up, knocking into Zachariah, causing him to drop one of the coins.

"Lady Vivienne, you need to get them out of here. I have work to do." Zachariah's patience was thinning fast.

"Well, I have work to do, too," she answered. "I liked Fanny, and I will do whatever I can to help find and convict her murderer."

"This looks like one of the coins that Adder used to have," said Mouse, picking up the coin and studying it in his hand.

"Adder had gold coins? From whom did he get them?" asked Vivienne, talking about the bad man who trained orphans to be thieves, that they'd dealt with on their last mission in Whitstable.

"I don't know who the man was. But he always wore a cloak with a hood. And he always gave Adder a gold coin just like this one every time he came to town." Mouse handed the coin back to Zachariah, but before he could take it, Cassandra snatched it away.

"Cassandra, give it to me," warned Zachariah. "I told you, that is evidence at this point so it needs to stay with me for now."

"I need something to live on since I won't be working until I get back home." She slipped the coin in between her trussed up breasts.

"Don't think that is going to stop me. Now hand it over."

"If you want to know who gave the coins to Fanny, then you're going to have to let me keep them." She pulled out the coin and held it up in the air.

Vivienne could see the anger growing in the sheriff's eyes and knew that there was going to be trouble between him and Cassandra. She hadn't wanted to bring the children here, and didn't even know until they approached town that Mouse had followed them. Silently as usual. Like a mouse. She had told Maleine to inform her aunt where she'd be, but had sneaked out of the castle without a guard, not wanting her uncle to know. Not just yet.

"Isaac, take Lady Vivienne and the children back to the castle immediately. I need to speak with my sister in private," instructed Zachariah.

"Me? I'm your deputy." Isaac's hand slapped against his chest. "I can't leave until we're done with our questioning. It's my job to be here to assist you since the constable is away on other business."

"You're not my deputy. You're just in training," said Zachariah. "And Lady Vivienne will be questioning the towns-people with me, now that she's here, so you won't be needed."

"What?" Isaac's head snapped up. "But you just told me to take her back to the castle."

Zachariah shook his head. "Nay. I changed my mind. Take the children only. Lady Vivienne is just going to keep sneaking back to Rotten Row, so I'd rather keep a good eye on her," he said with a sigh.

"Well, I'm not going anywhere," said Adrian. "I'm here as my sister's escort and will stay at her side to protect her."

"Me too," said Martin. "I'm here to protect my mother."

"Really." Zachariah looked over at Mouse. "And what about you, Mouse? What are you here for?"

"I'm here for...to watch over Grunt." Mouse dropped back down to his knees and threw his arms around the hound. Grunt decided to lick the boy's face, making him laugh.

"Martin, I think it might be better if you and Mouse take

Grunt to the sheriff's house and waited for me there," suggested Vivienne. "That way, you can get something to eat from Nairnie and also spend the day with Starah."

"Oh, all right. I'd like to see Starah and Midnight," said Martin.

"I'd like some food," said Mouse, licking his lips.

"All right. We'll go. Come on, Mouse." Martin put his wooden sword back into his belt.

"Wait a minute," said Zachariah, stopping them. "I never said anyone should go to my home, but it might be a good idea for now. But you two are only children. I am not going to let you walk down Rotten Row without an adult."

"Uncle Adrian can take us," said Martin, looking over to Vivienne's brother who was sixteen, taller than Vivienne, and had red hair.

"Nay, I can't," said Adrian. "I'm the man of the family and I'm going to stay at Vivienne's side to protect her." He stubbornly crossed his arms over his chest.

"Adrian, it would be better if you took the boys to the sheriff's house," said Vivienne. "They need to be looked after. I have the sheriff here to protect me. Please, do it and don't cause us any trouble."

"Well, all right. I guess. If you're sure," said Adrian, agreeing to the idea but still not seeming to like it.

"Isaac, you go with them too," said Zachariah. "And wait out in the hall for Cassandra since she will be joining you in a minute as well."

"This is hardly what I'd call the duties of a deputy-in-training," grumbled Isaac. "Come on, boys," he said with an outstretched arm. "Mayhap I can steal a little of Nairnie's cooking while I'm there and when she's not looking, since I am hungry too."

"You're always hungry," said Martin, trailing Adrian out of

the room with the dog and his new friend Mouse right behind him. Isaac followed.

"Now, Cassandra, tell me who gave these coins to Fanny," said Zachariah, once the door had closed.

"I don't know who it was, but the man was a good client of hers," answered the sheriff's sister.

"What did he look like?" asked Vivienne, searching for clues.

"Well, he was tall. And...that's all I really know. Whenever he came to the brothel, he was covered by a cloak and had his hood up. I never saw his face."

"Didn't you ever ask Fanny about this man?" Vivienne asked curiously.

"I did. But Fanny said she was getting paid not only for her services, but also to keep her mouth shut."

"About what?" asked the sheriff.

"I'm not sure," answered Cassandra with a shrug. "I suspect this mysterious man didn't want his identity known. And Fanny was greedy, so I'm sure she didn't want him going to anyone else but her to fulfill his carnal needs. That is probably why she'd been so upset for a while now."

"What do you mean? Upset about what?" asked Vivienne.

"She said her best client stopped coming to her and she was going to do something about it."

"What does that mean?" asked Zachariah.

"I'm not sure," said Cassandra, starting to put the coin in her pouch, but Zachariah cleared his throat and held out his hand.

"You said I could keep the coins if I told you what I know," protested Cassandra, holding tightly to this one.

"Nay, I never agreed to your silly deal. Besides, you said you'd tell me who gave the coins to Fanny and I've yet to get an actual name."

"I told you, I don't know his name."

"Then go back to my house with Isaac and think really hard about it. Mayhap something will come to you. Even if it's not a name, it could be a voice or any other identifying factor of some sort."

"But I don't want to leave. I want to help find Fanny's murderer. Lady Vivienne?" The whore looked over to her for help.

"I'm sorry, Cassandra, but the sheriff is right. That coin is evidence for now."

"And what will I live on?" Cassandra's eyes narrowed as she scowled at her brother.

"I'm giving you room and board, so why do you have need for money?" Zachariah asked her.

"For...other things."

"Such as?" Zachariah looked at his sister and waited.

"Oh, all right." Cassandra slapped the coin into his hand and pulled her cloak tightly around her. Her eyes went to the hook on the wall where Isaac had returned the whore's cloak. "Just don't give Fanny's cloak away. I could use a new one."

"You keep talking like that, little sister, and I'll start suspecting you had something to do with your *good friend's* demise."

"Zachariah, how can you even say such a thing? Fanny was my best friend. I'd never do anything to hurt her."

"Are you sure about that?" he asked, making Vivienne cringe at how insensitive he was being toward his sister right now.

"You were always an ass, Zachariah, and I can see now that nothing has changed. I don't know why I even returned to Mablethorpe in the first place." Cassandra looked as if she were about to cry.

"Neither do I. Why *did* you come back, Cassandra? Were

you really expecting me to welcome you home with open arms?" asked the sheriff.

"Believe me, it wasn't my idea to reconcile with you. It was all Fanny's." Cassandra took Fanny's bag, turned and left the room, closing the door behind her.

"Zachariah, you don't really believe that your own sister had anything to do with Fanny's murder, do you?" asked Vivienne.

"I'm not sure what to think right now," he told her, putting the coins into his pouch and closing it up. "All I know is that in this business, you have to think with you head and not be ruled by your heart. I can never exclude anyone from being a suspect without first knowing all the facts."

"God's eyes, Zachariah! She is your sister. What is the matter with you?"

He slowly looked up to her with sad eyes, looking so forlorn that it almost made Vivienne want to cry.

"Nay, she's not my sister, Vivienne. Not anymore. Cassandra stopped being my sister the day she abandoned me, deciding that instead of staying home with me, she'd rather leave and become a Winchester Goose."

Chapter Seven

"I'll speak with the proprietor next," said Zachariah, opening the door to the room and calling the man inside. They'd been questioning people most of the day, but hadn't had a single real lead yet. There was only the proprietor and a few whores left to talk to. Isaac was out in the hallway, having been sending in people one at a time since he'd returned from delivering the children and Cassandra to Zachariah's home. "Orvyn, we have a few questions we'd like you to answer."

"Why am I being questioned? I didn't do nothing," said the man, coming into the room, being followed inside by Isaac. Orvyn was a tall man and strongly built. He was a little older than Zachariah but didn't have a wife or family. Vivienne figured he used the tavern whores when he needed to find his release.

"Please, have a seat and make yourself comfortable." Vivienne motioned to the stool in front of the small table.

"Fine, but I don't know nothing," the man insisted, plopping his big body down atop the stool, causing the wood to creak.

"Orvyn, where were you last night?" asked Isaac, closing the door and walking over as he spoke. He was taking his turn now and then asking questions.

"This is my inn. I was downstairs in the tavern until closing as is expected," said Orvyn, looking around and tapping his toe on the floor in a nervous manner.

"What about after closing time?" asked Vivienne.

"I was up here. In a room all night with Dulcia and Sigga."

"With *who*?" asked Isaac.

"The whores," said Zachariah, making Vivienne wonder how he knew their names.

"Let me call them in," Isaac offered, hurrying over and opening the door. "Girls, would you like to join me in here?"

"Would we," said one of the whores, as they both walked into the room swaying their hips.

"I hope this won't take long," said the tall girl with the red hair. "I want to wash my hair before tonight's clients. The men like it when I smell like flowers and herbs."

"And I need to get my beauty rest," said the shorter woman with the dark curly hair and lots of curves to her body.

"You both look just fine to me," said Isaac with a big smile, probably hoping to get lucky with one of them or possibly both later tonight.

"Dulcia, your hair is fine, and Sigga, you will have a chance to sleep after you've answered my questions," said the sheriff.

"If the question is if we'll be free later, then the answer is yes. For you only." Dulcia ran her fingers down Zachariah's chest but he pushed her hand away.

"Where were you two last night after closing hours?" continued Zachariah.

Orvyn looked up with a start. "I already told you, Sheriff, they were—"

"Nay! Let them answer." Zachariah held up a halting hand, causing Orvyn to be quiet.

"We were with clients, of course," said Dulcia.

"Which clients? I want names," insisted the sheriff.

"Well, the last one of the night was Orvyn," said Sigga, catching the proprietor's eye. Vivienne couldn't tell if the story was true or if Orvyn had given her a secret signal, warning her to say that.

"*Both* of you were with him?" asked Isaac with wide eyes.

"Yes. Orvyn likes two on one," cooed Dulcia. "I'd bet you would too if you gave it a chance, Sheriff." Once again, Dulcia had her hand on Zachariah's chest. Vivienne was ready to go scratch the whore's eyes out for even touching him.

"I'd be open to the idea," said Isaac with a shrug, but the girls completely ignored him.

"Did either of you hear anything out of the ordinary?" asked Vivienne.

"Like what?" asked Sigga.

"Anyone screaming perhaps?" continued the sheriff.

"Screaming in pleasure or in pain?" asked Dulcia with a giggle. "Because we like both."

"Enough!" Vivienne hurried to the other side of the room and stood in between the randy whore and the sheriff. "I know you didn't like the fact that the Winchester Geese were staying here last night, so just admit it."

"We didn't like the fact you were here either," said Sigga with her upper lip snarled. "This is our territory and we don't share it with Geese or noblewomen."

"So it made you angry, did it?" asked Zachariah.

"Of course it did." Dulcia crossed her arms over her ample breasts. "Orvyn never should have given them a room." She glared daggers from her eyes at the proprietor.

"Lady Vivienne offered me good money that I couldn't refuse," said Orvyn in his defense.

"But you let the Geese in here too," complained Sigga, her

hands waving wildly through the air. "The one was making eyes at some of our clients down in the tavern, I saw her. We didn't like that at all."

"Which one?" asked Vivienne.

"The dead one," said Sigga.

"So, did it make you angry enough to want to kill her?" asked the sheriff.

"What?" Dulcia's painted-on brows arched. "We didn't kill the hussy if that's what you mean, Sheriff. We make love, not war. You should know that by now."

"Should he?" asked Vivienne, looking over at Zachariah, not able to stop herself from wondering if he'd ever spent the night with either of these whores. He didn't look up or even meet her eye.

"They were with me all night, like I told you, Sheriff," said Orvyn. "Can we please go now? There is so much to be done."

"Go on," said Zachariah, nodding at the door.

Before they walked out the door, Vivienne stopped them. "Which men?" she asked.

"What?" asked Sigga.

"Which men were Fanny, the Winchester Goose, making eyes at in the tavern?"

"What's it to you?" Dulcia looked down her nose at Vivienne. "Hopin' to get lucky, mayhap?"

"Stop it! Have respect for a noble," warned Zachariah. "Now tell Lady Vivienne what she wants to know. It could help clear your names, so do it," he commanded.

Dulcia and Sigga exchanged looks between them and Orvyn slowly nodded as if giving them permission to speak.

"It was two men in general," said Dulcia. "One of them was cloaked and wearing a hood so I'm not sure who he was. I've never seen him in here before. Or at least I don't think so, since I couldn't tell for sure."

"We did recognize the other one since he is a regular here," added Sigga.

"Who was he? I want a name," said Zachariah.

"It was that stablehand from the castle," Sigga spoke up.

"Which stablehand?" asked Vivienne, her heart racing, hoping the woman wouldn't say it was Wymond. The last thing she'd want to know was that Wymond occupied a place like this and possibly enjoyed the tricks of whores. Not when the boy seemed so devoted to Maleine. Vivienne didn't want anyone to ever hurt her handmaid.

"His name is Castor," Orvyn supplied the information. "He is an odd man and doesn't speak much, but the girls like him."

"We don't like him," said Dulcia, wrinkling her nose. "He is obnoxious and smelly and wants to do odd things all the time."

"Then why do you service him?" asked the sheriff.

"He is a paying customer," Dulcia continued. "Isn't that reason enough?"

"And last night he paid very well indeed." Sigga pulled a gold coin out from between her breasts and held it up with a smile.

"Did you get that from the stinky cur?" asked Dulcia, with an edge to her voice.

"I certainly did," answered Sigga proudly.

"He likes what I do a lot better than your pathetic routine. Why would he pay you a gold coin?" Dulcia was furiously jealous about this.

"Well, mayhap you're not really as good as you think after all, and he tired of you," Sigga snapped at her friend.

"Did you take him to an upstairs room last night, Sigga?" asked Zachariah.

"I did. But when we got there he didn't want to do anything with me other than talk," Sigga told the sheriff.

"Because you're not good in bed like I am," said Dulcia, hiking up her breasts. Sigga glared at her friend for that remark.

"Talk? About what?" asked Vivienne.

"Nothing in particular, really. That I can recall, anyway," said Sigga.

"Sigga, you need to tell us everything if you don't want to be a suspect," the sheriff warned her.

"All right," said the girl, with a puff of air from her mouth. "If you must know, he was very interested in Lady Vivienne and the Winchester Geese that he heard were staying the night at the inn. He seemed especially interested in the one who died."

"You mean Fanny. The woman who was pushed out the window?" asked Vivienne.

"Yes, that Winchester Goose who died," she confirmed. "He was asking why she was here in Mablethorpe, but I told him I didn't know."

"What else did he want to know?" asked the sheriff.

"He kept asking if I'd spoken to her and what she said, but I hadn't so I couldn't give him answers." She shrugged. "Oh, he did ask which room they were staying in," said the whore. "I was tempted to lie to him since I figured he wanted a romp with Fanny, but when he pulled out the gold coin and I saw it, I didn't care and so I told him."

"Then what did he do?" asked Isaac.

"Well, once I told him, he didn't seem interested in me any longer and just up and left. But not before telling me he wanted the room we were in to remain empty all night long and that the gold coin should be more than enough to pay for it." She held up the gold coin once again and kissed it.

"Was that room number 6 by any chance?" asked Vivienne.

"It was. Lucky number 6," said the girl, still staring at the coin.

"That coin should be mine," whispered Dulcia, throwing Sigga a dirty look now.

"Thank you, that'll be all for now," Zachariah dismissed them.

"It's about time," grumbled Orvyn, getting up and leading the whores to the door.

Isaac held the door until they left, watching the whores shake their hips before he closed the door behind them.

"Shall I find more people for questioning?" asked Isaac.

"Nay," the sheriff answered, taking Fanny's cloak from the hook. "I want you to take another look around the place where we found the body, then check in with the coroner to see if he's discovered anything that we might have missed."

"And where will you be?" asked Isaac.

"We have to leave."

"Leave? But I just got here. Where are we going?" asked Vivienne.

"We're going to Mablethorpe Castle to question a stable-hand that I can almost guarantee had something to do with Fanny's murder."

"Zachariah, mayhap we should have brought the children back to the castle with us since it will be dark soon," Vivienne told the sheriff as they approached the castle, both riding atop his horse since she had walked to town with the children, and left her horse in the castle's stable. She was sitting in front and he had his arm around her to keep her from falling since she was riding sidesaddle.

"Nay. I'd rather they stay out of the way for now," he explained. "We need to focus on this investigation. We'll go back and collect them later."

"I see," she said, wondering how to initiate a conversation about him and his sister without causing him to become angry again. "I think we need to talk with Cassandra when we go back to town."

"Cassandra? Nay. Whatever for?"

"To find out more about Fanny, of course. She could be very helpful to us since she knew Fanny the best. Regarding this investigation, she could prove to be a very valuable asset."

"I don't think so. Cassandra is not needed," was his reply as they rode through the castle's gates.

"Oh no. I see my aunt and uncle."

"What's wrong with that?"

"I...might not have exactly told my uncle where I was going. Or where I really spent the night when I was on Rotten Row. However, my aunt knows."

"Vivienne, you didn't lie to Lord Mablethorpe, did you? I'd better tell him the truth."

"Nay, wait!" She turned so suddenly that she almost fell from the horse and he grabbed her and held her tightly up against his body. She liked the feeling of him holding her like this. His body heat emanated onto her and it was so intimate, making her feel safe and secure in his arms. Vivienne also noticed that she could feel the very rapid beating of Zachariah's heart. "Sheriff, your heart is racing. Why is that? Does it have something to do with...me, by any chance?" She looked up, their faces close together. Would this be the time he admitted his true feelings for her? And if so, how was she supposed to react? Should she admit that she had feelings for him as well or just play coy?

"Of course, it has everything to do with you, my lady."

"It does?" Excitement fluttered in her belly. So she was right. He was having feelings for her like she was having for him lately.

"You just gave me a scare by almost falling from my horse. That would cause anyone's heart to speed up. I'm just thankful you didn't break your neck."

Her excitement drained quickly when she heard him refer to a broken neck. She couldn't get the image of poor dead Fanny out of her mind. "Yes. Of course. That's why," she said, turning and trying to face forward, feeling silly now to have thought there was really anything intimate brewing between them at all.

"Lord and Lady Mablethorpe," said Zachariah with a nod, riding right up to her aunt and uncle.

"Sheriff? Vivienne?" Her uncle's look was not one of approval. "What are you two doing together? And on the same horse no less."

Zachariah hopped off the horse and reached up to help her to dismount. She saw Wymond running from the stable to take the reins. Castor stayed in the stable, but looked on from the shadows.

"Lord and Lady Mablethorpe, I am here on official business regarding the murder on Rotten Row." Zachariah handed the reins over to Wymond.

"Aunt Ellen. Uncle Gilbert." Vivienne smiled and nodded to acknowledge them. "I am helping the sheriff investigate the murder of Fanny."

"Not that Winchester Goose again!" snapped her uncle. "Vivienne, I told you I don't want you associating with whores."

"Uncle! Fanny is dead," she blatantly pointed out. "Please have some respect for those deceased, no matter who they were."

"There were two of them, weren't there?" her uncle continued.

"Yes, that's right," she answered. "Her name is Cassandra."

"Please don't tell me you have anything to do with that bawdy strumpet who was most likely raised by a harlot as well!"

"Uncle!" gasped Vivienne. "What are you saying?"

"Gilbert, you are speaking about the sheriff's sister and referring to his mother, too," said Aunt Ellen in a hushed but firm tone. "What is the matter with you?"

"Lord Mablethorpe, I can assure you that my sister, Cassandra, was not raised by a whore," said Zachariah. A throbbing could be seen from a vein in his neck. "And while I do not condone Cassandra's profession, she is still my sister and she will be staying with me until she returns to The Liberty of the Clink. Now if you'll be kind enough to allow me to call for your stablehand, I have questions for him."

"Well, there he is," said Lord Mablethorpe, nodding to Wymond. "Go ahead and ask him whatever you want."

"Nay, not Wymond, Uncle," Vivienne corrected him. "We need to talk to Castor."

Her uncle's head snapped up. "Castor? Why?"

"He was seen in the Hogg's Head Inn last night, and I need to question him about the murder," Zachariah informed him.

"Castor rarely leaves the grounds and usually only at my request," said Lord Mablethorpe. "You must be mistaken about having seen him in the tavern. I'm sure he was here inside the castle gates at the time of the murder."

"Gilbert, do you know that for certain?" asked his wife. "Perhaps he left without you knowing it. Let the sheriff and Vivienne do their job."

"Hrmph," sniffed Lord Mablethorpe. "It's not Vivienne's job at all, even if she thinks so."

"Yes, it is, dear," said his wife. "You remember that she helps the sheriff investigate murders now. Don't you?" Aunt Ellen put her hand on her husband's arm but Gilbert pulled it away abruptly.

"Do whatever you want. Vivienne will anyway," he said, his

hands flying in the air at his last comment. He turned on his heel and left in a huff, heading for the keep.

"Sheriff, I'm so sorry about my husband's improper behavior," apologized Lady Mablethorpe. "He just hasn't been himself lately. I don't think he is feeling well. Go ahead and question whomever you want, you have my permission. Now if you'll pardon me, I need to see to my husband."

"Of course, my lady," said the sheriff with a bow, as Lady Mablethorpe turned and left.

"Castor is in the stables," announced Wymond.

"Yes, I saw him watching us from the shadows," said Vivienne.

"Good. We'll speak to him there then." Zachariah turned to go. Vivienne put her hand on his arm to stop him as Wymond left to put the sheriff's horse in a stall.

"Zachariah, I'm sorry about what my uncle said. I'm sure he didn't really mean anything by it. He was just angry and started spouting off nonsense, not thinking."

"It sure sounded like he meant it when he called my sister a whore and my mother a strumpet. One might be true, but certainly not the other." Zachariah started to walk to the stables and she kept pace with him.

"You know as well as I that my aunt and uncle were good friends with your parents."

"It certainly doesn't seem that way now."

"Uncle Gilbert is just not himself lately, like my aunt said. As a matter of fact, Aunt Ellen seems to think he is going mad and I tend to agree with her."

"What?" Zachariah stopped and turned to face her. "Lord Mablethorpe is going crazy?"

Vivienne sadly nodded. "You must have realized for yourself that his demeanor is not the same as it used to be."

"I have. But I just thought it was because he blames himself for your parents being killed and that he wasn't able to do anything to stop it."

"I think it's more than that," she told him. "I have noticed for a while now that my uncle leaves on long rides by himself in the early morning hours."

"Why? Where does he go?" They continued walking toward the stables as they spoke.

"I believe he has a mistress. My aunt verified that my assumption is probably true."

"I'm not even sure who would want him," he told her, not sounding at all remorseful to hear the news. "Your aunt certainly doesn't deserve that kind of treatment at all. Your uncle is being a true bastard, Vivienne."

"Bastard? Did you have to use that word?" she asked, since everyone now knew that she was the bastard of King Edward III.

"Oh, I'm sorry, Vivienne." He stopped and turned toward her, gently reaching out to cup her cheek. "You know I never meant anything derogative toward you. I could never intentionally hurt you. I spoke out of turn as well. Anger makes one do and say things that they don't really mean."

"I know," she said, giving him a quick flash of a smile. The warmth of his hand against her face felt good. Too damned good for someone who might not really have true intimate feelings for her. If not, then why did he have to be so gentle and caring by his endearing touch? Their eyes met and interlocked, and for a moment, time stood still. Why did she feel as if she could see right through to his very soul? Zachariah usually guarded his feelings by putting up walls. Right now, she didn't see a wall at all. Only the love coming from him that he had seemed so hard to try to hide. His gaze traveled down to her lips and for one quick second she believed he might actually kiss her. It would be risky and not a smart thing to do out in the open, but she wasn't going to be the one to stop him since it is actually what she craved.

Sadly, that didn't happen. Instead, he removed his hand quickly and fidgeted with his weapon belt, continuing to walk to the stables, acting like that quick intimate moment between them had never happened.

When they got to the stables, Wymond was talking to Castor and looked up and pointed at them.

"Castor? We'd like to have a word with you," said the sheriff, heading inside with Vivienne right on his heels.

"Me? Why?" The stablehand took a few steps backward as if he were scared or possibly about to run.

"Where were you last night?" asked the sheriff.

"I was in the stables. Like always," said the man.

"Nay, not the entire night," said Wymond. "I looked for you after dark but couldn't find you anywhere."

"I tend to sleep covered up in the hay, so I'm not always seen," said Castor, shifting his weight from one foot to the other and staring at the ground.

"Were you on Rotten Row last night?" Vivienne asked him directly.

Castor's face reddened. "I don't know who said I was in the Hogg's Head Inn, but it's a lie I tell you."

"We never mentioned the Hogg's Head Inn," said Vivienne with a sly smile. "But since you just did, you more or less admitted your guilt."

"So when is it a crime to get a drink at the tavern?" asked Castor. "You can't arrest me for that."

"No one said we are going to arrest you," the sheriff assured him. "Or at least, not unless we feel you had something to do with Fanny's murder."

"I didn't even know the whore, I swear. I tell you, I didn't kill her."

"Why did you ask the local strumpet about me and my friends and what room we were staying in last night?" Vivienne blurted out.

"I only did it because I was paid to find out."

"Paid? Who paid you?" Wymond asked, and Vivienne gave him a shake of her head and held her finger to her mouth to warn him to stay quiet.

"Yes, who was it that paid you?" asked Zachariah.

"I don't know who he was. A man in a cloak. I was having a drink and he approached me and asked me to befriend the whore and find out what he wanted to know."

"What did he look like?" asked Vivienne.

"I couldn't tell you. He was hidden under his hood and cloak. He gave me a gold florin and told me the second gold florin was for the whore to keep a room open and unoccupied all night long."

"And of course he asked you to report that room number to him too," said the sheriff.

"Yes." Castor kicked at the straw. "I didn't see any harm in it. And I really needed the money. I've never had a gold florin before."

"You should have told us about this right away," the sheriff continued. "By holding back the information, you could be held responsible for being an accomplice to the crime."

"But I didn't know what the man wanted the information for, I swear," said Castor. "Please, you've got to believe me. I am innocent regarding the death of the Winchester Goose."

"Can you remember anything else about this mysterious man in the cloak?" asked the sheriff. "Like the way he walked, or how he spoke or maybe a smell about him?"

"Nay. I was drinking in a noisy tavern. I didn't notice anything," Castor insisted.

"All right, that is all for now," said Zachariah. "But if you remember anything about the mysterious stranger, please tell me or Lady Vivienne at once."

"Of course. Can I go now? I have work to do and Lord Mablethorpe will have my head if it's not done."

"Yes," said Zachariah, but Vivienne wasn't yet satisfied with Castor's confession.

"Wait," she told him. "What were you talking with Lord Mablethorpe about when he just returned?"

"My lady?" He looked up but didn't say a word.

"Tell her," said Zachariah. "And we'll know if you're lying."

"He just instructed me to tend to his horse," said the man, but Vivienne could tell it wasn't the truth.

"Where did my uncle go this morning?" She continued with her questions.

"He doesn't tell me that," said Castor. "I am just a simple stablehand. I saddle and ready his horse for him when he calls for it, and that is all."

"Then you don't know where he goes when he leaves in the mornings to go riding?"

"He is a noble and I am a servant, my lady. I am not privy to that information, and neither do I want to be. I do my job without asking questions since it wouldn't be proper to ask a noble such personal information."

"Nay, I suppose it would not," she said, realizing they were not going to get any more information or confessions out of Castor today. This was the most the man had ever spoken to her, and she was surprised they got as much information as they did.

"My lady, there you are." Maleine hurried into the stables, stopping when she saw Wymond. "Hello, Wymond," she said, her face lighting up in a blush. She turned suddenly shy.

"Hello, Maleine. Are Snuff and Chomp giving you any trouble?" Wymond asked about his ferrets that were recently used to hunt rats when Wymond worked for the Pied Piper.

"Nay, Chomp and Snuff have been so good that I let them out of their cage for a while to explore the room."

"Maleine, did you take the ferrets to our chamber?" asked Vivienne.

"Yes, my lady. I hope you don't mind. But they were almost getting trampled by the horses in the stable so I told Wymond I'd help him out."

Wymond chimed in. "They need to roam, and can't really do that in the stable unless there aren't many horses here. They tend to spook the horses, my lady. And when that happens, the ferrets could end up underfoot and that's dangerous for them, as Maleine said. "

"I understand. Just don't let Lord Mablethorpe know there are ferrets inside the castle," Vivienne told them, knowing she couldn't be mad at them for only wanting to protect Snuff and Chomp.

"Yes, my lady," both Wymond and Maleine answered together.

"You were looking for me, Maleine?" Vivienne got back to the matter at hand.

"Yes, Lady Vivienne," her handmaid answered, with a slight curtsy out of respect. "Cook and Maria really want to be married, since Maria is getting heavier with their child. I told her I'd speak to you about possibly asking permission from Lord Mablethorpe, since they are afraid to do it themselves."

"Why are they afraid to talk to him?" asked Zachariah.

"Sheriff, if you don't remember, my uncle doesn't have much love for the two since the day his good friend, Lord Gainsborough, was found murdered inside the keep."

Zachariah nodded. "Oh, yes. I understand. Lady Vivienne, we need to go back to town. I want to have another look around the murder site before we pick up the children and return them to the castle."

"Of course," said Vivienne. "Maleine, tell Cook and Maria that they will have their wedding and I will plan it personally."

"Oh, thank you, my lady. They'll be so elated to hear that." Maleine curtsied. "They will be so excited to finally have permission to marry." She ran off but not before waggling her fingers at Wymond in a playful and flirtatious manner.

Wymond smiled at Maleine and slowly raised a hand and waved back, but then quickly lowered it again and cleared his throat.

"My lady, do you think it is wise to give permission and even plan the wedding without first consulting your uncle about this?" Zachariah looked truly concerned.

"I'll handle it. I'm not worried. Now, let's get back to town because it'll be dark soon. Wymond will you please saddle my horse for me?" She didn't want to ride double with Zachariah again since she would be in his arms and wasn't sure that is what she wanted. If she had feelings for the sheriff and he didn't reciprocate those feelings, then it was wiser for her to keep her distance. At least for now. She didn't have any regrets about that. Or did she?

Chapter Eight

Vivienne saw Zachariah look down into the horse trough, thinking that he must have seen something thru the semi-murky water, lit up by the last rays of the setting sun. Dipping in his hand, he dug around and pulled something out.

"Did you find something?" asked Vivienne, joining him.

"I'm not sure." Looking at the object in his hand, she realized it was a pair of wooden dice used for gambling and playing games. "It's just some dice."

"Do you think it's a clue?" asked Vivienne. "After all, anyone from the tavern could have accidentally dropped it in there."

"True. But I'll keep it just in case." He shoved it into his pouch.

"Zachariah." Isaac met them at the trough. "I found out a few things since you've been gone."

"Good job," said the sheriff. "What did you learn?"

"It seems a few people did see the man in the cloak, but no one could identify him or say what happened to him either. He just sort of disappeared. However, I learned that Torsten was drinking in the tavern last night and he was well in his cups and pinching the whores on their bottom ends. And he followed one of them upstairs as well."

"Torsten? The coroner's scribe?" asked Vivienne. "I don't see him as the killer type at all."

"Never dismiss someone as a suspect, no matter how crazy it seems to suspect them," said Zachariah. "That's rule number one in my business. And you should know that from some of our past investigations."

"You're right," she answered.

"It would make sense," said Isaac.

"How so?" asked Vivienne.

"Well, the Goose had a written note in her hand, right?"

"And Torsten is a scribe and would have pen, paper, and ink on him at all times," said Vivienne with a nod, seeing what Isaac meant.

"That's true," agreed Zachariah. "Most men wouldn't be walking around with the means to write a note. Especially since in town, there are not many who can even read or write to begin with. These are just commoners and not learned people."

"Yes. Just some of the proprietors, the merchants, and visiting nobles mainly are the only ones who can read and write," said Isaac.

"Now that you mention that, it does make sense." Vivienne had been too distracted to even figure this out herself and felt embarrassed that it had slipped right past her. "The commoners don't have these skills. The only reason why Fanny could read is because Cassandra taught her. Anyway, the murderer must be someone who is learned."

"Or it could be that the killer hired someone to write that note for him," said Isaac.

"Good job once again, Brother." Zachariah slapped Isaac on the back. "You are really starting to do well in your training."

"Are we going back into the tavern to question some more people?" Isaac seemed tired and not really eager to do so.

"Nay." Zachariah looked up at the setting sun, narrowing his eyes. "It is time to head back home."

"Actually, I was hoping you'd say that." Isaac had his horse as well, and quickly mounted. "I saw Nairnie whipping up a thick stew earlier, and my mouth is salivating just thinking about eating it."

"Lady Vivienne, won't you and the children join us for a meal?" asked the sheriff.

"Oh, I'm not sure Nairnie will have enough food for all of us," said Vivienne, not sure she wanted to be spending yet more time with Zachariah. As much as she longed to be close to him, it would only make it harder to watch him and his family and know that she could never be a part of it. She was a noble and he was a commoner. They didn't belong together. He knew it, and so did she. It was probably why he always had his walls up while around her.

"Nairnie said she made a double batch since there were so many in the house and because...because I eat so much," Isaac admitted under his breath.

"Then there is no reason not to join us. My lady?" Zachariah held out his hands to help her mount her steed. Not wanting to feel the warmth of his touch again, she quickly mounted her horse on her own.

"We'll just have a quick bite to eat and then I'll take Adrian, Martin, Mouse, and Grunt back to the castle."

"You mean, *I'll* take you back," said Zachariah, pulling himself up into his saddle. "Now that your life has been threatened, don't think you're ever getting out of my sight again until we catch and imprison Fanny's killer."

"Whatever you say," she told him, feeling her heartbeat picking up. Was it because he'd just reminded her that her life was in danger? Or was it because he said he wasn't going to let her out of his sight? Either way, this was never going to work. Seeing so much of Zachariah was only going to tempt her to want to kiss him the way he'd kissed her when she was passed out once before. Even if he refused to admit to her that he had done so. "Keep focused on the case," she muttered to herself, trying to push any other thoughts from her head.

"What did you say, my lady?" Zachariah rode up next to her, looking handsome, back-lit by the setting sun.

"Nothing."

"Oh, I thought you were telling yourself to keep focused on the case. Is there something that is distracting you?" He smiled in a way that made her think he could read her mind. "Something to do with...me?"

"Nay," she blurted out. "Nothing to do with you. I was just distracted thinking about planning the wedding for Cook and Maria. And wondering what I'm going to say to my uncle to convince him to let me go ahead with my plan."

"Oh. The wedding," he said, the words almost seeming to upset him. "Yes. Cook and Maria will be very happy together, I'm sure."

"Yes. I agree." She didn't know what else to say.

"They've known each other for a long time, haven't they?"

"They have. But not nearly as long as we've known each other. I mean, we've been friends since childhood."

"Yes. Yes, we have." His eyes were on her again, and she swore they were sultry. He paused for a moment before responding further. "They are a good match, Maria and Cook. Both of them the same status and all."

She paused now before answering. "Even if they weren't of the same status, it wouldn't matter, since they are so much in love."

He looked at her from the side of his eye and swallowed

deeply. She'd give anything at that moment just to read his thoughts. "I'll race you to the house," he said, surprising her, since that is the last thing she thought he was thinking. He kicked his heels into his steed, just like when they used to race their ponies as children. He passed up Isaac, taking him by surprise.

"Whoa, what's the hurry?" ground out Isaac with a jerk.

"Don't think you can beat me, because you know I will always win, Zachariah Fitch." Vivienne took off like an arrow being shot from a bow, causing Isaac to pull his horse to the side so he wouldn't get run over.

"You two need to grow up!" Isaac shouted after them.

"Now what's the fun in that?" Vivienne yelled back over her shoulder, feeling so alive and happy. She was actually living a memory of the past and in the present, all rolled in one. Just sadly, not one of the future.

~

"Eat up, lassie," said Nairnie later, as they were all joined around the sheriff's table having a meal together. "Ye've barely had two bites. Dinna ye like my stew?" Nairnie ladled more stew into Vivienne's nearly full bowl.

"Oh, it's wonderful, really it is, Nairnie. I'm just not that hungry today, I guess."

"Why not? We've worked up a powerful hunger with the investigation." Zachariah reached across Vivienne to grab a slice of crusty bread from the platter on the table. When he did, he caught the scent of rose water wafting from her silky blonde hair. Damn, she smelled good. He felt an undeniable attraction to her and now regretted sitting next to her at the table. Her presence was more tempting to him than even the apple cinnamon pie that Nairnie had cooling on the windowsill.

"I just...miss Fanny," said Vivienne, reaching down to pet Grunt who had wedged his way between them under the table. When she petted the dog, her hand brushed against Zachariah's leg, causing his heart to jump for some reason.

"I miss her, too," said Cassandra, who was sitting across from Vivienne. "Zachariah, did you bring me her cloak like I asked you to do?"

"We have it, but it's still evidence so you can't have it," Isaac answered for him, reaching out for more bread and getting a nasty look from Nairnie.

"Isaac! Let the children have more first," spat Nairnie.

"Nairnie, there is plenty of bread, so what's the difference if I have more?" complained Isaac.

"Dinna make me get my ladle out of the stew to use it on ye, because ye ken I will." Her hands went to her hips which meant she wasn't fooling around but meant business.

"Fine. Just a small piece then." Isaac took the bread and looked over at his sister next to him. "Did you want more bread, Cassandra?"

"It's no' for strumpets," sniffed Nairnie, picking up the tray of bread and putting it at the other end of the table with the children. Zachariah understood how Nairnie felt, but still she shouldn't be so crude since Cassandra was his sister. He almost felt sorry for Cassandra.

"Mother, can we spend the night here?" asked Martin. "I like it here better than at the castle."

"So do I," said Mouse, eating a piece of cheese. "Nairnie is a better cook than Cook."

"Why, thank ye, child," said Nairnie with a chuckle, reaching down and ruffling the boy's hair. "Ye boys remind me of my great-grandsons."

"You have great-grandchildren?" asked Adrian.

"I do," said Nairnie. I have ten in all. Five girls and five boys. And that's no' countin' future ones."

"My, that is a lot of great-grandchildren," said Vivienne. "You are lucky to have such a large family."

"Why aren't you with them?" asked Adrian. "I know if my great-grandmother were still alive, I'd want to spend all my time with her."

"Aye, I do miss them dearly." Nairnie let out a sigh and settled her round rump atop the bench, squeezing in next to Starah.

"Nairnie, any time you want to go back home, you're free to do so," said Zachariah, giving her permission to leave and not feel guilty about it.

"Are ye tryin' to get rid of me, Sheriff?" The old woman squinted one eye and he realized he'd offended her somehow. "If ye dinna want me here, then just say so and I'll go."

"Nay, that's not the case at all," said Zachariah. "We love having you here, Nairnie."

"I love your cooking," said Isaac, taking a huge spoonful of stew into his mouth.

Zachariah continued to try to smooth things over with Nairnie. "I just know how important family is, and realize that you've been away from yours for a long time now. I figure you'd be eager to get back home."

"I miss Bear," said Martin. "When is he coming back?"

"He's no'," said Nairnie softly.

Grunt whined, almost as if he were saying he missed the man too, since Bear had always given the dog more food than anyone.

"I miss Bear, too, and all the pirates," said Starah. "Father, can we go sailing on Bear's boat again soon?"

"It's a ship, no' a boat," Nairnie corrected the sheriff's

daughter. "And they are ex-pirates. Bear willna be comin' back, so there will be no more rides, I'm afraid."

"Who is Bear and these pirates you speak of?" asked Cassandra.

"Bear is Nairnie's husband. He sails a ship for the King," Vivienne explained. "His work keeps him away for long periods of time."

"I heard that the King is your birth father," said Cassandra. "If that is true, can't you ask the King to let Bear stay with his wife more often? I mean, Edward is your father so you should have some influence on him."

"Nay! I dinna want to be with Bear. It's over between us, so just hush, all of ye." Nairnie jumped up and started collecting the dirty dishes. "I dinna want to hear anyone talkin' about Bear or my family again. A damned whore has been murdered and we should all be focusin' on her and findin' her killer. Just forget about me, it's no' important," said Nairnie. Zachariah knew the old woman was trying to act strong and like it didn't bother her to be away from Bear and her grandchildren and great-grandchildren, but he could see the loneliness in her eyes and hear the hurt in her voice as well. It was starting to take a toll on her and even making her sharp and ornery. At least, more so than usual.

"Cook and Maria are to be married," Vivienne announced, obviously trying to change the subject as well as the mood in the room.

"Who are they?" asked Cassandra.

"They work in the castle kitchen," Vivienne explained.

"Maria is pregnant," added Zachariah.

"Oh, that sounds so nice." Cassandra had a dreamy look in her eyes as she pushed her food around in the bowl.

"What did you say?" Zachariah felt confused to hear his sister say that.

"I hope someday I can get married and have children, too."

She smiled at Mouse sitting next to her, placing her hand over his, atop the table. Mouse looked up and smiled back.

"I hope someday I'll have a mother and father again," he told her. "Do you want to be my mother, Cassandra?"

"Oh, my!" exclaimed Cassandra with tears in her eyes. Her hand slipped away from the boy's. "I wish I could, but you don't want someone like me for your mother."

"I'll say," mumbled Zachariah, getting a kick in the leg under the table from Vivienne.

"Why not?" asked Mouse. "You seem like you're really nice. And I want Nairnie to be my grandmother."

"Och, child, I have grandchildren who are old enough to be yer parents," said Nairnie.

"Then be my great-grandmother," said Mouse, with all the hope in the world in his eyes.

"Sure," said Nairnie, nodding her head. "I'd be happy and proud to be yer great-grandmother, Mouse."

"Yay!" shouted Martin. "Now Cassandra has to be your mother, too."

"Martin, hush," scolded Vivienne.

"I couldn't be your mother before finding a man to marry," Cassandra tried to politely suggest that it wouldn't be a good idea.

"Don't you know any men?" asked Mouse, causing both Zachariah and Isaac to almost choke since they were drinking from their cups at that moment.

"Mouse, Cassandra will never marry," said Zachariah.

"Why not?" asked Mouse.

"Oh, she must be like the sheriff's other sister, Magdalena," said Martin. "She's a nun and there are rules that they have to marry God."

"Yes, I know all about that, Martin," said Cassandra. "Magdalena is my sister too. But I don't think God would smile on me like He does her." Her smile faded and she looked like she was about to cry.

"Cassandra and Nairnie, I'd like to invite you to Maria and Cook's wedding at the castle," said Vivienne, only making things worse in Zachariah's opinion. "You too, Isaac and Zachariah."

"When is it?" asked Cassandra.

"Oh, I don't know. But I'd say the sooner the better. I think it'll be in three days' time."

"Three days?" asked Isaac. "That soon?"

"Vivienne, you haven't even cleared it with your uncle yet," Zachariah reminded her. "And I'm sure it takes a lot longer than that to plan a wedding."

"No, it doesn't. I'll help to cook the food, lassie," offered Nairnie.

"And I can help too," said Cassandra.

"You?" Zachariah chuckled. "I don't think your services will be needed or appreciated, Cassandra."

"Nonsense. Of course you can both help," said Vivienne. "Cassandra can help me with the decorations." Vivienne stood up and shook out her gown. "Children, come along. It is time for us to return to the castle."

Grunt barked and led the way to the door. Thankfully Starah's cat was locked away upstairs.

"Wait for me," said Zachariah, taking one more drink of ale, not wanting to go yet since he wasn't finished eating. Still, there was no way he was about to let Vivienne and the children step out into the dark streets unescorted.

"Oh, can I go along for the ride?" asked Cassandra. "I'd love to chat with Vivienne some more about the plans for the wedding."

"Nay," growled Zachariah. "Most definitely not. And I don't want to hear any more talk about weddings."

"Why not?" Vivienne looked him directly in the eye. "Do you have something against weddings, Sheriff?"

Egads, why was she asking this? And how was he supposed to answer? He'd been having thoughts about Vivienne lately and feeling like mayhap she was the one to fill the void in his life, since he was feeling lost and lonely after the death of his wife. But Vivienne was a noble. He wasn't. Even though they were good friends, that was all they would ever be. All they *could* ever be. And even if Vivienne was entertaining the crazy idea of them...possibly marrying someday...her uncle would never condone it. It wasn't right. Plus, it wasn't what he wanted.

Or was it exactly what he needed but he was listening to his head instead of his heart? He was so damned confused around Lady Vivienne Harlowe that he really wasn't sure of anything anymore.

Chapter Nine

Vivienne tossed and turned all night long, not able to sleep because of the many thoughts crowding her head. Who killed Fanny? Did they really mean to murder her instead of the whore? Why would someone want to kill either of them? Then again, why would anyone want to kill her parents? Seven years ago, the nightmare started, and to this day Vivienne felt no closer to knowing who murdered her parents than she had on that awful night that changed her life forever.

The heaviness of her lids caused her eyes to close, and before she knew it, she was reliving that horrible night all over again and there wasn't a thing she could do to stop it.

Lying in the back of a wagon filled with trunks and hay, sixteen-year-old Vivienne held her newborn baby boy close to her chest. Her nine-year-old brother, Adrian, was asleep in the hay next to her. Her parents drove the team of horses pulling the wagon down the bumpy road. They were heading north from Somersby. She watched the positioning of the stars in the sky above her as they trundled along on their way to Mablethorpe, where her aunt and uncle lived.

They'd left their home in a hurry after packing most of their belongings. They were going to live with her aunt and uncle in Mablethorpe this time, not just visit. She'd overheard her parents talking about it earlier.

Her mother was a noble, but her father was a commoner. He was a foot soldier in Somersby, and was being sent overseas to fight for the King. He was about to join an army of others, all of them boarding a ship that would take them across the Channel to France. She had heard him tell her mother that he would be gone for months this time, or possibly never even return.

With the new baby and her young brother as well, Vivienne and her mother were going to need all the help they could get, since her father would be gone. Vivienne realized that she was actually the reason they had to leave their home. She was to blame, and could only hope that someday they'd be able to return to Somersby with her entire family.

Vivienne lay in the hay of the wagon, too exhausted from giving birth earlier that day to even sleep at all. She smiled down at the newborn, who had a tuft of blond hair, the same color as hers, and clear, bright blue eyes. He was a cute little baby. Everything was perfect about him. Well, almost everything. Opening the blanket, she ran her fingers over the brown, heart-shaped birthmark on the bottom of her son's left foot. Her mother said he'd been kissed by an angel. Vivienne smiled, wrapping him back up, knowing that indeed he was an angelic child. She had been blessed to be given a son, and she just wished her late husband could have seen him before his untimely death.

Suddenly, Vivienne felt her stomach twist into a knot. She couldn't help feeling that something was horribly wrong, or perhaps about to happen. The twisting feeling inside her gut felt like the sharp blade of a dagger, such as the one she had strapped to her side. The last time she felt this way was six months ago when she'd lost her husband, George, after he was kicked by a horse and died. She reached down to touch the hilt of her blade, *feeling odd. The thought flashed through her mind that she'd need it tonight for protection, although she had no idea where this thought came from. The feel of the cold, sharp metal in her hand was so opposite to the warmth of new life from her baby pressed up against her.*

Holding her newborn baby boy to her chest, Vivienne stretched out in the hay along with her younger brother, Adrian. It was hard to sleep, since the baby's crying kept her awake.

"Vivienne, allow me to rock your baby to comfort him," offered her mother, Flanie, from the bench seat of the wagon in which they traveled. "Mayhap then you can get some rest."

"We should be at Mablethorpe soon," her father, Abiathar Harlowe, assured them. "Once there, you'll have plenty of people to help you with the baby."

"All right, Mother. You take him for a while," agreed Vivienne, handing the newborn to her mother over the side of the wagon and to the bench seat. "Perhaps you'll have the calming touch that I have yet to learn."

"My grandson is so precious." Her mother smiled down at the baby in her arms, giving him a kiss on the forehead. "What have you decided to name him? Will you name him George after his father?"

"No, Mother. I won't do that," Vivienne answered with a yawn. Her husband, a stablehand at Somersby, had died by being kicked by a horse shortly after they'd married. George had been a kind lad even though he had no money. Vivienne's family, although they were poor as well, strangely always seemed to have whatever they needed. It broke her heart when George died, but she promised herself she'd stay strong for their baby. She had to be strong now, since her poor child would grow up without a father. "I don't want to curse my baby by using the name of his dead father. I'm afraid if I do, my baby might die as well."

"That's nonsense," scoffed her mother. "No name is cursed. I'm sure your baby would love being named after his father."

"My baby's already cursed since he'll be growing up without a father," she told her parents. "I cannot even imagine how awful it will be to never know the man who sired him." Her parents became quiet all of a sudden, and Vivienne thought it was an odd thing for them to do in the middle of a conversation.

"He'll need a name, sweetheart," her father finally spoke up from the front seat. "You should give him one before much longer."

"He'll get a name," she promised. "Mayhap I will name him Abiathar after you, Father. That way he can follow in his grandfather's footsteps instead." Once again her parents became quiet.

"Nay, I'm not sure that is a good idea," her father finally answered. The clip-clop of the horses' hooves on the road was the only sound in the night, now that her mother had managed to get the baby to sleep. She'd swaddled him tightly and placed him into a wicker basket she carried at her side, using it like a crib after she'd removed the food. "I am sure you could name your son after someone more honorable and respected than me," her father continued.

"What do you mean? You are the most honorable and respectable person I know," she told him. "Besides, I don't know anyone else who fills those qualifications, do you?"

"Oh, I don't know. How about...the King?" asked her father.

"Abiathar," scolded her mother. "Hush."

"Edward," Vivienne said the King's name aloud, pondering the suggestion. "I kind of like the name, actually. Still, I'm not sure. I will decide soon, but right now I am just too tired to think straight."

"You get some rest then, sweetheart," came her mother's beautiful voice from the front of the wagon. "And don't worry about a thing. Your baby is sleeping safely in my care. He seems *to think that basket is a cradle and he likes it. I will protect him, I promise. Sleep now, and save your strength, Daughter."*

Vivienne had finally dozed off, but was abruptly awakened after too long. What roused her was the sound of neighing horses and the jerk of the wagon as it halted, coming to a complete and sudden stop. She heard voices, and they sounded menacing, if she wasn't mistaken.

"Off the wagon," commanded a gruff male voice.

"Nay. Leave us alone. We just want to pass," her father replied, doing all he could to protect his family, she was sure. Vivienne's heart sped up. She realized these roads were filled with bandits and perhaps they were about to be robbed. Her fingers closed over the hilt of her dagger strapped to her side. She would fight to help protect her family if need be.

The next thing she heard sounded like a sword being drawn from a scabbard, followed by the sounds of a struggle. Slowly, she pulled her blade from its sheath and rolled over in the hay, trying to see what was happening.

"Abiathar!" shouted her mother. "Nay!" she screamed and started crying.

Before Vivienne could get to her knees to look over the back of the bench seat, she heard the sickening sound of a body hitting the ground.

"Kill her, too!" commanded another man.

"Nay," Vivienne mumbled to herself, pushing up to a half-sitting position to see what was happening. She saw her mother struggling with a man as he pulled her off the wagon and to the ground. The basket with her baby in it was still on the bench seat. Vivienne started to panic. She needed to get to her baby as well as to help her poor mother. Since her father was so quiet and not protecting them, she was sure he'd been killed.

"Sister, what's happening?" Her brother rubbed a sleepy eye, looking up at her from under the hay.

"Adrian, stay down," she warned her brother in a hushed voice. "We're being attacked by bandits. Keep quiet, so they don't know you are here."

"Who won't know?" he asked, and she silenced him with her finger to his lips.

"Mother is in trouble. I have to help her, as well as to protect my baby." Not wanting to be seen, Vivienne quietly flipped over the far side of the wagon, letting her feet silently drop to the ground. She hoped to be able to sneak up to the front of the wagon and grab the basket with her baby, without the ruffians noticing her. It was night and very dark, so that would give her cover. Only a partial moon lit the sky, but was mainly hidden by clouds.

Gripping her dagger tightly, she crept around to the front of the wagon, scared because she knew she was still weak from giving birth. How would she fight off a full-grown man? Especially in her condition? Her toe hit something on the ground. When she looked down she saw the bloody, lifeless body of her father lying in a crumpled heap. Biting her tongue so as not to cry out, she quickly hunkered down to check for signs of life. His throat had been slit and there was no hope he could survive such a heinous act. He was no longer moving. It was too late for her father, but mayhap she could still save her mother and her son. She was their only hope now. Slipping her dagger back into her waist belt, she reached down and took her father's sword from his hand. Since he was only a foot soldier, he didn't own one of the longer, heavier swords mainly used by knights. His was a shorter, lighter blade, devised for closer, hand-to-hand combat. Therefore, Vivienne was able to lift it, having even learned from her father how to use it, at her insistence.

Gripping the hilt of her father's sword with two hands, Vivienne slowly stepped around the front of the wagon, just in time to see a shadowy figure stab her mother with his sword and then throw her body to the ground. Too scared to even speak, she froze.

Standing in the dark, fear consumed her, making her feel as if she were in hell.

"Someone's coming. Hurry, let's get out of here," came the voice of another shadowy form atop a horse. The man who stabbed her mother withdrew his sword and headed toward his waiting horse.

"Mother! Nay!" screamed her little brother. Vivienne's head snapped around to see Adrian standing in the hay in the back of the wagon, looking over the edge, terror on his face.

"Dammit. There's someone else," shouted the first bandit to the second.

"Kill him, too," commanded the ruffian's companion. "Leave no witnesses."

The first man rushed over, but Vivienne wasn't about to let him kill her brother too. Guilt already ate away at her that she wasn't able to save her parents. She stepped out in front of the attacker, wildly swinging her father's sword in the air. Mayhap it was her anger controlling her actions, but somehow she managed to stab the man in his right shoulder with her blade. The tip stuck into his flesh, and she was sure she felt the blade meet his bone. Quickly she pulled the blade back, seeing the blood oozing from the man's wound.

"Aaaaah!" the attacker screamed, one hand gripping at his bleeding shoulder from where Vivienne had struck him.

"Dammit, there's a girl here too," shouted the other man from his horse.

The fighting frightened the horses, causing them to rear up and paw at the air, whinnying loudly. The wagon jerked and her brother fell back in the hay with his feet in the air. Then the horses took off down the road at a run, pulling the wagon along with them. The sound of Vivienne's crying baby from the bench seat inside the basket caused her to panic and become furious all at the same time. Even in her weakened state from just having given birth, Vivienne's motherly instincts kicked in and she fought like a lion. She started swinging the sword wildly at her attacker as she lunged forward, stabbing at him over and over again. All the while she gritted her teeth. No one was going to kill any of her family and get away with it! She was so angry right now, that she wasn't even scared. She wanted both of these bandits to die.

"You bastard! I'll kill you for what you've done," she shouted, causing him to actually back away from her now. His sword dangled from his fingers as he gripped his bleeding sword arm which she had injured. God's eyes, she wished she had severed his arm altogether.

"Let's go," called out the man's friend from his steed. "Some-one's coming."

The man she'd struck mumbled something under his breath that she couldn't decipher, but it sounded as if he said the words, 'too soon.' He then turned and ran, mounting his horse, and taking off with his friend, leaving her stranded all alone.

"Vivienne," came her mother's soft cry from the ground. Vivi-enne spun on her heel and ran to her mother, dropping the sword and falling to her knees at her mother's side.

"Mother!" she cried, cradling the woman's head atop her lap. "They killed Father. And the horses ran off with Adrian and my baby." Tears gushed from her eyes as she looked down at her mother bathed in the scant light of the partial moon that broke through the clouds. "Mother, please don't die too! Do not leave me, I beg you. I need you!" Vivienne said the words, but knew that all the wishing in the world wasn't going to change what happened here tonight. Blood covered her mother who clutched her abdomen and moaned in pain. There was no use denying that she was not going to live. Her mother lifted her hand, yanking at a chain around her neck until the chain released. Then she slowly held out her closed fist to Vivienne.

"Take...this...Daughter. For you...and the baby."

"Mother, what are you doing? What do you mean?"

"Listen...to...me."

"I need to get you help. I think I hear horses coming down the road. I'll signal to the riders." She started to stand, but her mother's hand on her arm stopped her.

"Too...late," came her mother's soft reply as her eyes started to close. "Go to...your father. He...will protect...you...and the...babe."

"Mother, didn't you hear me? Father is dead!" she screamed. "I can't go to him for help. It's too late! I need to find Adrian and my baby."

"Wait." Her mother opened her fist and Vivienne looked down to see a gold ring with a ruby gemstone embedded in it dangling from the chain. It was something her mother had been wearing around her neck, although Vivienne had never known it. "This is...your father's."

"Mother, what you saying?" Vivienne cried. "You are delirious from the pain. Father doesn't have a ring like this. He is only a poor foot soldier." She picked it up with two fingers, taking a better look at it in the moonlight. "This is gold. With a ruby! It must belong to a very rich noble, or mayhap even a king."

"Yes. King...Edward. He's your...father. Don't...tell...a...soul."

"M-my father?" Vivienne thought for a moment that she had heard wrong. "Mother, what did you say? You are hurt and talking nonsense. Mother, can you hear me?"

Her mother became deathly still. When the light of the moon broke through the clouds once again, spilling over her, Vivienne saw that she stared up at her with open eyes that held no life at all within them. Just like her father. Now her mother was drained of all life too. There was no doubt in Vivienne's mind that she was dead. She had just lost both her parents in a matter of minutes. This couldn't be happening. She had to find Adrian and the baby. Bid the devil, her stomach ached and her body started shaking.

She looked down to see blood on her gown and it wasn't from her parents or the man she'd stabbed. It was a result of giving birth and still not being healed. Her head dizzied. The sound of approaching hoofbeats pounding on the earth echoed in her head. Then she felt as if she couldn't breathe and everything went black around her.

"My lady?"

Vivienne was pulled from her horrendous dream and her eyelids slowly flickered open. Her handmaid, Maleine, stood over her with a gown in her arms. Grunt was atop the bed with his chin resting on Vivienne's chest.

"Maleine?" Vivienne blinked several times, finally focusing. The dream slowly faded away. Through the open shutter, sunlight streamed in through the window. "Oh, thank goodness, I am here safe and sound in my bed at the castle." She tried to still her racing heart as well as catch her breath.

"Were you having that nightmare again?" asked Maleine, putting the gown down on the bed and pulling back the covers. Grunt jumped off the bed, landing with a thump once his feet hit the floor. His ears flopped around, hitting him as he shook out and stretched and prepared to start the day.

"Yes, I had the nightmare again, and it doesn't get any easier to accept as time goes by." Vivienne sat up and yawned, stretching her arms above her head.

"You need to get dressed, my lady. You have overslept again."

"Why do I have trouble falling asleep and then just as much trouble waking up, too?" Vivienne stood up and removed her nightshift. Maleine helped her don her clothes. She had just sat back down on the bed to put on her shoes when the door burst open and Martin and Mouse ran in, followed by Adrian.

"Get back here!" shouted Adrian, coming to an abrupt halt

when he saw Vivienne sitting on the bed. "I'm sorry, Sister. They are uncontrollable."

Martin and Mouse both jumped up on the bed. It did Vivienne's heart good to see her seven-year-old son alive and with her, as well as her brother who had been missing for years. Thank goodness the dream was nothing but bad memories of the past. All was good in her life right now and she never wanted to forget it.

"Come up on the bed, Grunt. It's all right," Martin beckoned the dog to join them.

"Nay, it isn't all right," scolded Adrian, storming all the way into the room. For a sixteen-year-old boy, he acted much more mature and Vivienne was proud of him. "Martin, I'm your uncle and you need to listen to me," continued Adrian. "You cannot go barging into your mother's room with a friend, jump on her bed, and then proceed to call a hound up there too."

"It's all right, Adrian," said Vivienne with a giggle, fixing the buckles on her shoes. "It's what they always do, and actually...I kind of like it."

"You do?" asked Adrian, sounding confused, sitting on the edge of the bed.

"I do. You see, I spent so many years with it being too quiet. I felt so alone. I like the noise and the bustle because it reminds me that I have my family back again. I was convinced that I had lost you two forever. I am so glad that things have changed." She pulled Martin onto her lap and kissed him atop his head. Then she reached out for Adrian and she pulled him over and kissed him as well.

"I want a hug and a kiss, too," said Mouse, sounding so sad and left out that Vivienne had to pull him onto her lap and kiss him as well. Grunt wanted in on the action, of course, being the sociable dog that he was. Before she knew it, the hound was knocking her back on the bed and licking her face with his slobbery dog kisses. She laughed, loving every minute of it. Life was truly good. Martin and Mouse squealed with laughter when the dog started licking their faces, too.

She heard someone clearing their throat and sat up to see her uncle and aunt standing in the doorway.

"Oh, good morning," she said, still laughing.

"Vivienne, I'd have a word with you. In private," said her uncle in a deep resounding voice.

"Of course, Uncle," she answered, getting up and putting the two young boys on the floor. Martin, you and Adrian and Mouse go to the great hall with Grunt and wait for me there. I'll only be a moment."

"I'll take them, my lady," offered Maleine, going with them so as to give her some privacy. Vivienne's uncle and aunt entered the room, and the others left. But when Grunt started sniffing Uncle Gilbert's leg, her uncle had the audacity to kick the dog away.

"Get away from me you mangy mutt," complained her uncle, acting as if he didn't like dogs when she knew for sure that he did.

"Gilbert, please!" came Aunt Ellen's remark. "There is no need for that."

Grunt growled lowly at Vivienne's uncle.

"Martin, take Grunt," Vivienne called out, running over and pushing Grunt out the door. "Go on, Grunt." When Martin took the dog, she turned back to her uncle. "I don't know what's the matter with that dog, I'm sorry."

"You can't blame the poor dog from growling at him," said her aunt. "If I were being kicked at, I'd growl, too. I'd actually bite him. Gilbert, there was no need for you to be so mean to Vivienne's hound."

"There is no need for you to tell me what to do. Now hush,

woman, before I take the back of my hand to you." Her uncle was acting so mean that it was shocking.

Vivienne was convinced now that he truly was losing his mind. Her mouth dropped open. She had never heard her uncle threaten her aunt before now. If he really was going mad, then she didn't like what it was doing to him and how it affected those around him. Her aunt and uncle had always seemed to be so much in love. Now they acted as if they almost despised each other. She wondered if having a mistress was the reason her uncle was changing so much lately.

"Did you want to talk to me about something?" asked Vivienne, wanting nothing more than to get back to spending time with her son and brother. The more she was around her uncle, the more it filled her with anxiety.

"Yes. Did you give that fat cook and the sleazy serving girl permission to be married?" asked her uncle.

"There is no need for name calling," retorted Vivienne. "And yes, I told Maria and Cook that it was all right for them to marry and that the wedding will take place right here at the castle. I've decided it will happen in three days' time."

"Oh my, that is fast," gasped Aunt Ellen with her hand to her mouth. "Please, let me know how I can help you to prepare things."

"Thank you, Aunt Ellen. I've had a lot of people offer to help. Nairnie and Cassandra will be assisting me as well," Vivienne told her.

"Cassandra?" Her uncle's craggy brows dipped together. "Not that Winchester Goose. I don't want her inside my castle walls."

"She is the sheriff's sister," Vivienne reminded him. "And Cassandra is a very nice woman, I assure you. I want her here and so she will be."

"Who are you to make such a decision?" snapped her uncle. "This is *my* castle. I make all decisions, not you."

"I see," said Vivienne, purposely pulling out the King's gold and ruby ring she wore on a chain around her neck usually hidden by her clothes. She looked at the ring and then breathed on it, rubbing it on her sleeve to shine it. "I was thinking of inviting my father as well."

"Your father is dead," snarled Lord Mablethorpe.

"I am speaking about my birth father. King Edward III." She held out the ring to remind him of who begot her.

Her uncle suddenly became silent. "King Edward is busy ruling our country. Do not bother him with such trivial things, Vivienne. Surely not for the wedding of two mere servants. That is preposterous to even think he'd want to attend."

"I beg to differ," she told him. "My father knows Cook and Maria from when he visited for the joust, and I believe he likes them. Besides, I'd like another chance to see him," said Vivienne. "Our last meeting was so rushed. I would love some time just to talk with him and get to know him. To let him get to know me. We need to find out about each other's lives."

"Well, I think it's a wonderful idea, Vivienne." Her aunt was so sweet to support her decisions. Vivienne had always thought of Aunt Ellen as a second mother. She was also becoming braver being around Vivienne. Especially supporting her in front of her domineering husband. "I'll send for the scribe to write a note, and a messenger to deliver it to the King right away." Lady Mablethorpe picked up the hem of her skirt and hurried across the rushes and out the door.

"I don't like this. Not at all," her uncle complained with a menacing stare.

Vivienne knew it probably wasn't a good idea to directly confront her uncle about his latest behavior, but for her aunt's sake she decided she needed to mention it. "Uncle, can I ask you a question?"

"You will, even if I say no."

"You're probably right," she agreed. "Tell me, where do you go in the mornings when you go riding by yourself?"

His head snapped up and he perused her in a way that told her that the question upset him. Or that she had no right to even ask.

"Why should that concern you?" He was cautious with his words.

"I, as well as Aunt Ellen, believe you are leaving to meet with your mistress."

"My mistress?" His brows arched and he chuckled lowly. "I hardly think so."

"Then if it's not a mistress you are hiding, what is it?"

"What makes you think I'm hiding anything?" His walls were up again. Much like the way Zachariah acted when he was trying to hide his feelings and emotions, her uncle showed all the signs as well.

"Oh, I don't know. It's just that you're so secretive all the time. And you are acting so strangely lately."

"I am not."

"Yes, you are. Even Adrian noticed. Sometimes we feel as if we don't even know who you are anymore."

"You're all crazy! Besides, Adrian has been gone for seven years so you can't go by that. He was young at the time of his disappearance and doesn't know the first thing about blasted riddles."

"His answer to the riddle was correct," she said softly. "You told that same riddle to me when I was his age. Don't you remember?"

An odd look contorted his face and he shook his head like a

dog trying to rid himself of wet fur. "I don't have time to remember silly nonsense or to talk about rubbish that is not even true. Now get out of my way, because I have things to do." He pushed past her into the hall, knocking into the sheriff in his hurry to leave.

"Oh, I'm sorry Lord Mablethorpe, I didn't know you were in there," said Zachariah, stepping back and holding up his hands.

"What are you doing up here by Lady Vivienne's chamber?" asked her uncle. "If you want to see her, you wait in the great hall and a page gets her. You know the rules. You aren't allowed up here."

"Martin was going to summon her for me, but he was having such a good time with Grunt and Mouse that I told him not to bother," said Zachariah. "I decided that I'd make the trip myself."

"You are making yourself a little too comfortable at the castle lately, Sheriff, and I don't like it."

"I'm not here courting your niece, if that is what you're insinuating. I am here on official business."

"Did you find out anything more about the death of the whore?" asked Lord Mablethorpe.

"Nay, not yet, but we're working on it," Zachariah answered.

"Then don't bother me with frivolities! Don't even speak to me again unless you can tell me the name of the whore's killer." He stormed away, leaving Zachariah and Vivienne watching him in utter confusion.

"I think you're right. He's losing his mind," said Zachariah. "And now all I've done is to manage to upset him."

"Don't worry about my uncle." The last thing Vivienne wanted was for her uncle's actions to affect Zachariah, too. "I'll handle him. Now tell me, why are you here?"

"I'm here to escort you to town so we can continue with the murder investigation. Isaac found some more people who were in the tavern the night Fanny was murdered. We're hoping one of them can give us some information on the mysterious cloaked man. Plus, I had Orvyn keep the room where Fanny was pushed out the window free of customers. I'd like to take another look in case there is something we missed."

"I agree," said Vivienne. "If there is a clue we've missed, then I want to be sure to find it. And the sooner we catch this killer, the faster I will feel at ease."

"Yes. Especially since the killer might be after you, and could be the same person who murdered your parents."

"We have to find him or her, Zachariah." Her gut twisted into a knot, remembering her awful nightmare about the horrible night when her parents' lives were taken right in front of her very eyes. "We have to do everything in our power to hunt down whoever killed Fanny...and whoever seems to be after me. Not until we find them and convict them, and put them behind bars will I ever rid myself of my nightmares and finally get a good night's sleep."

Chapter Ten

Zachariah watched Vivienne as she inspected the area around the window where Fanny had been pushed out. Grunt sniffed around the floor. A sick feeling engulfed him. It could have been Vivienne who died here. He'd been so scared to look at the dead woman's face because he thought he had lost her this time. None of this was right. Vivienne didn't deserve to die, but yet it seemed as if that note had been meant for her. That the killer was targeting her and not the whore.

"What is it, Grunt?" he heard Vivienne ask, and looked over to see the dog pawing at something on the floor beneath the window. "Oh, good boy." She took something from the dog's mouth. "Sheriff, I think I found something," said Vivienne, looking at something cradled in the palm of her hand.

"What is it?" he asked, hurrying over to the window.

Vivienne stood up, holding up a cloth tie that was used to fasten a tunic. It seemed to be ripped off. "Grunt found it, actually. I think Fanny must have ripped this off of the killer when he was struggling with her and throwing her out the window."

"We can't know that for sure, Vivienne. This room is used

for patrons to bed the whores. It could just be from one of those encounters."

"No, I don't think so." She bent closer to look at the tie. "I think I see a splotch of blood on here. Why would it be there? Nay, I'm sure this belongs to the killer." Grunt barked in agreement.

"All right. Give it to me. I'll log it as evidence." He held out his hand.

Vivienne gave it to Zachariah and he stuck it in his pouch.

"My, that is a long way down." Vivienne put her hands on the sill and leaned out the open window, looking downward to the trough where they'd found Fanny's body.

Zachariah's heart beat faster. He didn't like her being in that position. "Come away from the window, my lady," he said, putting his hands around her waist. "It is dangerous and I don't want you to fall out."

She turned to face him and when she did, their faces were close together once again. The breeze blew her silky blonde hair across her face and he gently reached out and pushed a strand out of her eyes. Her focus was on his mouth. His gaze moved to her lips. And then before he could have the sense to stop himself, he leaned forward and gently kissed her on the mouth.

Vivienne's arms went around his neck and the kiss deepened. Damn, this felt good. So right. But then again...it was so wrong.

"I'm sorry, my lady," he said, slowly releasing her. "I didn't mean to do that."

"Why not?" she asked in a breathy voice. "We both enjoyed it, didn't we?"

"Vivienne, we are good friends, and we both know that is all it can ever be."

"Why?"

"Because, isn't it obvious? You are a noble and I'm a commoner. We don't belong together and can never be."

"I think you're forgetting something, Sheriff. My father was a commoner even though my mother was a noble. Also, I was married to a stablehand. Your position is much higher than my late husband's. Never say never. I believe that...love shouldn't be conditioned by silly rules. Don't you agree?"

Zachariah's mouth went dry and he didn't know how to respond to that! She'd just said the word *love*. Is that what she was feeling between them? He wasn't feeling love. Or was he? Right now his mind was muddled and he didn't really know the answer to that.

"Vivienne, what the hell are you doing?" came a gruff voice from down in the street.

Vivienne looked back out the window and saw her uncle standing there watching them. She groaned inwardly. He had most likely seen the kiss between them since they were standing in the window on display. Mayhap it had been a bad idea after all.

"Uncle, what are you doing here?" she called out the window.

"I'm here to see what is going on and I don't like what I just witnessed."

Vivienne looked back at Zachariah. "I think he saw us kiss," she whispered.

"Oh, great!" Zachariah ran a hand through his hair. "Not what either of us need right now."

"Don't worry. It'll be fine," she assured him, even though she wasn't sure how much trouble her uncle would make for them since he was losing his mind.

"Let's go down into the tavern. Isaac is there and we have witnesses to question. We need to stay focused on our work."

"Yes," she agreed. "I don't think we're going to find any more clues here. Let's go, Grunt," she called out to her dog.

Once they arrived in the tavern, her uncle was already there talking with Orvyn, the proprietor.

"Sheriff," said Lord Gilbert with a glare.

"Lord Mablethorpe," Zachariah answered with a nod and slight bow, but thankfully nothing was said about the kiss. Or at least not for now.

"Orvyn tells me some of the patrons saw a man in a cloak the night of the murder."

"Yes, I'm conducting the investigation on that now," the sheriff answered.

"I want to know who he was."

"We are working on finding out, Uncle Gilbert." Vivienne wished her uncle had stayed at the castle instead of trying to get involved.

"I want to talk to everyone who was here last night." Lord Mablethorpe looked around the room.

"My lady," said Zachariah, pulling her to the side and whispering to her. "You need to get him out of here. I can't work with him interfering."

"I agree," she whispered back. "Let me see what I can do."

Vivienne walked over to her uncle and took him to the side. "Uncle, are you here to mayhap meet the woman you're having an affair with?"

"What?" He looked at her and scowled. "I told you, I don't have a mistress."

"Really. And what if someone in this tavern has seen you with another woman?"

"Who said that?" His face turned red with anger. "I want to know who is lying so I can strangle them with my own hands."

"No one has said that, so calm down. I am only trying to make a point. I know you mean to be helpful, but honestly, you shouldn't be here at all. Please, let the sheriff conduct the investigation and don't get involved," she told him. "You are a noble and shouldn't even be on Rotten Row."

"And neither should you, Vivienne. You need to come back to the castle with me right now."

Vivienne looked back at Zachariah who was talking with Isaac. There was a small crowd of men around them. She wanted nothing more than to be in on the investigation, but she knew that the only way to get her uncle out of there was to agree to return to the castle with him.

"All right, let's go back to Mablethorpe Castle together," she told him. "I have a lot to do to prepare for Maria and Cook's wedding, so mayhap that is a good idea."

"I still haven't agreed to that marriage, Vivienne," he told her.

"Nay, and neither have you agreed to tell me where you disappear to when you leave early in the mornings to go out riding." This had nothing to do with the conversation, but she knew if she brought it back to his secrets, he'd forget about little things like the marriage of two servants.

"I won't hear another word about that, Vivienne, now let's get out of here before one of these vagrants gets too close to me again."

Vivienne looked over to Zachariah and smiled and nodded and gave him a little wave of her fingers as they headed to the door. Zachariah seemed very serious. And concerned. He returned the nod and then turned back to Isaac and the witnesses they were about to question.

As Vivienne stepped out the door, she knocked into the coroner's scribe, Torsten. "Oh, I'm sorry, I didn't see you there," she told him.

"It's quite all right, my lady." Torsten bowed. She could see he had his pouch attached to his side and his quill was sticking out.

"Is Gandalf here too?" she asked.

"Nay. Well, he was with me, but didn't want to enter the tavern. He has a lot to do and is going back to the coroner's office." He nodded with his head and Vivienne looked across the street to see a tall man in a cloak with his head covered by a hood walking down the street.

"Is that Gandalf? In the cloak with his head covered?" she asked.

"Where?" asked Torsten.

"There," she said, pointing, but by the time Torsten turned around it was too late. The man in the cloak had gone around the corner and was now out of sight.

"It could have been, I suppose. Gandalf was wearing his cloak. Excuse me, my lady. I'd like to give a message to the sheriff."

"Message? What message?" asked Vivienne. "Is it something to do with Fanny's murder?"

"I am here to tell the sheriff that I think Gandalf..."

"Vivienne, let's go," commanded her uncle, coming back to get her.

"Just a moment," she said, but her uncle was not having any of this.

"I said, *now!*"

"Yes, Uncle," she answered, turning to talk to Torsten, but it seemed he had already entered the building. She sighed, knowing now she'd have to wait until she saw Zachariah again in order to find out what Torsten was about to tell her. Something was going to have to change regarding her uncle, because with him interfering every few minutes, she was never going to be able to participate in the murder investigation. She realized her uncle was only concerned with her safety, but she was used to doing what she pleased whenever she wanted. This was really going to slow her down.

ONCE BACK AT THE CASTLE, Vivienne immediately forgot all about the investigation when she saw her aunt, Maleine, and Cassandra walking into the keep together. She wanted to keep her uncle away from Cassandra since he was so adamant about not wanting whores inside his castle walls. Perhaps meeting with the women behind closed doors was the best idea.

"Excuse me," she said, and hurried out of the stable and to the keep, quickly catching up with the women. Grunt went ahead of her and disappeared inside the keep.

"My lady," said Maleine, noticing her. "We were just making plans for Cook and Maria's wedding."

"Yes, we were just headed to the kitchen to talk to the both of them," said her aunt.

"Allow me to join you then." Vivienne cherished the thought of taking time to help the two servants. She wanted to make them happy with the wedding plans since, in her mind, they deserved a fitting ceremony. Even if her uncle wouldn't agree.

"That would be wonderful," said Cassandra. She walked alongside Vivienne as they made their way to the kitchen. "Did you find out anything else regarding Fanny's murder?" she asked in a soft voice.

"Not really," was Vivienne's answer.

"Where are my brothers?" asked Cassandra, looking behind them. "Didn't at least one of them escort you back to the castle?"

"Nay. They stayed in town to work on the investigation. My uncle escorted me back here. He is starting to interfere with my participation in finding the killer, and it doesn't make me happy."

"Why do you think he is being so pesky?" she asked.

"I'm not sure," Vivienne answered. "But I intend to find out. Plus, I would like to speak with you. Privately," she told Cassandra.

"Of course," answered the Winchester Goose. "Should we go to your chamber?"

Grunt ran out of the kitchen with a sausage in his mouth.

"Get back here you mangy mutt!" Cook ran after him, his hands waving. Maria was right behind him. So were Martin and Mouse.

"Oh, my lady." Cook stopped in his tracks and Maria about ran into him.

"My lady, you're back," said Maria with a rushed curtsy.

"Is Grunt causing trouble again?" asked Vivienne.

"Grunt was just hungry, Mother," Martin announced.

"And Cook wouldn't give him a bone," added Mouse.

"Cook and Maria, we'd like to speak with you concerning the wedding plans," interrupted her aunt.

"Of course, Lady Mablethorpe. Right away," said Cook, looking over his shoulder at the dog.

"Let Grunt have the sausage, Cook," begged Maria. Then she leaned in and whispered. "We don't want to upset the nobles since they are being so generous and allowing us to be married. Right at the castle, too."

"You're right," said Cook with a nod. "Grunt can keep the sausage."

Vivienne looked down to see her hound licking his lips and it made her giggle. "I don't believe that you'd be able to get it back if you tried."

"Not until Grunt poops it out," said Martin, always coming right out and saying whatever was on his mind.

Vivienne heard her uncle's loud voice from the door to the keep. She figured he'd be angry as soon as he saw Cassandra so she'd save a lot of trouble if she got the girl out of here quickly.

"Aunt Ellen," called out Vivienne. "If you'll carry on without us, Cassandra and I have to make a quick stop somewhere."

"Where?" asked her aunt.

"I think it's time that Cassandra reunites with her entire family."

"Oh, Lady Vivienne, nay," said Cassandra, her cheeks blushing. "I couldn't go there."

"Where?" asked Martin. "I want to come too."

"We'll be at Mablethorpe Abbey visiting Sister Magdalena," Vivienne told her aunt.

"With us. We want to come too," said Martin, tugging on her skirt to get her attention.

"There you are, Martin," said her brother Adrian, hurrying down the corridor to join them. "Vivienne, I'm trying to keep an eye on the boys, but they keep on disappearing. Plus, Martin has been avoiding his training to become a squire."

"Martin, is that right?" asked Vivienne.

"I don't want to train to be a knight anymore. I just want to play with Grunt and Mouse."

"We will talk about this later," said Vivienne.

"Adrian, we're going to the abbey now. To talk to a nun," said Martin.

"Really." Adrian looked up with a start. "Then I'll escort you."

Vivienne sighed. While what she wanted was time alone to talk with Cassandra, she also realized that she needed and also wanted time to spend with her brother and son too. Mayhap she would just combine them all.

"I think that's a wonderful idea," said Vivienne. "Lady Mablethorpe, they will all be joining me."

"What about me, my lady?" asked Maleine. "I am your handmaid. I should be with you."

"I won't require your services right now, Maleine, but thank you."

"But I can watch over the young ones since they seem to keep disappearing from Adrian."

Adrian scowled. "I can handle it. Plus, I will be watching over my sister at the same time."

"Maleine will be joining us as well," Vivienne told her aunt. "We'll be back before dark, so please don't worry."

"Be careful, my dear," called out her aunt with a wave of her hand. "You never know where that killer might be hiding."

Chapter Eleven

"Where were you last night?" Zachariah asked Torsten, as he and Isaac conducted questioning inside the tavern of the Hogg's Head Inn.

"Sheriff, you don't suspect me of murdering that whore, do you?" asked Torsten, seeming more than nervous. He sat on the bench with a tankard of ale clutched between his hands, acting like it was a lifeline.

"We are simply questioning people who were in the tavern last night, and you were said to have been here," explained Isaac, making Zachariah want to hit him. Zachariah wanted to find out if Torsten would lie, but now the information was clear that they already knew he'd been here so his plan was ruined.

"Yes. I was here. For a short while," said Torsten, picking up the tankard in two hands and downing most of the ale.

"Was anyone with you?" asked the sheriff.

"What do you mean?"

"Was Gandalf here too?" asked Isaac. "Or did you come here alone?"

"Oh. Nay, Gandalf wasn't with me. He said he had something to do, so I came by myself."

"What did he need to do?" asked Zachariah, searching for more information.

"I...I'm not sure. I didn't ask and he didn't say. He just put on his cloak and left."

"You are his scribe, so I find it odd that you didn't ask if your services were needed to assist him," said Zachariah, watching the man squirm even more.

"I'm sure if he needed my help he would have asked for it." Torsten downed the rest of the ale, his eyes constantly scanning the room. "If you must know, I sometimes come here for a quick game of cards or dice. With the nature of my work, I like to be around live people sometimes too."

"I see." Zachariah dug into his pouch and brought forth the dice he'd found in the trough. "Do these look familiar?"

"Those look like Orvyn's dice. He had two sets, but said he lost one. Where did you find them?" He reached for the dice, but the sheriff pulled his hand away.

"They were found in the horse trough. Why would Orvyn's dice be there?"

"I...I don't know. I saw Orvyn out by the trough that night, so mayhap he was cooling off in the water and dropped them."

Zachariah turned to see Orvyn watching them from the drink board. Sigga and Dulcia watched from atop the stairs.

"And what time was that?"

"I'm not sure. It was still early."

"Did you happen to see a mysterious man hiding his identity beneath a cloak in here last night?

"Nay. Aye. Oh, I don't know, there were an awful lot of people, so mayhap, but I really don't remember." Torsten stood. "Sheriff, am I free to go now? I'd really like to leave."

"You seem in a hurry to go," commented the sheriff's brother.

Zachariah followed Torsten's gaze and saw Dulcia coming

down the stairs with Sigga right behind her. The whores were probably looking for a customer, even though it wasn't yet evening.

"You had relations with one of the whores last night, didn't you?" asked Zachariah, taking a wild guess by the man's actions.

"Me?" Torsten's head snapped around so fast that Zachariah wouldn't be surprised if he pulled a muscle. "Why would you say that?"

"I can call the girls over here and ask them, if you'd rather," continued Zachariah, raising his hand in the air.

"Nay! Don't do that." Torsten's hand shot up to block him. "I mean, please, I'd rather you didn't."

"Then tell us what you're hiding," stated Isaac. Zachariah nodded to his brother, liking the way he was catching on quickly to the process of questioning.

"I would rather not say."

"If you don't, it could be taken as admission of guilt to a crime that's been committed," Zachariah warned him.

"Nay, I'm innocent," Torsten tried to convince him.

"I'd beg to differ," said Isaac. "So, which of those two whores did you bed last night? Or was it perhaps the Winchester Goose?"

Torsten looked like he was about to run, so Zachariah stepped in front of him to keep him from going.

"All we want to know is if you saw anyone suspicious while you were here," said the sheriff.

"My wife doesn't know I come here, Sheriff Fitch. And I'd rather keep it that way if you know what I mean."

"I see." Zachariah nodded. "Did you bed Fanny by any chance?"

"Fanny?" Torsten was acting stupid now.

"You know who we mean. The whore who was murdered,

and is lying on a slab in the coroner's office at this very moment." Isaac was starting to lose his patience with the man.

"Nay, I didn't. I admit that when I saw her upstairs, I wanted her instead of Sigga, but I didn't think I'd have a standing chance to actually couple with a Winchester Goose. Neither did I think I could afford her, so I didn't bother to ask."

"She was in the corridor? What time was this?" asked Zachariah.

"I'm not sure. It was late. Mayhap about midnight."

"What was Fanny wearing when you saw her up in the corridor?" asked Isaac.

"She was wearing a cloak. Like she was going to go outside."

"Was it Lady Vivienne's cloak?" asked Isaac. "The cloak that was found on Fanny's dead body?"

Torsten screwed up his face as if trying to think. "I'm not sure, but I don't think so. I think she wore that cloak with the striped hood. Then again, mayhap I'm wrong. I wasn't looking at her outerwear."

"Nay, I don't suppose you were," said Isaac.

"Thank you, Torsten, that'll be all for now," said Zachariah, dismissing the man.

The scribe wasted no time in turning around and all but bounding out the door.

"Sigga didn't mention that she was with Torsten last night, did she?" Isaac asked Zachariah.

"Nay, she didn't. Mayhap she was trying to protect Torsten so his wife wouldn't find out," Zachariah answered his brother. "Either that, or mayhap she has something to hide."

"Do you think Torsten's lying?"

"I'm not sure, but it does give him an alibi, as well as Sigga. However, I'd like you to question Orvyn about the dice, and mayhap we should question the whores again, too."

"I wonder where Fanny was going?" Isaac's gaze wandered

up to the stairs where the two tavern whores were now perched like birds of prey, looking over the side railings at the men below.

"We might never know." Zachariah shook his head. "Isaac, let's get back to the house. Nairnie is making goose tonight. She's been so irritable lately that I don't want to be late for supper. Plus, I'd like to spend time with Starah. My daughter has been a bundle of nerves ever since she heard that someone is trying to kill Lady Vivienne. The poor girl is frightened that the killer is going to be after her next."

"Goose, did you say?" asked Isaac with a smirk on his face as they headed for the door. "You don't think this meal has anything to do with the fact that Nairnie hates Winchester Geese, do you?"

"I don't know and neither do I ever want to find out." Zachariah held open the door for his brother and looked back into the tavern, noticing the whores whispering to Orvyn behind the drink board. They were also giving Zachariah a daggered look. It was most likely because they hated Cassandra and they knew she was his sister. "All I can say is that the sooner we catch this killer and send Cassandra on her way, the better things will be for all of us."

Vivienne dismounted her horse, helping Cassandra to the ground since they'd been riding double. Maleine was atop a horse with Mouse, and Adrian and Martin rode together on another. Grunt led the way.

"Sister Magdalena is a nun, Mouse," Martin told his friend. "I've already met her and she's really nice." He jumped off the horse and Mouse did the same. "Maleine was gonna be a nun before she turned into a sleuth like my mother."

"Yes, that's true, but I wouldn't have made a very good nun, at all." Maleine also dismounted. "I like being a sleuth much better."

"Hrmph," grumbled Adrian from the ground, taking hold of the reins of all three horses. "You're not a good sleuth, Maleine. If you were you would have already caught the bloody killer."

"That wasn't a very nice thing to say," Vivienne scolded her brother.

"But it's true," Adrian continued. "I bet I can catch the killer faster than she can even find a clue."

"You don't know the first thing about how a murder investigation works," Maleine retorted. "These things take time and you can't rush them."

"Adrian, Maleine has been very helpful to me where investigations are concerned. Now, stop all the squabbling, you two," Vivienne told them. "Here comes Mother Superior now. Oh, I see Magdalena is with her. Good. That will save us the trouble of hunting her down."

"Hello, Sister," called out Cassandra, waving her hand over her head at her sister Magdalena.

Mother Superior, with her hands hidden beneath her cassock, hurried over with a firm, turned-down mouth instead of a smile. "What is all this commotion about? And why are all of you here?"

"Mother Superior, I am Lady Vivienne Harlowe from Mablethorpe Castle." Vivienne wasn't very familiar with the nuns at Mablethorpe Abbey, although she knew most of them from Maltby le Marsh where they'd had a past murder investigation. She'd had no real interest or reason to come to her own town's abbey before now.

"I know who you are," said Mother Superior, not seeming at all impressed. "You're that out-of-control noblewoman from the castle who thinks she is a constable and sticks her nose where it doesn't belong."

"Well, that's not really true," said Vivienne, thinking this woman was a bit harsh for being a nun. After all, weren't women of the cloth supposed to be kind and loving? "I do assist the sheriff on murder investigations, but I assure you our work is warranted on both our parts."

"I help them, as well," added Maleine with a proud smile.

Grunt barked once and when Mother Superior glared in the dog's direction, Grunt whined and ran back to Vivienne and lay down silently at her side.

"Dogs are not allowed in the abbey. They are much too distracting."

"We are just here for a short visit, Mother Superior. I hope you don't mind," said Vivienne.

"What I do mind is a woman with *her* reputation shouting out to me and calling me Sister in such a familiar manner when she doesn't even know me. She should have respect and call me Mother Superior like everyone else."

"You?" asked Cassandra. "Oh, I wasn't shouting a greeting to you," she explained. "I was calling out to Magdalena." She nodded to the nun standing behind Mother Superior.

"You know Sister Magdalena?" Mother Superior arched one brow.

"Well, I'd surely hope so." Cassandra giggled. "After all, she is my older sister."

When Mother Superior looked as if she were about to faint, Vivienne realized she needed to quickly step in. "Hello, Sister Magdalena. It's nice to see you again."

"Hello, Lady Vivienne. And Martin and Maleine," said Magdalena with a nod. Grunt whined and sat up and wagged his tail. "And good to see you again too, Grunt," she added. "I don't know who the other boys are, but hello to you, too."

"This is my friend, Mouse," said Martin, putting his hand on the smallest boy's shoulder. "He's part of the family now since he doesn't have his own family anymore."

"Well, that's very nice," said Magdalena in a kind tone, smiling at little Mouse.

"Don't you recognize me, Magdalena?" Adrian broke in. "I know you haven't seen me since I was a child, but I'm back now."

The nun cocked her head and looked hard and then her eyes opened wide. "Adrian? Is that you?"

"Yes. It's me and I'm not dead like everyone thought."

"Oh, dear child, I'm so happy." Magdalena actually ran over and gave Adrian a hug. "Let me look at you," she said, holding him at arm's length. "My you have grown up over the years. You have turned into a full-fledged man."

"That's right." Adrian stood taller and pushed back his shoulders. "I'm the man of the family now, and it's my job to protect all of them."

Magdalena finally looked over at Cassandra. "Hello, Cassandra. It's been a long time since I've seen you." She seemed hesitant at first, and Vivienne could only hope that Magdalena didn't hold the same grudge against Cassandra as their brother Zachariah did.

"I'm sorry, Sister Magdalena, I didn't know she was your sister," said Mother Superior. "But I must tell you that it is not proper for her to be here. Nuns do not associate with...with...her kind." She stuck her nose up in the air.

"Mother Superior, would I be imposing upon you if I asked if the children could see the abbey?" asked Vivienne, trying to bring the conversation away from Cassandra. She'd have to be sure to give the poor woman some different clothes to wear soon so she wouldn't be so easily identified by her profession. "I don't believe they've ever been here before." Vivienne reached down to scratch behind Grunt's ears. The dog cocked his head and smiled.

"Do you have a kitchen?" asked Martin. "Or don't nuns eat? At Maltby le Marsh Abbey, they barely gave us any food at all."

"Maltby le Marsh Abbey?" That took Mother Superior's interest. "We are a much better and more equipped abbey than that!"

"So you have food here then?" Little Mouse spoke up.

"Of course, we do. Plenty of it, too."

"Could you show them the kitchen, please?" asked Vivienne. "That will give Cassandra and me a few minutes to visit with Sister Magdalena. After that, I promise you that we'll leave."

"Well, I don't see any harm in showing them the kitchen, I suppose." Thankfully, Mother Superior agreed. As if understanding the word *kitchen*, Grunt ran over to join them. Mother Superior looked over to Maleine and Adrian. "You'll both come along to control the children and the hound." It was more of a statement or command than a question.

"Go ahead," said Vivienne with a nod. "I'll alert you when we are ready to leave. We'll all be safe within the abbey's walls," she added when she noticed the hesitant look on Adrian's face, not wanting to leave her.

"Come on, Grunt, we're going to get you a nice bone." Martin ran across the courtyard with Mouse. Grunt followed, barking like crazy.

"Quiet, please. You need to remain quiet." Mother Superior picked up the hem of her habit and ran after the children.

Adrian looked at Maleine and shrugged. "I could go for a bite to eat."

"Me, too," said Maleine with a smile. "The sleuthing will have to wait." The two of them ran off after the rest.

"Cassandra, I'm so happy to see you." Magdalena pulled her sister into her arms, giving her a big hug.

"You are? I wasn't so sure," said Cassandra.

"I'm sorry but I really couldn't show my enthusiasm in front of Mother Superior." Magdalena's face lit up with a smile. "It's good to have our family back together again. Are you in Mablethorpe to stay this time?"

"I'd like to stay, but I'm not sure. Zachariah doesn't want me here."

"Zachariah will get over it, just give him time," said Magdalena.

"He told me he wants me to leave and go back to the Southwark district as soon as we find Fanny's murderer."

"Fanny? Murder?" The nun blinked in confusion.

"Cassandra's good friend was murdered on Rotten Row just last night," Vivienne explained.

"Nothing good ever came from Rotten Row." Magdalena's smile faded. "But I assure you, Cassandra, that our brothers will find and lock away that killer. It is their job and they're good at it. Even Isaac, even though he is still in training."

"With Lady Vivienne's help, mayhap they will find the murderer quicker." Cassandra nodded to Vivienne.

"Yes, Lady Vivienne was so helpful in solving the murder at Maltby le Marsh. I just hope there won't be any ghosts involved this time." Magdalena faked a shudder.

"Sister Magdalena, I admit I wanted to bring Cassandra here so you two could reunite."

"Lady Vivienne is good at bringing people back together," said the nun, turning to Cassandra. "She brought me and Zachariah back together again, and even convinced our stubborn brother to forgive and accept Isaac, too."

"And I'll do the same for Cassandra, if it's the last thing I ever do," promised Vivienne.

"Let's go to the cloister by the crypts to talk," suggested Magdalena. "We won't have to speak in hushed tones there, since no one ever goes there."

"I don't blame them," said Vivienne, not really liking graveyards or crypts of any kind.

After securing their horses to a hitching post, they walked across to the far end of the abbey, and sat on a bench outside of the crypts.

"So, do you have any leads on the murder investigation yet?" asked Magdalena.

"Nothing substantial," answered Vivienne. "Of course, if I would be able to investigate without so many distractions, we might be a lot farther along by now."

"What's holding you back?" Magdalena wanted to know. "I've known you for a long time, my lady, and you never let anything get in your way once you've make up your mind to do something."

"It's my uncle, mainly," Vivienne told her. "He is acting odd lately. My aunt and I think he has a mistress. And that he's going mad."

"Oh, that's not good. Not good at all." Magdalena held her hand to her mouth. "I feel so bad for Lady Mablethorpe."

"Well, none of it is actually confirmed yet, but we have a pretty good suspicion we are right," said Vivienne. "But enough about Lord Mablethorpe. We have a killer to find. Have there been any travelers here lately, seeking lodging?" Vivienne realized this could be possible, since the abbey was known to take in those in need and to give lodging and food to travelers passing through.

"Not anyone suspicious, if that's what you mean," said Magdalena. "But I'll keep my eyes open in case anyone shows up. If so, I'll be sure to let you know."

"Thank you. That would be very helpful."

They chatted a while longer, and then Vivienne saw Mother Superior leading the children back across the courtyard. The boys were all holding chunks of bread and Maleine gave something to the dog to eat as well. The church bells rang out, calling the nuns to prayer.

"Oh, it's time for the evening prayers." Magdalena stood as well. "I'm afraid you'll have to leave now."

"Magdalena, I think I want to come back home for good." Cassandra started crying. "But I am sure Zachariah will never permit it."

"Oh, Cassandra, please don't cry." Magdalena gave her sister a quick squeeze. "I'll do my best to help convince Zachariah to accept you back, if Lady Vivienne doesn't already do it on her own."

"Thank you." Cassandra sniffled and hugged her sister once again.

Vivienne thought she saw something from the corner of her eye by the entrance to the catacombs. She turned quickly, blinking several times since it was already dusk and she wasn't sure her eyes weren't just playing tricks on her.

"What is it, Lady Vivienne?" asked Magdalena. "Is something wrong? You look startled."

"I'm not sure. I could be mistaken, but for a second I could have sworn I saw someone over by the entrance to the catacombs."

"Not a ghost I hope," said Magdalena.

"Nay, I don't think so. It looked more like...a man. In a cloak."

"No, that can't be," said Magdalena. "No one comes here anymore, and the crypts are closed up and haven't even been entered for years. There is no reason for anyone to be here. Since there are so many rats down in the catacombs, the dead are now buried in the graveyard right outside of the church."

"Oh. I see." Regardless of Magdalena's explanation, Vivienne couldn't get the thought out of her mind that mayhap she really did see someone. Or perhaps a ghost. Still, there was no time to ask more questions. The church bells were ringing out, calling the nuns to evening prayer. Plus, it was dusk and she needed to get everyone back to the castle safely since she promised her aunt they'd be back by dark.

They all mounted their horses and left the abbey and once again Vivienne looked back over her shoulder at the crypts. Was her mind playing tricks on her to think she had seen a mysterious man in a cloak? Perhaps she was going mad like her uncle. She decided not to think about it again tonight because she had so many other things to concern herself with right now. A wedding, a murder investigation, and a reunion between Zachariah and Cassandra were at the top of her list.

Family was the most important thing of all, and she hoped she could convince the sheriff to forgive and accept his sister back with open arms. It wasn't going to be easy, so she'd have to work hard and fast at it before Zachariah ended up sending poor Cassandra away again forever. Vivienne wanted Zachariah's family all reunited, and wouldn't stop trying until she succeeded.

Chapter Twelve

Zachariah had just sat down at the table, ready to eat the sumptuous meal of roasted goose, root vegetables, and herb-encrusted buns, when the door to the house slammed open and Martin, Mouse, and Grunt ran in. The dog barked and the boys squealed with excitement. Cassandra, Adrian, Maleine, and Vivienne were right behind them.

"What's all the noise about, laddies?" grumbled Nairnie, looking up from the table.

"It looks like we'll need a few more plates, Nairnie," said Isaac.

Nairnie mumbled to herself and pushed up from the table to get them. As soon as her back was turned, Isaac reached out for another slice of goose.

"Isaac, don't even think of taking more food until the others are served," warned Nairnie.

Isaac slowly pulled back his hand and looked at Zachariah and mouthed the silent words, *"How does she do that?"*

Zachariah responded with a shrug.

"Hold tightly to Midnight so Grunt doesn't chase her,"

Zachariah instructed his daughter. Then he looked over at Vivienne. "What's going on? Why are you all here?"

"I'm escorting the others back to the castle," Adrian spoke up, with his hand on the hilt of his father's sword that was strapped to his weapon belt.

"We're not staying, Sheriff. Just dropping off Cassandra on our way home," Vivienne told him.

Nairnie put down the stack of plates and threw her hands in the air. "Well, make up your minds. I'm a nursemaid, not a kitchen servant." She waddled over to the bench and sat back down.

"I'll get my own plate, Nairnie, don't worry about it." Cassandra walked over to where Nairnie had left her plate, obviously not wanting to serve a whore.

"Why are you all in town this late? It's already dark," Zachariah pointed out.

"We're coming from the abbey," said Adrian, once again answering before Vivienne had a chance to do so. He walked over and sat down at the end of the table, helping himself to an herb-encrusted bun and taking a big bite.

"I want one too," said Martin, hurrying over and sitting next to his good friend Starah. Mouse silently squeezed in between Martin and Isaac on the bench, his eyes devouring the goose. Maleine sat in the open space at the far end of the table.

"God's teeth, why dinna ye all just stay for the meal," said Nairnie with a sigh. "Goose, make yerself useful and bring over plates for the rest of them. And don't forget the cups and pot of spiced cider."

"Nairnie, she has a name!" gasped Vivienne, not able to believe how the old woman had just insulted the sheriff's sister. "It is Cassandra."

"Aye, I guess it is," said Nairnie, taking the plates from

Cassandra and proceeding to put food on them and pass them around. "Sit down, Lady Vivienne. The food is gettin' cold."

"I really think we should get back to the castle. My aunt is expecting our return before dark."

"Too late for that," said Zachariah. "And I'm sure by now she doesn't really expect you to do what you say."

"Sheriff Fitch, that was uncalled for." Vivienne couldn't get angry with him since she knew that what he said was true. She also didn't want to be a burden to the sheriff or Nairnie. Especially since Nairnie was so grouchy lately ever since she and her husband Bear split up. If the old woman continued to stay so irritated, she might just leave, and then Zachariah wouldn't have anyone to care for his daughter.

"Mother, I want to stay," said Martin, getting up on his knees on the bench and reaching over the table to take the plate of food from Nairnie. He gave it to Mouse and waited for the next one. Mouse looked up at him with big brown eyes and a cute little grin crossed his face.

"Please, Lady Vivienne? Can they stay? I feel safe with Martin here," said little Starah, burying her nose into the cat's fur as she hugged Midnight closer.

"Sit down, my lady," said Zachariah over his shoulder. "I'll be sure to escort all of you home right after the meal. I'll even apologize to your aunt and tell her it was all my idea that you stayed."

"Well, if you insist." Vivienne was about to sit next to Zachariah when she saw Cassandra standing by the fire with her empty plate in her hands. "Cassandra, you take this seat next to your brother. You two have so much to catch up on."

"What?" Zachariah looked up in surprise. He wanted to sit next to Vivienne and had hoped she'd want to be close to him as well. The last thing he wanted was to talk to Cassandra since he really had nothing to say to her.

"Oh, thank you," said Cassandra, shyly settling in next to her brother.

"Ye gave us the cups but forgot the cider," Nairnie said to Cassandra.

"I'll get it, Nairnie. Everyone just stay seated." Vivienne hurried toward the fire to get the pot, being sure to put on the padded mitt first to keep herself from being burned.

"Oh, my lady. I'll do that." Maleine jumped up and took it from her. Vivienne went and sat between Cassandra and Nairnie, and Zachariah figured she planned on acting as a wall between them should a fight break out.

They ate in silence for a few minutes and Zachariah decided to speak up to break the awkwardness. "So what were you doing at the abbey?" He picked up his cup and took a sip of cider.

"We were visiting with Magdalena," said Cassandra, almost causing Zachariah to choke on the hot liquid.

"Were you," he said, glancing over to Vivienne. "And I wonder why that is."

Vivienne didn't answer him. Instead, her eyes interlocked with his and then she quickly looked away. "Did anyone want another bun?" she asked, picking up the tray of buns in the center of the table.

"I do," said Isaac, hurriedly taking the tray from her, but not before Mouse and Martin could grab the last two buns. "Damn it, make more food, Nairnie," scowled Isaac putting the empty platter back on the table. Grunt laid his chin on Isaac's lap and looked up with a slight whine. "If I didn't get any more, then neither do you," Isaac told the dog.

"Come here, Grunt," said Vivienne, calling her dog over and handing him a slice of roasted goose under the table.

"I saw that. I'm no' cookin' for hounds, Lady Vivienne," scolded Nairnie, giving her the evil eye. "And I didna ken I'd have so many mouths to feed or I would have made more," she said, now glaring at Isaac.

"So...what is new with Magdalena?" asked Zachariah, wondering how the reunion went between his two sisters.

"Magdalena wants me to move back to Mablethorpe for good," Cassandra announced. "And I'm going to do it."

"What?" That surprised Zachariah, and he almost dropped his cup. He didn't think a nun would want to reconcile with a whore. Even if they were sisters.

"I agree with her. I think you should stay here, too," said Isaac, talking as he chewed. "It's not safe for you to return to Southwark. Stay here in Mablethorpe where we can protect you. Right, Zachariah?"

"Now, wait a blasted moment." Zachariah didn't like where this was going. The last thing he wanted was to have both his mercenary brother and his whore sister living here with him. This was going to be nothing but a bad influence on his daughter. "I never said Cassandra could stay."

"Zachariah, don't be silly," Vivienne spoke up. "This is Cassandra's home. If she wants to stay and start a new life in Mablethorpe, then of course she should be able to do so. It's a step in the right direction."

"It's too crowded here," complained Zachariah. "And I'm sure Nairnie doesn't want to keep sharing her room with Cassandra." He had hoped Nairnie would start a fuss and come to his aid. Instead, she just blew a puff of air from her mouth, shrugged and said nothing.

"I won't be living here for long, Brother," Isaac assured him. "As soon as I can afford to move out, I will."

"You're not the one I want out of here," mumbled Zachariah, finishing off his food.

"Mother saw a ghost by the crypts today in the abbey," Martin spoke up.

"Not again. Is that true, my lady?" Zachariah leaned forward to look around Cassandra to talk to Vivienne.

"I'm not sure." She leaned forward to see him. "I thought I saw something or someone from the corner of my eye, but it was dusk and it could have just been my eyes playing tricks on me."

"She thinks it is that mysterious man in the cloak. You know...the murderer," said Cassandra, taking a bite of food.

"Nay!" screamed Starah, tears in her eyes. "Father, don't let anyone kill Lady Vivienne or Martin or any of us. Stop him!"

"Starah, you heard Lady Vivienne. Her eyes were just playing tricks on her. There is no reason to be scared," Zachariah told his daughter, trying to calm her down.

"Just the same, we'd better make sure all the windows and doors are locked up tight tonight," said Isaac, only managing to make Starah cry out again. She got up and left the table with the cat in her arms, and ran up the stairs to the bedroom.

"I think I'd better go try to calm her down." Zachariah stood to go, but Cassandra jumped up and put her hand on his arm to stop him.

"Nay, Brother. I'll do it. After all, I never should have mentioned the killer in front of the children."

"We're used to it," said Martin calmly.

"Yes. It doesn't bother me either," Mouse spoke up.

Sadly, hearing that didn't make things better. Zachariah felt it was time to end all this. "Nairnie, you'd better comfort the girl, while I escort the others back to the castle."

"Aye, Sheriff." Nairnie started to get up, but Cassandra stopped her too.

"Nay, Nairnie. I want to do it." Cassandra picked up her skirts and ran after Starah before Nairnie could even go.

"You're going to put up with that?" Zachariah asked Nairnie.

"I've got dishes to do and Isaac is goin' to help me. Besides, my old legs canna outrun a whore, so why even try?" Nairnie got up and started to collect the plates, seeming to have lost her spirit ever since Cassandra showed up.

"Me? I'm not going to do dishes." Isaac looked at Nairnie and then over to Zachariah. "It's not a deputy-in-training's job."

"Just help her," Zachariah told him. "After all, you're still earning your keep while you're staying here and eating me out of house and home."

"Fine," said Isaac, grumbling about it as he started to collect the dirty plates.

"Come on, Grunt," Maleine called out from the door, holding it open.

"Wait!" shouted Adrian, running to the door. "I'm the protector. What are you doing opening the door at night? It's not safe. I need to do that, not you."

"Oh, stop it, Adrian," said Maleine with a roll of her eyes. "I might be a girl but I assure you, I am far more capable than you think I am."

They left the house squabbling, with Grunt leading the way.

"Come along, Martin and Mouse," called out Vivienne. "It's time to leave."

"But I didn't get to say goodbye to Starah." Martin pouted as the boys headed to the open door.

"I'm sure Nairnie will let her know that you said goodbye." Zachariah walked Vivienne to the door as the boys stepped outside.

"Why dinna ye just let the Goose do it?" was Nairnie's snide reply. "After all, we ken she is skilled in far more than me." Nairnie banged the plates around and managed to accidentally step on Isaac's foot. He cried out and dropped a stack of plates that went clattering to the floor. "Ye clumsy fool," yelled Nairnie. "Ye're only makin' more work for me."

"Let's get out of here, fast." Zachariah took Vivienne's arm and escorted her from the house and closed the door behind them.

"It seems that Nairnie is pretty upset about Cassandra staying here," Vivienne mentioned once they were outside.

"She's not the only one," he mumbled. "Nothing is ever going to be the same again, now that Cassandra has decided to stay in Mablethorpe...where she no longer belongs."

ONCE THEY RETURNED to the castle, the sheriff offered to apologize to Vivienne's aunt, but Vivienne told him she'd probably already be in bed and convinced him just to leave. Thankfully, they didn't come across her uncle. The boys went directly to their room, and Maleine and Vivienne made their way to the kitchen with Grunt.

"I like Cassandra," said Maleine making small talk. "Even if she is a...Goose."

"I like her, too," said Vivienne.

"Why do the sheriff and Nairnie both seem to hate her?"

"The sheriff doesn't hate her. Not really," said Vivienne. "He is just not used to change. But I'll bring him around. In time."

"Well, what about Nairnie? Why doesn't she like Cassandra? Is it because she's a whore?"

"Part of it is, I suppose," Vivienne answered as they neared the kitchen. "However, I think Nairnie is just very unhappy with everything lately since she and Bear went their separate ways."

"Do you think they'll ever reconcile?"

"Not according to Nairnie, they won't. However, I wish they would."

"Mayhap they just need help," said Maleine. "You are good at bringing people back together, my lady. Can't you do something to bring Bear back to her so they would at least have a chance to talk and make up?"

"I'm afraid not," said Vivienne. "Part of the reason Nairnie pushed him away is because Bear is always out at sea for the King and never around for her."

"Then talk to him."

"I don't even know where to find Bear, so that's impossible."

"Not him. I mean the King. After all, he is your father. I'm sure there is something he could do to help."

"Cassandra mentioned that too, and I think that's a wonderful idea, Maleine." Vivienne took the King's ring out from under her clothes, toying with it in thought. It hung from a chain around her neck. This was the ring her mother had given her when she'd divulged the information that King Edward was Vivienne's birth father. She often held it when she was upset and somehow, crazy as it sounded, it tended to calm her down. Mayhap it had more to do with the fact that her mother used to wear it, rather than it being from the King.

Grunt ran after a mouse, knocking into people as he barked and chased the rodent.

"Nay, Grunt," Vivienne called after her hound. "Oh, he's going to cause trouble. It's too late to be so noisy."

"I'll fetch him and bring him back to your chamber, my lady." Maleine ran after the dog. Vivienne turned and headed into the kitchen, surprised to find her aunt still there. She was at a table talking with Cook and Maria.

"Aunt Ellen? What are you still doing up?" she asked. "I figured by now you'd be in bed."

"Hello, Vivienne," said her aunt with a nod. "Aren't you a little late?"

"I'm sorry," she apologized. "We dropped off Cassandra at

the sheriff's home and he asked us to stay for a meal. The children were hungry and I know we shouldn't have stayed...but we're all home safely now. The sheriff escorted us."

"You should just be happy that your uncle isn't here since he wouldn't be as understanding as me."

"Thank you," said Vivienne. "Aunt Ellen, what is going on here?"

"I have basically completed the plans for Cook and Maria's wedding the day after tomorrow." Aunt Ellen let out a satisfied sigh.

"I'm sorry I wasn't here to help you. That must have been so much work on your own."

"We recruited some of the servants to help out," Maria told her.

"Where did you want us to put the garlands, Lady Mablethorpe?"

Vivienne turned around to see Leif, the jongleur, and Wymond, the stableboy, walking through the kitchen with their arms filled with garlands strung together made of pine boughs and other natural plants.

"You two helped?" Vivienne giggled.

"We were told we had to," complained Leif, making a disgruntled expression since they were doing such work. "Even though I wanted to practice the new song I wrote for the wedding, I helped anyway. But you know, the lute isn't going to play itself."

"Nay, I can't say it will," she chuckled. "Oh, nay." She hurried over to inspect the garland. "You boys used ivy when you should have used holly."

"It all looks the same to me," said Wymond with a shrug. "What difference does it make?"

"You need to get those garlands out of the castle at once.

Bringing ivy indoors is bad luck," said Lady Mablethorpe rushing over to them.

"It is?" asked Leif as he and Wymond looked at each other in a confused nature.

"Since ivy is frequently found in graveyards, it is linked to death," Vivienne explained.

"It also has ties to pagan traditions," added Vivienne's aunt.

"It's bad luck indoors for sure," Cook spoke up from over by the fire.

"Oh no." Maria rubbed her very pregnant belly. "We don't want bad luck or anything to go wrong for us regarding the baby or the wedding."

"Plus, if Lord Mablethorpe sees it, he'll be blaming anything that does go wrong on you two, since you wove the boughs with ivy and brought them indoors," said Vivienne. She looked around, hoping not to see her uncle. "Did Uncle Gilbert already pass through the great hall?"

"Don't worry about him, dear," said her aunt. "He wasn't feeling well and has been in his chamber sleeping for hours now."

"Nay, he hasn't," said Wymond. "His horse was gone from the stable for most of the night and he just returned about an hour ago."

"Are you sure?" asked Vivienne.

"Aye. I saw him rushing up the stairs to his room, pulling off his cloak in his hurry to get up there," Wymond explained.

"His cloak," repeated Vivienne, wondering if mayhap she had seen someone in the crypts after all. But what on earth would her uncle be doing there? Nay, this had to be an unrelated incident.

"Oh, Vivienne. Gilbert must have sneaked out to see his mistress again," whispered her aunt so the others couldn't hear her.

Vivienne looked over at the boys. "Wymond, Leif, you did nice work but please take the boughs outside for tonight."

"Lady Vivienne, please don't tell us that you want us to remake them tomorrow," said Wymond, looking scared at the thought.

"I'll never get my song prepared if we have to re-do them." Despair showed in Leif's eyes.

"Well, we can't have bad luck at our wedding," said Cook. "Nay, I'm afraid we can't use them."

"I really want everything to go well." Maria rubbed her belly again. "But it is a shame since the garlands look so nice and the boys worked so hard on them."

"Vivienne, there is no time to remake the boughs. We still have much to do to prepare for this wedding." Her aunt looked distraught. Vivienne felt bad, realizing she hadn't been doing her part to help.

"I'm sure we could still use the boughs if we just have the wedding out in the courtyard," suggested Vivienne.

"But the weather is already turning colder." Her aunt shook her head.

"Then we'll all wear an extra cloak if we have to, but I'm sure this wedding will be blessed and we'll have a sunny day so I wouldn't worry." Vivienne tried her best to make the situation better but wasn't sure it was working.

"What if it rains?" asked Maria with a slight moan. "Then what will we do?"

"If it does rain and we're all outside, the food I've planned will be ruined. Ruined!" Cook threw his hands up in the air and turned in a half circle.

"Everyone, please calm down. I assure you that this wedding is blessed and that everything will be just perfect," Vivienne told them.

"Lord Mablethorpe still hasn't agreed to the wedding, has he?" asked Maria with a worried look in her eyes.

"He won't make us cancel it after all this work, will he, my lady?" asked Cook.

Vivienne exchanged worried glances with her aunt. While they had proceeded to make plans, it is true that the lord of the castle never really approved this wedding between two of his servants.

"I'll smooth things out with Lord Mablethorpe tomorrow, I promise," said Vivienne, finally managing to calm everyone down. The boys left with the boughs, and Cook consoled Maria softly from over by the fire.

"Do you really think that you'll be able to talk some sense into your uncle regarding the wedding?" asked Lady Mablethorpe. "After all, we've both seen how angry, odd, and unstable he is lately."

"Don't worry about that," said Vivienne. "I'll handle my uncle. Don't forget, after all these years he's never been able to stop me from doing what I pleased, so why should this be any different?"

"I hope you're right, Vivienne. But something tells me you might have trouble this time."

"Believe me, getting Uncle Gilbert to agree to Cook and Maria's wedding is the least of my problems right now, Aunt Ellen. What I really should be focusing on is finding Fanny's killer." And also keeping herself safe from being murdered, although she didn't think it'd be a good idea to say that to her aunt right now.

Chapter Thirteen

Vivienne was up early the next morning, meaning to help finish the preparations for Cook and Maria's wedding so she would have time to join the sheriff in town this afternoon and continue searching for Fanny's killer.

"My lady, how does this look?" Wymond was atop a ladder, hanging the garland out in the courtyard, attaching it to a wooden arch that he and Leif had constructed so that the couple could stand beneath it while taking their vows. Leif was at the other end, holding on to the opposite side of the garland.

"A little higher, Leif," she called out.

"Yes, my lady," said Leif. It was barely light enough to see and they worked by the flame of handheld lanterns.

"And me?" asked Wymond. "What about my side?"

"Lower," said Vivienne, holding her hand to her chin. "Nay, on second thought, a little higher. We don't want any of the tall knights to get caught up in it if they walk through."

"Knights are coming to the wedding?" asked Maleine walking over to join them. Grunt was with her. "Nobles are really going to attend the wedding of two servants?"

"Well, I'm not exactly sure who all will be here but

everyone is invited," said Vivienne. "We'll play it safe just in case and hang the garland a little higher."

"My lady? Are we done yet? I really need to string my lute." Leif yawned, not being used to getting up so early. Usually the servants were awake and working before anyone else, but Leif was a musician. They played late into the night and had no real reason to wake up early. Before now, anyway.

"Well, I'm not sure." Vivienne saw someone in the shadows heading toward the stables, and recognized the man as her uncle. "Yes, that's good." She turned to Maleine. "I see Lord Mablethorpe is heading to the stables. I'm going to try to follow him to see where he goes."

"Oh no. Lord Mablethorpe?" Wymond descended the ladder so quickly that he nearly fell. "I let Snuff and Chomp out of their cage to catch mice in the stable this morning since the horses were half asleep and basically still. But Lord Mablethorpe doesn't like them to be out of their cage. I need to collect them quickly before he discovers them and kills them."

"Snuff and Chomp are in danger?" asked Maleine, talking about Wymond's ferrets. "We've got to help them. Quickly, let's get to the stable."

"I'll try to distract my uncle while you two put the ferrets back into their cage," said Vivienne.

"But, my lady," said Maleine. "Won't that ruin your plan of trying to follow him to find out if he has a lover on the side?"

"It will, but the ferrets right now are more important. I'm sure I'll have another chance to follow him later. Now go."

While Wymond and Maleine ran to the stables, Vivienne hurried toward her uncle.

"Good morning, Uncle Gilbert!" she called out, but he didn't stop walking. "Going for your morning ride?" she asked, knowing that would get a reaction out of him.

He stopped and slowly turned toward her. "Vivienne, what

on earth are you doing up before the sun? Everyone knows how late you like to sleep."

"I usually do, that's true." She ran to catch up to him. "However, today I woke up early to finish preparing for Cook and Maria's wedding tomorrow." She waited for his explosion of anger, but it never came.

"Yes, that is tomorrow, isn't it?"

"Aye. It is."

"What time?"

"It is planned for noon."

He nodded and continued to walk but Vivienne had to give Maleine and Wymond more time to catch the ferrets and to put them back in their cage.

"You'll be attending, won't you?" she asked, causing him to stop and turn around once more.

"What difference does it make if I'm there or not?" he asked her. "It is merely the wedding of two simple servants. It's not as if nobles were being married."

"True, but you are usually fair and giving, Uncle. Why do you even object to this wedding?"

"You know the tarnished past of those two kitchen servants," he sniffed. "They were not actually innocent in the death of my good friend, Lord Gainsborough, yet they are free to walk around as they please."

"Please, my lord. You know as well as I do that they were both cleared of any charges."

"I still don't like it. Why are we rewarding people who did wrong?"

"I'll make sure the ceremony is over with as quickly as possible. I'm doing this because I consider both of them friends. You aren't going to object to the wedding, are you?"

"Would it make you change your actions if I did?"

"Well...nay. I suppose not. We've already done so much work and the plans are in motion."

"Then I've proven my point. Now if you'll excuse me, I'm on my way to the stable."

"Are you going for your morning ride?" she asked him.

"That depends."

"On what?" She figured he was going to complain that she was pestering him too much, but his answer surprised her.

"On whether Castor has taken my horse again without my permission. I swear, I don't know why I put up with that man."

"Castor has taken your horse before?"

"Not just my horse, but I've also caught him wearing my cloak at times." He continued to walk.

"And you haven't dismissed him for that?" Vivienne didn't understand why he'd put up with such actions from a servant.

"He's been with us for many years, Vivienne, you know that. He is loyal and a good worker, but sometimes he pushes me too far. I probably should have dismissed him by now, but your aunt feels sorry for him since he has no family. So, to suffice her, I let the issue slide."

"Aunt Ellen knows what Castor has done yet she agrees to keep him?" Vivienne found it interesting that her aunt was now acting odd too, and wondered why.

"Vivienne," he said, turning toward her. "In case you haven't realized it, your aunt and I have not been so compatible for quite some time now."

"Oh, really? I didn't notice." She lied, of course, but was trying to get her uncle to open up to her. "Is that why you've decided to take a mistress?"

"Damn it, how many times do I need to tell you that I don't have a mistress?"

"If not, then where do you go in the mornings and why are you away from the castle for so long by yourself?"

"I usually go riding alone just to get away from her, to be honest. But I know we need to make amends. I've known it for years now and have been doing something that she'd never expect."

"I'll bet you are," she said. "So what is it?"

"Why don't I just show you instead of telling you?"

"You are going to let me ride with you? Really?" She couldn't believe her ears.

"If you want to come along, then do so. If not, stand here and continue to accuse me of having a mistress and of being crazy, since I know what is being said behind my back. I don't really care."

"No one thinks you're crazy," she said, running after him as he entered the stables. He stopped and turned around and crossed his arms over his chest.

"No?"

She couldn't go on lying to him because he'd always been able to see right through her. Therefore, she figured she might as well admit it. "Well, mayhap just a little addled. You tend to forget things a lot or say or do things that don't make sense."

"Vivienne." He grabbed her arm. "I don't know why that happens, but honestly, I think somehow, someway, someone must be slowly poisoning me. Perhaps it's somebody who wants to take over my position as lord of the castle once I'm dead."

"Poisoning you? You must be jesting."

"Nay, I'm not. And since you were almost poisoned not long ago, you must know how much this concerns me."

"I'll look into it, if you'd like."

"Nay." He held up a halting hand. "I don't want you to do anything of the sort. Just focus on your murder investigation. If someone is really after you, then it is important that you catch them before you end up dead like your parents."

"Oh, so you're aware of my death threat?" She was surprised that he knew.

"I've heard rumors and just figured they were true."

Vivienne made a mental note to ask if Zachariah or Isaac shared the news with her uncle. They were supposed to keep it a secret.

"Lord Mablethorpe, good morning," said Wymond, stopping in front of them. Vivienne could see Maleine off to the side, locking the ferrets into their cage.

"Where is Castor?" asked her uncle.

"I...I'm not sure." Wymond looked around. "I've been busy with hanging garlands and wasn't paying attention."

"Well, is my horse here?"

"Yes. Yes, your horse is in the stall, my lord," Wymond answered, stretching his neck to look.

"Well? Are you going to saddle it for me or stand here all day acting like a dolt?"

"Right away, my lord." Wymond ran to saddle the horse.

"Saddle my horse as well, Wymond," Vivienne called out. "I'll be riding along with Lord Mablethorpe this morning."

"Aye my, lady," he answered.

"And hurry! I haven't got all day," ground out her uncle, once again not seeming able to control his anger.

Vivienne was in shock. She never thought her uncle would actually invite her to ride with him. Finally she was going to find out to where he always disappeared. And hopefully after they returned, she'd be able to assure her aunt that he didn't have a mistress after all.

They rode toward town at breakneck speed, and as they approached, her uncle finally slowed their pace.

"Have you and the sheriff got any ideas regarding who might have killed Fanny and threatened your life?"

"Just a few suspicions we want to follow up on, but not a whole lot of evidence," she told him.

"Well, certainly you must suspect someone."

"We've seen a mysterious man in a cloak, but that's it."

"Tell me more about that."

"Some of the patrons said they saw him in the tavern the night Fanny was murdered and his presence seemed suspicious."

"What did he look like?"

"He was totally concealed by his cloak, so no one knows. Actually, we don't even know at this point if the cloaked person was a man or a woman. All we know for certain is that they were tall."

"Ah. Tall like Castor," he said.

"Castor? Are you trying to say you suspect he could kill someone?"

"He does disappear with my cloak and my horse and never gives me an explanation as to why he takes such liberties or where he goes."

"Yes, that is suspicious. You shouldn't put up with such behavior, Uncle."

"I am starting to see that mayhap I have made a mistake in being so lenient with the man. I will change that soon, I promise."

"Good idea," she told him.

"Is there anywhere else you've seen this mysterious cloaked man?"

"No. Well, mayhap. I thought I saw him at the entrance to the crypts in the abbey, but it was getting dark and my eyes could have been playing tricks on me."

"Vivienne, you are imagining things since your life has been threatened. Those crypts are closed up and haven't been entered by anyone for many years."

"You're probably right," she agreed, feeling foolish now. "I admit that the thought of someone possibly watching me and trying to kill me has shaken my nerves."

"Here we are." Her uncle stopped at a house at the edge of town, away from most of the others. She recognized it as the home of the old, blind carpenter, Wallace.

"This is Wallace's home, isn't it?" She didn't really know the man but had heard about him.

"It is," he told her, helping her to dismount. "Wallace is blind, but he is still a very good carpenter."

"Yes, that's what I've heard. And he must also be efficient since he lives alone. Didn't his wife leave him for another man?"

"Yes."

"Did they ever find out where she went or who she is with now?"

"Not that I've heard of, but that's none of my concern. Finding people is the job of the sheriff, not a noble."

Vivienne got the feeling her uncle was insinuating that Zachariah wasn't doing his job. Instead of arguing with him, she let it go. "I'm glad that Wallace can still live by himself." Vivienne felt sorry for the old hermit. "I've heard it said that Wallace and his wife moved here years ago and only lived in Mablethorpe for about a month before his wife left him. He must have really loved her since he never remarried."

"It's none of my business and neither is it yours."

Vivienne didn't know much about the blind man since he was such a hermit and barely left his house and rarely had visitors. She realized, albeit belatedly, that she should have taken it upon herself to visit him now and then. "I also heard they once had a son, but he died. Apparently, they moved here from Northumbria to forget the pain."

"Vivienne, enough!" snapped her uncle.

"I'm sorry," she said, seeing that she was irritating him with all her questions and comments. However, for poor Wallace, the pain just seemed to continue and that didn't seem right at all. The man tended to have bad luck indeed.

They walked up to the house and her uncle softly knocked on the door and then opened it without waiting for a reply. "Wallace? It's me, Lord Mablethorpe. I came to see if you've finished the project for my wife yet." It was dark in the house, but she supposed that a blind person didn't need to open a shutter or light a candle to see.

"Ah, Lord Mablethorpe, come in. I am happy to say that I am almost finished."

"Hello, Wallace," said Vivienne, just to make her presence known. "My name is Lady Vivienne. I am Lord Mablethorpe's niece."

In the daylight now coming through the door, Vivienne could see the blind man cock his head as he listened. "Lady Vivienne, I've heard of you but we've never met, have we?"

"Nay, I don't believe I've had the pleasure before now."

"Of all people, I never expected you to be here. I hear you are usually busy helping the sheriff solve murders and different crimes."

"Yes, I help him with his murder investigations. I'm sorry about your wife." She didn't know why she said that, but was trying to be friendly and uplifting. However, when she saw the dark shadow cross the man's face, she instantly regretted her words.

"Wallace is making something for me to give to your aunt," said her uncle. "I want to reconcile with her and hope this will help."

"What is it?" she asked, wondering what her uncle was doing.

"I was trying to keep it a surprise and I didn't tell you since I didn't want you to accidentally tell her, but it's a throne."

"A...throne, you say?" Vivienne surely wasn't expecting to hear that!

"Yes, I hope it will win back Ellen's admiration."

"I see." In Vivienne's mind, she was thinking he would have better results with a bouquet of flowers or mayhap some special fruit tarts from the baker's shop. But, she supposed, at least he was trying. That was all that mattered.

"I should be finished in the next day or two," announced Wallace.

"How long have you been working on it?" she asked him.

"Oh, let me see." Wallace put a hand to his chin. "It's been mayhap a few years now, I'm thinking."

"That long?" she gasped.

"I'm sure it hasn't been that long," her uncle whispered to Vivienne, pointing a finger to his temple and tapping his head to let her know he thought the man was addlepated. "A year at the most, but I'm not rushing Wallace since I want a good job."

"Can I see it?" asked Vivienne.

"I'm going to light a candle so we can view your progress," announced her uncle lighting a tallow candle by the door. The room lit up in a soft glow, illuminating a huge throne chair that was so large it looked ridiculous. It was ornate in every way possible. It appeared to be made from several kinds of wood layered together to make it look like the chair had stripes. Big claw feet like eagle talons grasped ball shapes which she could only imagine were supposed to symbolize worlds. Vines and wild animals were carved into the wood leading up to the backrest where more carvings showed dragons and wild boars and what she could only imagine was some kind of water monster. The craftsmanship was phenomenal, but it was so big and manly-looking that she was sure her aunt would hate it.

"My, that's...something," she said, at a loss for words.

"Do you like the dog?" asked Wallace.

"What...dog?" Her eyes searched up and down the chair but she couldn't find a cute little dog anywhere.

"Right here," said Wallace, making his way over to the chair and tapping his finger against the front leg. A beast with an open mouth and sharp fangs took her aback. "It's Grunt," he said, with a chuckle. "I carved his image into the wood. I love to carve things," he told her.

"That's Grunt?" she asked. "Do you mean...my dog?"

"Yes, your dog, my lady," he said, sounding very proud. "I've heard his barking in the streets and although I've never met him, I have heard he helps to solve mysteries with you."

"Yes. Yes, he does do that." Suddenly, Vivienne realized that for as long as she'd known about Wallace, he'd always been blind. In his mind, Grunt must look like some kind of feral beast since he'd never even seen him. She glanced up at her uncle and he motioned for her to agree that she liked it. "Yes, I do see Grunt now. How nice of you to include him, Wallace. I am...honored." This had to be the ugliest, gaudiest, most despicable chair she'd ever seen in her life. Even if it was well constructed and the carvings were realistic.

"Do you think your aunt will like it?" asked Wallace.

Vivienne didn't want to lie, but then again, she didn't want to hurt the man's feelings either. Not when he'd been working on the project for such a long time. "I'm sure she'll find it to be one of a kind," she said, wanting nothing more than to get out of there right now before she lied to a blind man any more than was necessary. This had to be one of her lowest times and she didn't feel good about her behavior at all.

"Did you bring the gold leaf for the back of the chair?" asked Wallace.

"I did." Her uncle dug into his pouch and pulled out a box and put it in the man's hand.

"You're going to gild the chair too?" she asked with a gasp, not having thought it could get any gaudier, but now she could see that she was wrong.

"Nothing but the best for dear Ellen," said her uncle with a chuckle.

"And the money. Where's the money?" Wallace held out his open palm. "I need to buy food and supplies."

"Calm down, I've got it." Her uncle pressed a small pouch of coins into the man's hand. Wallace quickly opened the pouch, felt the contents, and frowned.

"That's not what we agreed upon, and you know it."

"You know I give you the fee in payments," explained her uncle. "The rest of the money will be delivered to you when you finish the damned chair."

"That wasn't our original agreement. If you don't keep our deal than neither will I." Wallace threw down the pouch and coins spilled onto the floor. Vivienne's eyes opened wide in surprise when she saw how many were there. "And these are not gold. You promised me gold florins."

"You did?" Vivienne looked over at her uncle, knowing now that he truly must be crazy to promise gold florins to a blind man.

"I don't have any gold florins right now," growled her uncle. "They've been stolen from me, but I'll have them for you when the chair is finished. Now get working."

"I'll start talking, I will," the man spouted off. "I'll let everyone know just what kind of a man you are and pretend to be."

"Enough!" shouted her uncle. "You cannot speak that way to a noble. Do it again, and you'll be punished. Come along, Vivienne, we need to leave."

"What does he mean he'll start talking?" she asked, feeling confused.

"Nothing. Let's go!"

"Let me help him pick up the coins first," she said, getting down on her knees to do so, feeling sorry for Wallace. But before she could do so, her uncle's rough grip dragged her to her feet and hauled her out the door. "Goodbye, Wallace," she called out, but the man was on his knees feeling around for the coins, grumbling, and didn't respond.

"That man is greedy," complained her uncle as they left his house and mounted their steeds.

"I've always heard that Wallace was just a simple man. And appreciative of everything and anything that anyone gives him or does."

"Time changes everyone, Vivienne. Never forget that."

"Uncle, did you really promise to give him gold florins? Even though you have already been making payments to him for years now?"

"Only one year, Vivienne. I told you the man has no sense of time, being blind and holed up in that little hovel all by himself with barely any outside contact."

"Yes, I suppose he's confused," she said. "After all, his wife left him and that is so sad. I am sure he's lonely and that he really loved her."

"Not as much as I love Ellen. That is why I commissioned the throne to begin with. I'm sure this will make things better between us."

"Yes. I'm sure," she said, really thinking it was only going to make matters worse. Her uncle knew that Ellen didn't like anything too big and bulky or overly ornate. She wondered if deep down he was only having Wallace make something that *he* really wanted, and not what her aunt would desire, after all. "But gold florins? Why would you pay him so much?"

"I don't intend to give him gold florins at all."

"So...you lied then? Were you hoping he wouldn't know the difference? I assure you, even though he's blind he will know."

"Don't get me wrong, I was going to give him a few, but it no longer matters since I don't have any to give him."

"I heard you say they've been stolen?"

"Yes. They were."

Vivienne's mind went to the gold florin that Castor gave Sigga and also to the story Cassandra told her, that Fanny had a regular mysterious customer in Southwark that would always pay her with gold florins. "How long ago did this happen?"

"A while ago. I don't remember."

"You don't know?"

"I had them in a secret chest in my chamber and never looked at them much. I don't know if they've been gone a year or ten years. I should have checked once in a while, but I was saving them for some special day and had no need for them until now."

"Did you know that Castor said that the mysterious man in the cloak paid him a gold florin to get information out of the whores at the Hogg's Head Inn regarding the Winchester Geese and where I was staying with them?"

"What?" His head snapped around. "He said that? Really?"

"Yes. Mayhap Castor is the thief who stole your gold coins since it seems he thinks nothing about taking your cloak or horse whenever he wants either."

"Dammit, if that's true, I'm going to kill him."

"Don't say that, Uncle. And honestly, don't ask him about it or do anything right now. Let the sheriff continue to investigate. If Castor is a thief, he could be a murderer too. I'll tell Sheriff Fitch about this."

"Do you think Castor is Fanny's murderer? Really?" asked her uncle.

"I didn't say that, so please keep this between us. This is how gossip starts. I don't know anything yet," said Vivienne, as they rode through town.

"Aye, you're probably right. We need to keep this to ourselves until the sheriff can investigate further."

"I do think that whoever threatened my life is also the person who hired those two men to kill my parents seven years ago."

"Hired? Don't you mean the ones who killed them?"

"Nay, Uncle. Don't you remember that assassin at the joust? He said someone hired him. And the night my parents were murdered, there were two attackers on the road."

"So, mayhap the second man on the horse was the man who hired this assassin."

"Perhaps. Or there might be another assassin on the loose yet, and also the man who hired the both of them to kill Mother and Father."

"Vivienne, I think I'd better bring you back to the castle where you'll be safe."

"Nay. I see the sheriff's and Isaac's horses up there by the coroner's office. You go back to the castle, and I'll join them. I need to help them with this murder investigation."

"I should escort you inside."

"It's right here, Uncle. I'll be fine. Please, just go back to the castle without me."

"Have it your way. As usual," said her uncle with a sigh. "Now remember, not a word about Wallace and the throne to anyone. Not to your aunt, your handmaid, or even the sheriff. I want to keep it a surprise."

"I promise," she said, parting ways with her uncle, then riding up to the coroner's office and dismounting.

"Lady Vivienne, up here!"

She looked up to see Isaac sticking his head out the window on the second floor and waving his hand.

"Is the sheriff with you?" she asked, as she tied up the reins of her horse.

"I am," came Zachariah's voice and then his face appeared at the open window as well. "God's eyes, don't tell me you came here unescorted? How many times do I have to tell you not to do that?"

"My uncle escorted me, but has just gone back to the castle."

"We found something on the body that we've missed before," Isaac relayed the information.

"I'll be right there," she said, hurrying up the stairs, eager to be away from the gaudy throne and the crazy blind man, not to mention an angry uncle. Finally she was back to investigating with Zachariah and where she belonged. It was the only thing, besides being a mother, that she wanted to do for the rest of her life.

Chapter Fourteen

"What were you doing with Lord Mablethorpe in town?" Zachariah asked Vivienne, once she had joined them in the coroner's office. He hadn't seen much of her lately and it really bothered him. Especially since they had a murder investigation in process. Vivienne seemed distracted. He had the feeling something was really bothering her, and he would have to find out later just what it was.

"It's nothing worth mentioning," was her answer. She headed directly over to the table with the corpse, covering her nose with a hand cloth since the body was starting to decay and stink. "Tell me. What did you find?" She looked around the room. "And where are Gandalf and Torsten?"

"They were here," Isaac spoke up. "But it seems someone died in town so they were called away to collect the body."

"Really? Another murder?" Her brows raised in suspicion.

"Nay, I don't think so," Zachariah answered. "It sounded like a natural death. Someone who had been ill for some time now."

"Why didn't they call for the priest and physician then,

instead of a coroner?" she asked. "After all, if it wasn't a sudden, unnatural, or suspicious death, why are they even there at all?"

"I don't know, Vivienne," Zachariah answered, sounding impatient. "I didn't ask."

"Well, why not? You are the Sheriff of Mablethorpe and need to know everything that is going on in town."

"Oh, like where you've been and why your uncle was in town this morning?"

That shut her up. She changed her focus to the murder now, thankfully.

"What did you find?" she asked once again.

"This," said Isaac, holding up a white feather.

"A goose feather?" Vivienne looked confused. "I don't understand. Fanny had lots of feathers attached to her hair and clothes."

"Yes, but not any white ones," Zachariah explained. "Also, this feather wasn't on her dead corpse when we fished her out of the horse trough."

"What do you mean?"

"We, along with Gandalf and Torsten, found it when we came up to this room to view the body this morning," Isaac explained.

"It was atop Fanny's chest," said Zachariah. "And it wasn't there before."

"Well, mayhap Torsten or Gandalf dropped it there."

"Nay, we asked them and they didn't," Isaac broke in.

"So what are you saying?" Vivienne inspected the feather. "That the killer sneaked in here just to place a white goose feather atop Fanny's body? That doesn't make any sense at all."

"Exactly." Zachariah walked over to the table and picked up a gold florin and held it up in the air. "This was also found in Fanny's mouth."

"It wasn't there before," Isaac added.

Vivienne froze and her gaze settled on the gold florin in his hand. "That's odd. How did we miss it?"

"We didn't," said Isaac. "We, along with Gandalf, all looked into Fanny's mouth when her body was first brought here. It wasn't there. Until now."

"Oh." Vivienne stepped away from the table and wrapped her arms around herself. "So, it's almost like someone is trying to leave a message or a warning."

"Or their mark," said Zachariah, putting the gold florin back down. "Vivienne, I'm afraid the killer is still here in town and possibly watching our every move."

"Nay." She shook her head, almost as if she didn't want to believe it. "I'm sure they are long gone by now."

"Your life is still in danger." Zacharia walked up and put his hand on her shoulder. "I don't like you disappearing on me so often. Or going anywhere alone. I think until we solve this murder and find the killer, who might also be after you, that you'd better stay at my home where I can keep a better eye on you."

"I can't do that," she told him.

"Why not?" he asked. "Afraid you'll ruin your reputation?"

"Nay, that's not it at all. But I have a brother and son back at the castle whom I've been too busy to tend to lately. I also have Cook and Maria's wedding tomorrow. I am needed there."

Zachariah didn't like to hear this at all. Then again, he knew better than anyone that Vivienne had a mind of her own and was controlled by no one.

"At least promise me you'll stay around other people day and night and go nowhere on your own."

"I have things to tend to, Sheriff. I'll not be confined to rules and feel like a prisoner in my own home."

"Vivienne, this is serious." He picked up the note from the table that they'd found on Fanny. The note pertaining to Lady

Vivienne. "Someone is after you, whether you want to admit it or not."

"We don't know for certain that the note has anything at all to do with me."

"You are in denial. Your life is in peril, and I'll not let you wander off alone to be nothing but bait for some madman who might have killed your parents and who is out to do the same to you now."

"Sheriff, you know better than anyone that I want nothing more than to catch and punish the killers of my parents. However, I am not going to stop living in the meantime, and I refuse to live in fear."

Just like that brave and stubborn little girl he'd grown up with, Vivienne was still the same person, but now she was in a woman's body. With more means to go where she wanted and do what she wished on her own, he could see this was going to be a problem.

"Promise me, Vivienne. It's for your own safety."

"I can't make a promise that I might not be able to keep."

"Then at least agree that after the wedding tomorrow, you'll stay with me at my home until we catch the murderer."

She didn't seem happy with that idea. "What about Martin and Adrian? Am I supposed to leave them unprotected at the castle while I'm cowering in hiding, here in town with you?"

"Bring them along too," said Isaac, making Zachariah spin around on his heel and glare at his brother. How big did he think his home was? It was already cramped with Nairnie, Isaac, Starah, and now his damned Winchester Goose sister. Not to mention the pesky cat.

"Well, I suppose that might work," said Vivienne, with a hand to her chin in thought. "Then I'd be right here in town to investigate things closer, and my son and brother would surely be safe since they'd be in my care."

"Yes," said Zachariah, clearing his throat, not wanting to tell her he didn't want them to come with her. He supposed that since they were her immediate family, their lives could very well be in danger too. "That's fine. Bring Martin and Adrian with you then."

"Thank you. But you know I can't leave my handmaid behind."

"Maleine?" Zachariah's head snapped up. "Oh, I don't think she needs to join you."

"Why not? She is my handmaid and it is her job to tend to my needs. Not to mention, she's been a big help with the past few murder investigations. I think in this case we could use the extra eyes."

"All right, fine," Zachariah grumbled. "But no one else. My home is already overcrowded."

"No other people, I agree," she answered with a smile. "Just Grunt."

"Your dog too?" Zachariah was almost ready to explode. "You know that Midnight doesn't get along with him."

"And you know that Grunt is a bloodhound and has also been more than helpful in solving past cases."

"I think it's a good idea," said Isaac, getting another scowl from Zachariah.

"Vivienne, I don't know about this." Zachariah's head was already filled with visions of the cat and dog chasing each other around his house and Nairnie chasing after the animals waving her damned ladle in the air.

"If I must remind you, Sheriff, it was all your idea to begin with," she told him. "If Grunt can't stay at your home, too, then none of us will be there, I'm afraid."

"Fine, you win." He had no choice but to agree, and already regretted his decision.

"Good," she said, heading toward the door. "Since you want

to stay at my side, you can join me later today as I head out to the bakery, the butcher, and then over to the chandler's shop, to pick up the rest of the things needed for tomorrow's wedding."

"What are you talking about? We need to interview witnesses," he said, putting the coin back down on the table and hurrying after her. "Can't you have a servant do those menial chores?"

"I suppose I could, but since I have been too busy with the murder investigation to do much in helping with the preparations for the wedding, I want to do my part. For Cook and Maria, of course."

"Of course," he grumbled.

"I need to show them that I truly care. It's important. Now hurry up, Sheriff. We have a lot of work to do before tomorrow's wedding."

Zachariah didn't feel as if any of these things regarding the wedding were necessary. But Vivienne would be assisting him with the investigation first, and he supposed he needed to reciprocate by helping her afterwards. To him, Lady Vivienne Harlowe was one of the most important people in his life, and he didn't ever want to do anything that might possibly let her down.

AFTER SPENDING a good part of the day interviewing more people about the murder and not coming up with a single lead, Vivienne decided it was time to collect the things for the wedding and head back to the castle. She'd made sure to recruit Isaac and Zachariah to help her. Since the sheriff had refused to leave her side, she figured she'd put them to work.

"Lady Vivienne, I didn't expect you to show up personally to collect the candles," said the chandler, Miles, as he wrapped up the tapers made of scented beeswax that Vivienne insisted they had to have. After all, Cook and Maria didn't have much in life and she wanted them to feel important, and to have nice things for their special day.

"Neither did the butcher or the baker," said Vivienne, paying the man and taking the bag of candles from him.

"I just figured you'd send a servant for the candles, the way Lord Mablethorpe does."

"My uncle sends a servant for candles?" she asked, surprised to hear this. "But that is my aunt's responsibility, not his."

"He said he is trying to get on her good side by helping out. He's been doing it for years now."

"Really." If so, she wondered why her aunt and uncle hadn't reconciled yet. "I'm sure you were busy having my order for beeswax candles as well as his. That must be a lot to make."

"Oh, no. He always orders tallow candles," said Miles.

Vivienne figured that sounded like her uncle. Never wanting to spend more money than he had to. "Well, thank you, and have a good night." She turned and started for the door.

Isaac and Zachariah waited outside in the street for her since they were watching over the horses that were already loaded down with items they'd be taking back to the castle for the wedding. Thank goodness they had their horses to carry the supplies for them or she didn't know how they'd transport all the goods.

"I wish for a good night, but I'm afraid it won't be," said Miles, causing her to stop and turn around.

"Why not?" she asked. "Is something wrong?"

"I want to close my shop since my wife isn't feeling well," Miles told her. "However, I am still waiting for blind old Wallace to pick up his tallow candle order. He comes once a week, always at the same time and is usually never late. But he hasn't shown up today at all."

"Did you say Wallace?" she asked, thinking she had heard him wrong.

"Yes, that's right."

"Why on earth would a blind man need candles?"

"I'm not sure. Ever since his wife disappeared, he's been living alone as you know. Yet, he still comes in once a week right on schedule to pick up a shipment of jar candles."

"Miles, how long ago was it that Wallace's wife disappeared?"

"Seven years," he told her, putting the jar candles into a burlap bag.

"Seven years. Are you sure it's been that long?"

"I'm positive. It was right after our first son was born, and he is now seven." Miles made his way around the counter, blowing out candles as he went. "Well, I guess I'll just have to deliver the candles to Wallace myself. I'd better hurry if I want to get home before dark. I don't like to be out in the streets or anywhere near Rotten Row after sunset. Not with a killer on the loose."

"Nay, of course not," she said in thought. "Miles, go tend to your wife and children."

"I can't," he said. "I need the money from Wallace to feed my family since I've been down on my luck lately. I have to make this delivery."

"I'll pay you for his candles, and I'll deliver them to Wallace's house myself."

"You? Oh no, Lady Vivienne, I can't let you do that. It's not right and neither is it safe."

"Don't be silly. I like to help out when I can. And it is more than safe." She nodded toward the door. "I have the sheriff and his deputy-in-training with me. Here, this should cover the cost." She handed him a few coins and took the bag from him.

Miles looked down to his palm and shook his head. "This is too much money, my lady."

"Keep it," she told him. "Use it for medicine to heal your wife. Well, I need to go now."

She headed outside, being greeted by Zachariah, who took the things from her and gave them to Isaac to put in the saddle bags while he helped her mount her horse.

"Well, that's the last stop. Let's head back to the castle," he told her.

"Nay, we have one more place to go first," she announced turning her horse.

Isaac groaned. "Nairnie is going to be furious if we show up late for another meal."

"You can head on back to the house if you want, Isaac," said Zachariah. "I'll escort Lady Vivienne and then take her home and help her unload the supplies. Just tell Nairnie not to wait for me to eat. You might want to mention to her about our houseguests starting tomorrow, too, so she can prepare for them."

"Nay, I'll wait." Isaac settled himself atop his horse, looking the other direction.

"Go on, Isaac. There is no need to come with us," Zachariah tried to convince his brother.

Vivienne almost laughed since she could see what was going on here.

"I am not going to be the one to tell Nairnie anything of the sort," said Isaac in a huff. "And don't tell me it is part of my training, because it's not."

"This will be fast," Vivienne told them, not wanting poor Isaac to be put in that awkward position. "I just need to drop off some candles at Wallace's house at the edge of town."

"Old blind Wallace?" asked Zachariah with a chuckle.

"Why in heaven's name does he need candles? The man walks around constantly in the dark."

"I'm not sure, but he didn't show up to get his weekly shipment, and Miles needs to tend to his ailing wife and doesn't have time to deliver them. I promised him I'd deliver the candles for him."

"This sounds silly, but all right." Zachariah got atop his horse. "But as soon as we deliver them, you are going back to the castle and I'll not hear another word about it."

"Yes, Sheriff," she said with a roll of her eyes.

They rode through the streets in the near dark since the sun had just set. Vivienne suddenly felt cold and her stomach twisted into a knot.

"Oh, no," she said aloud.

"What's the matter?" asked the sheriff from atop his horse.

"It's my stomach. It is churning again."

"So is mine," complained Isaac. "It's called hunger, since we've barely eaten today."

"No, Isaac. This always happens to me right before something bad is about to transpire," she explained.

"I'm sure it's nothing. You're just tired," Zachariah told her. "Everything will be fine."

"I wish I could believe that, but my stomach tells me otherwise."

They arrived at Wallace's house and Vivienne dismounted before Zachariah could help her. As she looked at the blind man's hut, her stomach twisted more than ever.

"I'll take the candles in there. You stay here with Isaac," ordered the sheriff, heading to the house with the bag in hand. Vivienne was sure something was very wrong. Something that had to do with Wallace.

"Stay here and watch the horses and supplies so no one

steals them," Vivienne instructed Isaac. "I'm going inside and no one is going to stop me."

"Whatever you say, my lady," Isaac answered with a stifled yawn.

"Hello? Wallace? It's Sheriff Fitch, so don't be alarmed," Zachariah called out banging on the man's door. "Open up, we have your candles."

When no one answered, he knocked once more, but still received no reply in return.

"That's odd," surmised Zachariah, looking back at her. "Mayhap he didn't hear us."

"Sheriff, Wallace is blind, not deaf," Vivienne remarked. "Something is wrong, I just know it." Before the sheriff could stop her, Vivienne pushed open the door and stepped inside.

"Vivienne, what are you doing?" she heard Zachariah say from behind her.

"I am finding out why Wallace didn't answer us." She took a few more steps and her foot hit something, causing her to stop. At the same time, the sheriff lit a candle near the door.

The room lit up, and Vivienne looked down and screamed. There, on the floor, was Wallace. His blind white eyes stared up at her and he wasn't moving. His throat had been slit, and blood covered his body, running in rivulets on the floor.

"God's eyes, nay!" Zachariah rushed over and hunkered down to check for signs of life. "I'm afraid we're too late, Vivienne. Wallace is dead!"

"Nay," she cried, her eyes fixated on the poor man's face. "I just saw him today and he was very lively."

"You did?"

"Yes. I was here with my uncle earlier."

"What's all the screaming about?" Isaac rushed into the house and stopped in his tracks when he saw the dead man lying there. "Oh, ugh. Another murder, I see."

"And I think the killer is the same person who murdered poor Fanny," said Zachariah, plucking a white feather off the top of the dead man's chest and holding it up for them to see.

"It's a feather. A white goose feather." Vivienne's hand clutched her stomach. She truly felt as if she would retch now.

"Wallace doesn't have any livestock so there is no reason for a feather. This is the killer leaving his mark again, I'm sure," stated Zachariah. "Isaac, check his mouth."

Isaac bent over and stuck his fingers in the dead man's mouth and pulled out a gold florin. "Yep," he said. "Most certainly the same killer."

"I think I'd like to go back to the castle now." Vivienne's body started to shake. This was all getting to be too frightening. Now she understood the sheriff's concern for her safety. There was a killer out there, and for all she knew she could be the next victim on the list.

"Vivienne, I'll take you home," Zachariah said in a soft voice, standing up and putting his arm around her. "Don't look," he said, turning her so she wouldn't have to stare at all the blood. "Isaac, fetch the coroner. I'll return as soon as I know Lady Vivienne is safely home and locked inside the castle walls."

"I'm going." Isaac let out a deep sigh. "We're never going to get to eat today, are we?" he mumbled as he headed for the door.

"Not now, Isaac," said Zachariah. "We have another murder to investigate, and I'm afraid to say that this one might not be the last."

Chapter Fifteen

Vivienne hadn't slept well at all but it wasn't surprising, considering the circumstances. Every time she closed her eyes, she kept dreaming that she was being attacked and her throat was being slit by a man in a cloak. Just like poor old Wallace lying there bleeding to death, she seemed to be able to feel his pain and fear. Then, when she finally did drop into a slumber, she was quickly woken up once again.

"My lady, my lady, please wake up."

She opened her eyes to see Maleine wringing her hands together, standing above her with a worried look on her face.

"What is it, Maleine? Did something happen to Martin or Adrian?" Vivienne bolted up to a sitting position, her heart beating wildly. "Where is Grunt? What is happening?"

"Please, calm down, Lady Vivienne. Everything is fine," said Maleine, holding out her hands, trying to steady Vivienne's emotions. "It's just that today is Cook and Maria's wedding. It is very late and everyone is looking for you."

"Oh no!" she cried, bolting out of bed. "There is so much to do." She paced the floor. "What time is it?"

"The wedding will start in one hour, my lady."

"One hour?" Vivienne's eyes opened wide. "Why didn't you wake me earlier, Maleine?" She ran to the wardrobe to choose a gown to wear to the event.

"I tried to, honest I did, but you wouldn't get up." Maleine followed her to the attached room where her clothes were kept. She stood at the door and continued to wring her hands together. "You had such a restless sleep and kept whimpering and crying out in your sleep. I was worried for you. I figured you were having that nightmare again, and that you needed your rest."

"I don't need rest," she said, choosing a purple velvet gown and then pulling off her nightshift and throwing it to the floor. "What I need is two of me." She continued to dress, with Maleine's help.

"Two of you? That's silly," said Maleine, following Vivienne out of the wardrobe with a pair of shoes in her hand. "One is more than enough trouble."

"Maleine, that wasn't nice." Vivienne sat down at her dressing table and ran a boar's bristle brush through her long hair.

"I'm sorry, my lady. It's just that you seem so distracted lately."

"Well, I have a wedding to attend, and I wasn't done decorating yet. I need to get to the kitchen and make sure the food is being prepared correctly too. Oh, and I wanted to give Cassandra one of my old gowns to wear for the wedding so she doesn't stick out so much in a crowd." She threw down the brush and bent over to put on her shoes.

"Cassandra already has the gown."

"She does?"

"Yes. I had Wymond deliver it to her in town earlier, since I knew you wanted her to have it."

"Oh, good. Thank you, Maleine. That is one less worry."

"You don't need to worry about anything, my lady. Wymond, Adrian, and Leif have been helping Lady Mablethorpe all morning with the preparations. They even got Martin and Mouse involved although the boys wanted to watch the knights spar on the practice field. I was just down in the courtyard and everything looks beautiful."

"Remind me to thank them all. They are so wonderful. Especially my aunt. She shouldn't be going to all this trouble for mere servants."

"That's what your uncle keeps saying."

"Oh no. Is my uncle in the courtyard too?" This couldn't be a good thing. At least not for Cook and Maria since he didn't like them. "I need to hurry and get down there." Vivienne ran to the door.

"What about your hair, my lady? Don't you want me to plait it?"

"No time," she said, grabbing a cloak from the wall. Her hand wavered over her sword that was hanging there, but she decided at the last minute not to take it. Although she was concerned for her life right now and wanted a means to protect herself, showing up at Cook and Maria's wedding with the blade of that size at her side was only going to alarm them. Nay, she didn't need it. She was inside the castle walls and safe now. Therefore, she wouldn't need her sword until she went back to town. Still, something told her to take her dagger and so she stuck it into a band she wore around her hose to keep them up, under her skirt.

Hurrying down to the great hall with Maleine right behind her, she bumped into her uncle climbing the stairs.

"Good morning, Uncle Gilbert," she said.

"What's good about it?" he grumbled. "Two servants are using my courtyard to be married and everyone is acting like they are nobles. They don't deserve the attention, the expense, or all the fuss. I never should have allowed this to proceed."

Vivienne had never seen her uncle so angry toward any of the servants. He was usually such a fair and caring man. "Cook and Maria are very appreciative for the wedding, and want to start out their family right by being married."

"That's another thing. If that strumpet is going to lift her skirts so easily and get pregnant, she shouldn't even be working here at the castle at all. I should have her dismissed."

"Please, Uncle. Don't start trouble. Not today. The wedding will be over within a few hours. Just don't do or say anything to upset Cook or Maria, I beg you."

"I have no idea why I let you get away with all of your silly ideas. You need to be harnessed. I won't put up with this anymore, Vivienne."

"I am only trying to help two people that I care about. Is it too much to ask that poor servants have a little happiness in their lives too?"

"I no longer care to discuss this. I'm going to my chamber." He stepped around her and headed for his room.

"Lady Vivienne, hurry. Your aunt needs you in the court-yard," called out Leif from the bottom of the stairs. "She wants you to approve the way we decorated for the ceremony."

"I'm sure it's just fine," said Vivienne, walking down the stairs only to next meet the apothecary from town. "Mark? What are you doing here?" asked Vivienne, surprised to see him since he didn't usually come to the castle.

"I'm sorry, my lady. I didn't know there was a wedding taking place here today, or I wouldn't have come," said the man. "I am just here to deliver some potions." She could see that he had two small glass bottles clutched in his hand.

"Who are they for?" she asked.

The man hesitated before answering. "For...Lady Mablethorpe. But she wants it to remain a secret, my lady."

"My aunt wants potions and asks that no one knows about it?" This made Vivienne extremely curious. "Mark, please tell me. What are they for?"

Mark's eyes traveled to Maleine and then back to Vivienne. "I'm sorry, but I can't say. I need to keep that information confidential. Do you know where I can find Lady Mablethorpe?"

"I can fetch her for you," offered Maleine.

"Nay," Vivienne stopped her. "Maleine, you go out to help in the courtyard. I'll put the bottles in Lady Mablethorpe's chamber for now and let her know they are there later. She is much too busy to be bothered right now."

"Yes, my lady," said Maleine with a quick curtsy. She hurried away.

"I'll take those, thank you," said Vivienne with an outstretched hand but the apothecary was hesitant to hand them over.

"I'd rather give them to Lady Mablethorpe myself."

"Oh, I'm sure you need your payment. I can give you the money." Vivienne reached for her pouch but the man shook his head.

"Nay, my lady. She's paid for them. It has just taken me a while to make them, since it isn't an easy herb to find and she required so much of it."

"Mark, what is in those bottles? You need to tell me. Is my aunt ill?"

"Nay, I don't believe so," he said, looking down at the bottles. "This is meant for something else."

"Let me see them." She grabbed them from the man's hand, but they were not marked with the name of the contents. She popped open the bottle and took a sniff and felt as if she were about to be choked.

"Lady Vivienne, please close up the bottle. You shouldn't be doing that," the apothecary warned her.

"Tell me what's in it," she demanded to know. "And if you lie, I'll have you punished."

The man looked up and she saw fear in his eyes. "Nay, please don't do that. I am only filling an order."

"Then tell me."

"It is mandrake root oil, my lady. It is used as a sedative." He couldn't meet her eyes with his when he spoke.

"Mandrake root? Isn't that toxic?"

"Only if used in large amounts."

"What would happen if a large amount was taken?"

"It can make a person hallucinate and almost seem as if they've gone mad." He stared down at his feet.

"What?" Her head snapped up. "Why would my aunt even ask for this?"

"I can't guess her intentions. I told you, it is sometimes used as a sedative, so mayhap she is having trouble sleeping."

"I haven't heard of her having any trouble."

"Well, it is also considered by some to be good luck. Mayhap that is why she wants it."

"Good luck? How so?"

"Superstitious people believe it will protect them from evil spirits."

"How long have you been making this for my aunt?"

"It's been years now, I must admit. But honestly, I don't know what she is doing with it or why she requires so much of it. I don't ask questions of the nobles when they give me their orders. It is not my business, nor my position to do so, my lady. You must understand that I need to keep my clients and their needs discreet. If not, my job is at stake."

"Of course, I understand," she said, looking at the vials,

thinking that no one, no matter how superstitious they might be, could ever require that much oil as a talisman.

"I am glad to hear that, my lady."

"For years, you say?" asked Vivienne, looking at the bottles in her hand. "How many years, Mark?"

He didn't answer.

"Is it seven years by any chance?"

"Yes, I believe that's about right," the man finally answered.

"Why would she want this? Really?"

"I don't know." The man shrugged his shoulders. "I just supposed it was because...because she was so shaken up after the murder of her sister that she was adamant about warding away evil for the rest of her family, including you."

"She's never mentioned this to me."

"I believe she was embarrassed. Because she is so superstitious. Please, don't tell her that I told you about it. I don't want Lady Mablethorpe to know. I promised to keep her secret."

"It seems as if a lot of people have secrets around here lately."

"My lady?" asked Mark in question. "I don't understand."

"Never mind. I'll be sure to put these in her room."

"I really think I need to deliver them to her myself." He tried to take the bottles but Vivienne moved them out of his reach.

"Don't worry, she won't care if I know since I am superstitious as well. I won't reveal her secret to anyone, so you won't be in any trouble, I promise."

"But, my lady—"

"There is a wedding I need to attend, so you are dismissed now. Thank you."

"Yes, my lady." Mark hung his head and bowed. "Thank you. You are too kind." He bowed once more and headed away.

Grunt came running up the stairs to greet her, sniffing at the bottles.

"Well, hello there, Grunt," she said. "Nay, don't sniff these bottles. It could be fatal."

She turned and headed up the stairs with the dog following. This truly upset her. Why was her aunt getting mandrake root oil, and why so much of it? Did she really need that much sedative for her nerves? Or was she using it for something or someone else? The apothecary said it could cause someone to go mad if they took too much of it. That raised even more suspicions for her.

Vivienne approached her aunt's chamber door and was about to enter, but stopped. She glanced down the corridor to her uncle's room and started piecing things together. Hadn't it seemed as if Uncle Gilbert was going mad? Plus, he'd been very angry and acting strangely since the death of her parents. Well, mayhap her aunt had something to do with his condition, although she truly hoped not. None of this made any sense at all. Why would Aunt Ellen want to possibly harm her husband? They had always been so much in love.

Then again, Vivienne and her aunt believed that her uncle had a mistress. And her aunt had said their marriage hadn't been the same for a long time now. Had Vivienne misjudged her uncle? He had told her that he was trying to make amends with Aunt Ellen, and he even hired Wallace to create a throne for her, as odd as that seemed. Mayhap he wasn't the crazy one, but it was her aunt instead.

Rather than to enter her aunt's chamber, she decided to talk to her uncle about this first. She ended up going to his room instead. Vivienne wasn't even sure if Uncle Gilbert knew that Wallace had been murdered last night, and she wanted to personally inform him. She hadn't told anyone about Wallace, not wanting to spoil the high spirits of the wedding, but since her uncle had hired the man, she felt that he needed to know.

"Uncle Gilbert?" she called out, knocking on his door. "It's me, Vivienne. I need to talk to you. It's important. May I come in?"

Oddly, he didn't answer. She started wondering if mayhap her aunt had poisoned him, since her uncle had told her his suspicions. Mayhap right now he was lying dead on the floor. Just like poor old Wallace. That thought sent a shiver through her body. Her stomach started to clench and her heartbeat sped up uncontrollably. Grunt whimpered and she looked down at her dog.

"I'm not sure what to do, Grunt."

Grunt sniffed at the base of the door and pawed at the floor.

"Oh, I just have to take a look inside." She pushed open the door, but didn't see her uncle anywhere. Hadn't she just passed him on the stairs and he'd told her he was going to his chamber? So where was he? "Uncle Gilbert? Are you in here?" Leaving the door ajar, she entered his room.

She checked the entire chamber and also the wardrobe, but didn't find him anywhere. Then she noticed that his cloak was not on the hook. She saw a brass cup and some bottles on his table, all sticking out of a pouch. Picking up the cup first, she sniffed it, noticing a strong scent. Next, she popped the cork out of one of the bottles, then she took a sniff of that, as well. Sure enough, it was the same scent. God's teeth, was her aunt really slowly poisoning her uncle, just like he somehow suspected? Was he right about that, and if so, what should she do? With her thoughts muddled with this new finding, Vivienne decided she needed to talk to Zachariah.

Just then, she heard cheering from out in the courtyard through the open window, and then the sound of lively music as well.

"Oh no, the wedding has started." She shoved the small bottles into her own pouch and turned to leave. Just when she did so, she thought she saw someone in a cloak with their head covered, just outside the partially open door watching her. "Oh!" she cried, startled. Grunt looked up and growled lowly. She ran to the door and threw it wide open. Grunt sniffed the floor in a circle, in an eager manner. Glancing both up and down the corridor, she saw no one. "Come on, Grunt," she said, feeling very uneasy right now and wanting and needing to be around people. "Stalker or not, we have a wedding to attend."

Zachariah made it to the castle just as the wedding for Cook and Maria had started.

"Are you sure we should be here right now instead of back at the coroner's office?" asked his brother Isaac as they entered the stable where they would leave their horses. "After all, we have another murder on our hands and are no closer to solving the first one yet either."

"I want to be here for Lady Vivienne. This wedding is important to her, and I need to support her." Zachariah glanced out to the courtyard but didn't see her anywhere.

"You also want to keep a close eye on her since there are a lot of people here, don't you?" His brother was sharp. Zachariah couldn't fool him.

"Yes. That is part of the reason, too," he admitted, feeling worried to death about Vivienne's safety now.

"Sheriff? Are you and your deputy here for the wedding? Can I stable your horses?" It was Castor, the peculiar stable hand whom Zachariah didn't care for in the least.

"I suppose," he said, handing the man the reins. "And Isaac

is not my deputy yet, but is only in training." That's when he noticed Castor's tunic was not tied properly. "I'm surprised Lord Mablethorpe lets you walk around half undressed."

Castor's hand clutched the top of his tunic where only one string remained.

"You're missing a tie on your tunic," said Isaac. "You really need to fix that. It's not proper to look so shabby."

"Yes, one of the horses became high-spirited and ripped it off," said the man, taking the reins of Isaac's horse as well. "You'd better hurry if you want to make it to the wedding in time."

"Yes, we're on our way." Zachariah knew the stables of Mablethorpe like the back of his hand since he'd grown up coming here as a child. In all those years, there was a certain stall for each of the noble's horses and it never changed. He'd seen Vivienne's horse and also her aunt's horse, but the stall that held her uncle's horse was empty. "Is Lord Mablethorpe at the wedding too?" he asked over his shoulder, just to test Castor.

"Yes, I believe so."

"Then why is his horse's stall empty?"

Castor seemed to immediately grow nervous. He shifted his weight from one foot to the other. "His horse threw a shoe earlier. I had to take it over to the blacksmith's shop to get a new one," he answered. He couldn't look Zachariah directly in the eye when he spoke, and that made it seem like the man was lying.

"I see," he answered. "Well, we'd better hurry, Isaac, before we miss out on all the fun."

Once they were outside of the stables, he spoke to his brother. "Castor is missing a tie on his tunic."

"Yes, I noticed that too," Isaac answered.

"Vivienne found a tie torn off a tunic in the upstairs room

where Fanny was pushed from the window." He pulled it out of his pouch and held it up, the tie dangling from his fingers.

"That's right," said Isaac. "I almost forgot about that. It's the same color as Castor's tunic."

"It is." Zachariah replaced it back in his pouch.

"Then, let's go arrest him for the murder of the whore." Isaac started to turn around but Zachariah stopped him.

"Nay, not yet," he told him. "Castor could have just lost it while bedding a whore in that room. Any of the whores."

"But it has blood on it."

"He could have had rough sex, we don't know. We need more solid evidence first."

"True."

"Och, I hope we are no' too late for the weddin'."

"Nairnie?" Zachariah spun around to see his daughter and her nursemaid and also his sister Cassandra getting out of the back of a wagon that was being driven by a peasant. Cassandra was thankfully no longer dressed like a whore. However, she was wearing the gown of a noble, and it was one that Zachariah was sure he'd seen Vivienne wear in the past.

"Father, we're coming to the wedding too!" Starah ran over and wrapped her arms around him in a big hug.

"Nay, Starah. You shouldn't be here."

"Why not?" asked his sister. Cassandra walked up with her hips still swaying. It was going to take her a while to unlearn all that she'd learned to become a Winchester Goose in the first place. Nairnie waddled along behind her, with a canvas bag thrown over her shoulder. "Lady Vivienne invited us to be here. You know that, Brother. Just like she invited you and Isaac."

"Of course," he groaned, not wanting any of them there.

"Hope to see you again soon, Cassandra," said the man in the cart, his eyes scanning up and down the woman's body.

"Thank you for the ride, Stewart." Cassandra giggled and threw the man a kiss.

"Stop that!" Zachariah grabbed his sister and pulled her closer. "I don't know what kind of games you are playing, but I don't like the way you are acting around my daughter."

"Can I stable your horse and wagon?" Castor walked out of the stable, talking to the peasant driving the cart.

"Nay, I'm not staying," said the peasant. "I have a field to plow, but was just dropping off the womenfolk, that's all." He turned the wagon and left.

Castor was about to go back into the stables but stopped when he saw Cassandra.

"Hello. Don't I know you from somewhere?" Cassandra asked with a smile.

"No," mumbled Castor lowering his head and quickly walking back to the stables.

"Do you know Castor?" Zachariah asked his sister.

"I'm not sure. But he seems familiar. I swear I've seen him somewhere before."

"He was in the tavern the night Fanny was killed. Perhaps you've seen him there. Or mayhap you remember him from when you lived in Mablethorpe, since he's worked here for quite some time."

"Mayhap, but that is not where I recognize him from. I think, if I'm not mistaken, that I know him from the Southwark stew."

"You do?" asked Isaac with interest.

"Yes." Cassandra narrowed her eyes, drinking in the back of the man. "He's been there often, I'm sure of it."

"Cassandra, this isn't the time or place to be conducting business," warned Zachariah.

"Sheriff, I'll take Starah over to where I see Martin and the others," interrupted Nairnie.

"Oh, nay. Let me take her. I'll do it," insisted Cassandra, running after them. "After all, she is my niece."

"Well, she's my responsibility, Goose, so back away," snarled Nairnie, as the three walked over to the courtyard where the wedding had already started.

"Isaac, keep an eye on Castor," instructed Zachariah, spotting Vivienne, and wanting to be with her. He hurried over to where the musicians were playing their lutes, drums, and harps. Cook and Maria were standing together under an arch made of wood that was covered with garlands constructed of the elements of nature. It was a very pleasing scene and a delightful pine essence filled the crisp air. The priest was with them and they were about to say their vows.

"Vivienne." Zachariah joined her just as the music stopped. "I need to talk to you."

"Shhhh," she told him with a finger to his lips. "They're about to say their vows. Oh, isn't this romantic?"

"Huh? Sure. I guess," he said, standing next to her and watching as the priest married the servants. Just as they said their vows, he felt Vivienne slip her hand into his. He looked over at her and she had a big smile on her face. She glanced at him from the corner of her eye and winked. He cleared his throat and smiled back, hoping to hell that no one saw them holding hands. Then again, it was very crowded and everyone stood shoulder-to-shoulder, so mayhap they wouldn't be noticed. Hopefully.

The ceremony ended and everyone cheered to congratulate the newlywed couple. The music started back up in a lively fashion. Some of the onlookers clapped and started dancing. Zachariah spotted Gandalf and Torsten across the crowded courtyard. Gandalf looked around and raised his hood and then turned and walked away. Torsten was watching the girls and didn't seem to even notice that his employer had left his side.

Zachariah found Gandalf acting suspicious, since they'd been searching for a mysterious tall man in a cloak, and he seemed to be disappearing with no explanation lately. Then again, Castor's tunic tie was ripped off, and he seemed to be hiding the whereabouts of Lord Mablethorpe. Then he saw Orvyn, the inn proprietor, from town standing across the courtyard with Dulcia and Sigga. All three of them were wearing cloaks with hoods covering their heads. Still, he noticed Dulcia's gown and he was certain it was the same gown Fanny had been wearing the day she came to the docks of Mablethorpe. Sigga's hood was blown back by the wind and he noticed she had a feather in her hair. A white feather. Orvyn tossed something up and down in his hand and if Zachariah wasn't mistaken it was dice like the ones he'd found in the trough.

Everyone started to seem suspicious to Zachariah lately, and he shook his head to try to clear his mind.

"Isn't this a beautiful wedding?" asked Vivienne, drawing his attention away from the murders. Her hand slowly slipped from his and he was glad she'd let him go. The last thing he needed right now was trouble from Lord Mablethorpe for holding his niece's hand in public. He looked around and saw Lady Mablethorpe, but not her husband.

"Aye. I suppose so," he answered Vivienne, not paying attention at all to the wedding. He wiped the sweat from his palm against his leg. Being so close to her in a public place was making him anxious. Once again, he looked around, hoping no one had seen them holding hands.

"You *suppose* so?" Vivienne sounded hurt if he wasn't mistaken. "I worked hard with the others to make this wedding special. Look around you. It is a festive sight."

"Yes." He cleared his throat, not knowing what to say. "Well done."

She let out a deep sigh. "Zachariah, you could at least

pretend to be a little more enthused after all the work that went into the festivities."

"Vivienne, I've got two corpses lying as stiff as boards in the coroner's office right now, and a mad killer on the loose. I'm sorry if I'm not more excited about the wedding, but I have a lot on my mind."

"Oh, that reminds me, I need to talk to you about something." Her hand went to her pouch.

"I need to talk to you, too," he said, hoping that, finally, they'd be able to collaborate on what they'd learned regarding the two murders.

"Lady Vivienne, the King's messenger is here looking for you," announced her aunt, making her way through the crowd. "He says there is a missive for you from the King. He's waiting for you in the stable."

"Oh, good. I've been waiting for that. Excuse me, Zachariah. I'll be right back."

"You're going to leave? Now? Really?" Zachariah let out a big puff of air from his mouth, feeling as if they'd never solve these cases and or catch the murderer if they couldn't even find a few minutes to communicate. On past murder cases they'd worked much closer and things went smoother. This time, he felt as if he hadn't even seen Vivienne much at all. She was always so busy. Or distracted, in his opinion. He didn't really need her help, he supposed, but damn it if he didn't want it. Things just weren't the same without Vivienne at his side.

"Zachariah, come quickly," said Isaac, running through the crowd. "You're never going to believe this."

"What is it, Isaac? You're supposed to be keeping an eye on Castor."

"I was, but my attention waned when Cassandra called me over."

Zachariah looked behind Isaac to see his sister headed toward them, too.

"God's eyes, Brother, what does our sister want now?"

"I'll let her tell you herself." Isaac turned around. "Hurry up, Cassandra." He motioned to her.

"Zachariah, I remember where I've seen that man in the stable." Cassandra told him as she made her way to them after weaving through the crowd. "I remember how I know Castor and it is not from Mablethorpe at all."

"Where, then?" he asked, curious to know more.

"It was in the stew in Southwark, just like I said. I'm sure of it now."

"So you've said. Cassandra, I don't need to know, nor do I want to hear about your...clients."

"Nay, he wasn't my client, Zachariah. That's not it at all. But he was always there when that mysterious man in the cloak paid for some time alone with Fanny."

"What?" This took him by surprise. "Cassandra, are you sure about this?"

"Yes, I'm positive. I remember him by the odd way he always looks down to the ground when he doesn't want to be spoken to. Back in Southwark, I tried to lure him to my room on more than one occasion, but he'd never go with me. He just waited for that mysterious man in the cloak to finish with Fanny."

"That's good information," said Zachariah. "It's helpful. If the man in the cloak is our killer, than this proves Castor is somehow involved and working with him. We need to take Castor into custody right away."

"He should still be in the stable," said Isaac. "Let's go arrest him."

"The stable." Zachariah's heart sped up. "God's eyes, that is where Vivienne is headed! We need to hurry, Isaac. Lady Vivienne's life might be in danger."

Zachariah rushed through the crowd with Isaac right on his heels and Cassandra right behind Isaac. "Out of my way. Move!" the sheriff shouted, pushing his way through the horde of people who were celebrating the marriage and were hesitant to move. He had a bad feeling about this. Deep in his gut he felt as if Vivienne was in deep trouble, and that angered him to no end. Damn it, why hadn't he stayed at her side instead of letting her go to the stables without him?

He heard a woman scream from inside the stables and took off at a run. "Vivienne, are you in here?" he called out, bursting into the stable, then stopping suddenly when he saw Vivienne pulling her dagger out of Castor's gut. The stablehand gripped her by the hair, but slowly dropped his own dagger as his knees buckled as he fell to the ground, clutching his wound.

"Vivienne!" Zachariah ran over to her and pulled her into his arms. She was crying. "Are you all right?"

"I had to stab him, Zachariah," she wailed, holding her blade clutched in two hands. "He tried to kill me, I swear he did. But I caught him off guard. He never expected me to have a blade under my skirt."

"Dammit, Castor, why did you do it?" Isaac pulled Castor to his feet. Zachariah could see that Vivienne had stabbed the man in the gut, but was sure it wasn't a bad enough wound to actually kill him. Still, blood spurted out and Castor held his hands over the incision.

"I was ordered...to kill her."

"You're an assassin, aren't you?" growled Isaac.

"I am," he admitted.

"You were with that other assassin when he killed my parents seven years ago, weren't you?" Vivienne's voice trembled as she spoke. She still clutched her bloody dagger.

"Mayhap I was...but it was what I was paid to do. It was...only a job."

"What's going on in here? I heard someone scream," came the deep bellow of her uncle. "Let me through."

"Gilbert, did something happen?" asked her aunt, following on his heels. There was a large group of people right behind them, most likely having heard Vivienne's scream as well. Zachariah was surprised to see Lord Mablethorpe, and now realized that Castor must have been telling the truth about the lord's horse being at the blacksmith's.

"Castor just tried to kill Lady Vivienne," announced Zachariah. "Isaac, place him under arrest for the attempt to kill a noble."

"You tried to kill my niece?" Her uncle was livid and pulled his sword from his weapon belt.

"Uncle, he admitted that he was one of the two assassins who killed my parents," Vivienne told him.

"What else did he say?" Lord Mablethorpe wanted to know.

"That's all we were able to get out of him for now," Zachariah answered.

"Take him to the dungeon," shouted her uncle.

"Nay, not yet," said Vivienne. "First, I want him to tell me who hired him to kill my parents."

Castor wasn't talking, but everyone watching him, certainly was. Whispers went on from behind them.

"Vivienne, this is a wedding. There will be time for questioning him later," said Zachariah, feeling that he didn't want everyone witnessing a murderer confessing all his secrets.

"Nay, I want to know. Now!" she screamed, tears streaming from her eyes. "I've waited too damned long and I want answers."

"My dear, please," said her aunt, putting her hand on Vivienne's shoulder. "I know it is hard to bear, and I am angry too.

But let them put him behind bars for now. He'll be questioned after the wedding celebration is finished. This is supposed to be a special day for Cook and Maria. We don't want to ruin it."

Vivienne didn't want to let this matter go so easily, especially since the man had come after her with his blade right after the King's messenger gave her the missive and left the stable. She was glad she'd stabbed him, and hoped he would die for being involved in the assassination of her parents. But she was not going to let him walk away before she had the answers she needed.

"It'll be all right, Vivienne," whispered Zachariah, walking over and grabbing the man's other arm. "He'll be locked behind bars and we'll question him soon. Now go to Cook and Maria. They don't deserve to have their wedding ruined."

"Nay, they don't," she agreed, using one hand to wipe away the tears from her eyes. "Did you kill Fanny and Wallace too?" she asked Castor as they pulled the bleeding man toward the dungeon.

"Get him out of here," bellowed her uncle. "Everyone, go back out to the courtyard."

Castor stopped right in front of Vivienne and looked her in the eye. "I only do what I'm paid to do, my lady," he said softly. "I have nothing against you...or the others. I was only...doing my job."

"Why did someone want my parents dead? Tell me, I need to know."

"I said, get him the hell out of here. Now!" hollered Lord Mablethorpe. "Guards, help the sheriff take this man to the dungeon and lock him up and throw away the key."

"Did you kill Fanny and Wallace?" Vivienne asked once more, having to hear the man's confession.

Castor's eyes moved back and forth as he scanned the crowd

but still he didn't answer. Then, right before they hauled him away, she saw him nod slightly.

Vivienne looked down to see the bloody dagger still clutched in her hand. The man's blood was smeared all over the front of her gown as well. Her fingers opened and she dropped her blade in the straw on the floor. Vivienne had never killed anyone before, or even stabbed anyone except the other assassin after he'd killed her mother. Her stomach twisted terribly now, and she felt dizzy and ill. What had started out as a happy day had been ruined by this horrible assassin. If she hadn't had her dagger hidden under her gown, she would be dead right now, just like Fanny and Wallace. Just like her poor parents.

Damn it, this man had a hand in killing her parents and she'd never known it, all these years. It made her feel gullible and stupid. How many times through the years had she tried to befriend Castor? That thought alone made her feel like she was about to vomit. So many questions pushed through her mind and all of them still needed answers. Vivienne wanted a clear explanation and she wasn't willing to wait any longer to get it.

Her head dizzied and when she took a step, she swayed. Her stomach twisted into a harder knot, telling her that the trouble still wasn't over. With what little sleep she had gotten last night and now this, she wasn't feeling at all steady on her feet. She really needed to lie down.

"Come, Vivienne, we'll head back to my chamber and I'll clean you up, my dear. Then we'll go back to the wedding cele-bration," offered her aunt. "I have a tonic to give you that will help calm your nerves."

Vivienne's gaze flashed down to her pouch that contained the bottles of mandrake oil. Was her aunt involved in this attempt on her life? Was she going to try to poison her as soon as she got her alone in her chamber? Would the suspicions never end? Vivienne didn't know whom she could trust anymore, and that was the worst feeling of all.

"Let me through—move aside ye big oaf!" Nairnie made her way through the crowd, clasping the hand of little Starah. Cassandra followed right behind, stretching her neck, trying to see over the heads of the onlookers. Maleine was right behind her. "By the rood, Lady Vivienne, ye are bleedin'." Nairnie's gaze fastened to the front of Vivienne's gown.

"My lady, are you injured?" Maleine pushed her way through the crowd to get to Vivienne. Wymond and Adrian were there too. Next came the bark of Grunt, and he ran to her with Martin and Mouse following.

"Mother, you're hurt!" screamed Martin.

"I should have been protecting you." Adrian rushed up to her and slipped his arm around her waist when he noticed she wasn't steady.

"I'm not hurt," she assured them. "I stabbed a man who was trying to kill me and it is his blood you see."

"Someone tried to kill you? Who?" asked her brother. "Tell me, so I can have his head." His free hand went to the hilt of his sword.

"It was Castor," her aunt relayed the information. "Now boys, help me to get Lady Vivienne to my chamber so I can tend to her needs."

"Nay," said Vivienne, not wanting to go anywhere with her aunt right now. "I want to be taken to my own chamber instead."

"That's fine. I'll tend to you there then," said her aunt.

"I want to go with Nairnie and Maleine," Vivienne quickly added.

"What?" Her aunt's hand slipped from her shoulder and hurt shone in her eyes. "You don't...want me to help you? Vivienne, don't forget, that man murdered not only your mother, but she was also my sister." Tears formed in her aunt's eyes, making Vivienne feel bad for her now. But still, she remained cautious and suspicious.

"Ellen, let her go," said her uncle, putting his arm around his wife's shoulders. "And I think it is time to send everyone home. This is not the right time for a wedding."

"Nay, you can't do that to Cook and Maria," protested Vivienne. "They waited too long for this day and I won't have it ruined because of me. Please, Uncle Gilbert. Tell everyone to carry on," she begged him. "Aunt Ellen, I just need to rest for a while. I know you are upset and hurting too, but can I count on you to conduct the rest of the celebration? I know you will do the best job out of anyone here."

Her aunt took a minute to answer. She exchanged glances with her husband and then nodded. She sniffled and leaned her head back against her husband's chest. "Yes, Vivienne, I will do that. Our own woes shouldn't tarnish the happiness of others on their special day."

"Thank you," said Vivienne, glad she wouldn't have to be alone with her aunt right now. Her nerves were so shaken after being attacked by Castor in broad daylight, that she realized she really did need to go back to her chamber and lie down.

"I'll tend to yer needs, Lady Vivienne," Nairnie told her.

"As will I," offered Maleine, stepping forward.

"Let's go, Sister." Adrian helped her to walk.

"I'll help you get her back to her chamber," Wymond said, helping her from the other side.

"We'll come too, Mother." Martin reached out and took her hand.

"Where's my missive from the King?" Vivienne looked around the ground but didn't see it. "I must have dropped it. Someone, please find it for me."

"Go, Vivienne, you've had a rough day," said her uncle. "You need to rest."

Her head spun and she felt like she might pass out, and that was the last thing she wanted right now. Grunt licked her hand and she took a deep breath and released it. "Yes, I'll just rest for a while and then I'll be fine. But I'll not sleep tonight before I get the answers I need from Castor."

"Don't worry about a thing, my dear," said her uncle. "I have everything under control."

She realized that should make her feel better, but somehow it didn't. Honestly, there was something off about her uncle too, and right now she wasn't sure whom to trust...and whom to fear.

Chapter Sixteen

"I've posted your guard, Richard, outside your door. I don't want you leaving this room until I return for you in the morning." Zachariah made a trip to Vivienne's room after locking Castor away in the dungeon. His concern for her safety was great. How could Castor have tried to kill her right there in public? What was going on? "I've told the guard not to let anyone enter except for Maleine. And of course, Isaac and myself. We can't risk any more attempts on your life."

Maleine was with her and Grunt was on the bed curled up next to her. Adrian, Martin, and Mouse had been there, but just left to go down to the wedding to get something to eat.

"Thank you for your concern, but I don't think there is a need for a guard at my door," Vivienne told him, sitting up and letting Maleine fluff her pillows. "And you cannot keep my family from seeing me. That's not right."

"On the contrary, now there is more need than ever to see to your protection," he told her. "But I will tell Richard to allow your immediate family only into the room, since they are not a threat."

"Thank you. The man who tried to murder me is locked up behind bars, is he not?"

"Yes. Of course," said Zachariah.

"Then I should be safe."

"Not necessarily so. We have yet to get answers from him, and there is still the question as to who hired him in the first place. That person, probably the mysterious man in the cloak, is still at large. Isaac and I will be filtering through the crowd since everyone is still here and asking if anyone saw someone talking to Castor right before he made his attempt on your life."

"It happened right after I received the missive from the King. Do you think the murder attempt had anything to do with that?"

"I don't know. What did the missive say?"

"I'm not sure. I didn't have time to read it. When Castor attacked me, I dropped it. Did you find it in the stables by any chance?"

"We'll look for it," he told her. "Vivienne, it seems the mastermind of these murders is trying to keep something from being known. I get the feeling it might be something to possibly do with King Edward."

"I can't imagine what, if that is true."

"Nay. Neither can I, right now. Mayhap it has something to do with your parents having been spies for the King."

"Yes. It seems they had an important message for the King, but didn't live long enough to tell it."

"My lady, I feel we are moving closer to getting answers as to who hired the assassins to kill your parents. I swear, I will find out. But you need to stay put so I can focus on the case."

"Zachariah, you need to go to Cassandra and find out what else she might remember about the man in the cloak who paid Fanny to keep his identity a secret. She helped us by remembering Castor, so she is a big help."

"I just thought of something." Zachariah crossed his arms over his chest and stared at the floor. "Didn't my sister say that it was her friend Fanny's idea to come to Mablethorpe?"

"Yes, I believe she did. That's right."

"Mayhap Fanny knew the man in the cloak resided in Mablethorpe and she wanted to see him again," Maleine spoke up, while helping Vivienne get comfortable on the bed. "After all, it was said he paid her with gold coins, and mayhap she was greedy and wanted more."

"That's a very good point, Maleine." Vivienne reached out to pet Grunt. "You have a sharp mind. I don't know why I hadn't thought of that."

"I learned everything I know about investigating from you, my lady. You've had a lot on your mind lately, so it's not surprising that it slipped past you."

"Let me enter the room, ye fool. I'm Lady Vivienne's healer," came Nairnie's stern voice from the other side of the door.

"Zachariah, please tell Richard that is it all right to let Nairnie see me." Vivienne looked up at him with tired and pleading eyes. "We can trust her."

"Of course," he said. "I'll be back later, so stay put." He opened the door and spoke to the guard. "Let her in. It's fine. Nairnie, who is watching over Starah?"

"Dinna worry about yer daughter, Sheriff. She is with Cassandra who willna even let me get close to the girl lately. She keeps a good eye on her and says she wants to spend time with her niece and to get to know her." Nairnie sighed. "I swear Starah seems to like the Goose more than me. Martin and Mouse are with them too."

"All right, then. I need to get to work." Zachariah left.

Vivienne suddenly thought of something she wanted to tell the sheriff. It was about the bottles of mandrake oil in her pouch. "Oh, Sheriff," she called out, sitting up and stretching her neck toward the door.

"He's gone, my lady." Richard stuck his head inside the room. "Did you want me to fetch him for you?"

"Nay. It can wait, I suppose." She decided it wouldn't be a good thing to talk about her aunt possibly poisoning her uncle with Nairnie and Maleine in the room. In case she was wrong, she didn't want others to have a bad opinion of the lady of the castle.

"By your order, my lady." Richard bowed and closed the door.

"How are ye feelin' Lady Vivienne?" asked Nairnie, putting a big bag down on the bed. "I brought my bag of healin' herbs with me today since I had a feelin' it might come in handy."

"You did? Why?" asked Vivienne.

"I used to have visions that always came true," Nairnie explained. "This mornin' I had a vision of me havin' to tend to someone, but it wasna clear who. Now I ken it was ye."

"Thank you, Nairnie, but I'm fine, honestly. I am just a bit shaken from being attacked in the stable, but I am not hurt at all."

"You have good reason to be so shaken." Maleine tidied up the room as she spoke. "I can't believe Castor is an assassin. And that he was hired to kill your parents. He lives right here inside the castle walls and we never knew it. How scary is that?"

"Yes, it is frightening indeed," said Vivienne, feeling goose-flesh cover her arms. "Especially since Castor has been here since I was a child. I can't believe he was an assassin all that time. If so, why would he bother to work in the stables? This whole situation is odd, and I'm starting to believe that I can trust no one."

"Hrmph! It seems to me that people will do anythin' for money," sniffed Nairnie. "Mayhap he had a little job on the side from time to time, and was staying close to whoever it was who hired him."

"Castor has always been an odd man," said Vivienne. "The only one who has really befriended him through the years is my uncle."

"Lady Vivienne, ye have been through a lot today and the sheriff is right. Ye need to stay here under lock and key for yer own protection. I'll help Maleine get ye dressed in yer night clothes." Nairnie reached out and took Vivienne's pouch from her belt, the sound of the glass vials inside clanking together. "What's that noise? What have ye got in here?" Nairnie untied the pouch to take a look inside.

"Nay! Don't do that," said Vivienne, reaching for her pouch but it was too late. Nairnie had already lifted the small bottles from her bag.

"This looks like some kind of potion," said Nairnie. "Lady Vivienne, are ye ill?"

"Nay, I'm fine." She held out her hand. "Please, hand over the vials."

"What's in here?" Nairnie popped open the top of one of the bottles and took a sniff. "Och! I ken that scent. It's mandrake root. What on earth are ye doin' with this?" She wrinkled her nose as if the smell or possibly just the idea disgusted her.

"Mandrake root?" Maleine's interest was piqued, and she hurried over to take a closer look. "Lady Vivienne, aren't those the vials you got from the apothecary today?"

"This is a very dangerous herb," Nairnie continued.

"What is it used for?" asked Maleine, looking over Nairnie's shoulder.

"I've seen it used as a sedative," the old woman answered. "But if too much is taken, it can cause hallucinations, seizures, and even death."

"Oh nay! Please don't say that," said Vivienne, not wanting to hear this.

"Why did the apothecary give these to ye, my lady?" asked Nairnie, still holding the vials. "And so much of it, too?"

"Those bottles were delivered to the castle earlier today by Mark, the apothecary from town," Vivienne admitted. Now that both Maleine and Nairnie knew about it, she had to tell them the truth. If not, they'd think the wrong thing about her. "He was bringing them for...for my aunt."

"What?" Nairnie's head snapped up and her eyes narrowed. "What in the name of the devil would Lady Mablethorpe want with this?"

"Oh, Nairnie, I'm going to tell you and Maleine something that I've learned, but I don't want you to breathe a word of it to anyone. I haven't even had the chance to tell the sheriff yet."

"What do you mean, my lady?" Maleine sat down on the edge of the bed and leaned forward, eager to learn what she knew.

"Lately, my aunt and I have discussed the fact that we think my uncle might be going mad."

"Go on," said Nairnie pursing her lips and cocking her head.

"Lord Mablethorpe sneaks out of the castle gates early in the mornings to go riding alone. We think he has a mistress."

"I don't understand," said Maleine. "What does any of that have to do with the mandrake root oil?"

"It sounds as if Lady Mablethorpe is jealous and tryin' to control her husband through this." Nairnie held up the bottles.

"So she's poisoning Lord Mablethorpe?" Maleine's eyes opened wide at the thought.

"It sure seems like it," said Nairnie with a nod of her head.

"Oh, nay. I can't believe that. Not really," said Vivienne. "My aunt is concerned about Lord Mablethorpe, but I can't see her being so vindictive as to poison him or possibly want to kill him. She's not a mean person at all."

"Are ye sure about that?" Nairnie squinted one eye.

"Yes. I think." Vivienne swung her feet over the edge of the bed. "I mean, no. Mayhap not. Oh, I don't know anymore."

"Make up yer mind, lassie. This is a serious charge."

"All I know is that I was in my uncle's room earlier and I sniffed one of his goblets. It smelled like mandrake. Also, he told me that he thinks someone might be poisoning him somehow."

"Ye need to tell the sheriff, missy." Nairnie put the bottles down on the side table. "He will ken what to do."

"Not yet," she told them.

"Why not?" asked Maleine. "I agree that Sheriff Fitch should know about this."

"I will tell him. I promise I will. But right now he has a lot on his mind. And there is a wedding celebration in progress. It can wait until morning. Now, I am going to clean up and then we are all going back to the wedding. I will not let down Maria and Cook."

"Ye're no' goin' anywhere, my lady," said Nairnie. "No' with that guard watchin' over yer door."

"That's right, Lady Vivienne. You heard what the sheriff said," agreed Maleine. "You need to stay here for your own safety."

Vivienne realized that it was going to be more difficult to leave the room than she'd initially thought. She was being kept a prisoner in her own chamber and this did not sit well with her at all.

"You're right," she said, devising a plan in her mind. "You two help me clean up and change and then I'll take a nap. That way, you can both go back to the wedding."

"I dinna care to go to the weddin'," said Nairnie. "My old bones are tired."

"Me neither," said Maleine. "I'd rather stay here and help you."

"Nay," protested Vivienne. "If I can't go, then I need you two to be there to support Maria and Cook. It's important. I want you to tell them I am sorry I am being held prisoner and can't celebrate with them."

"Dinna say it that way." Nairnie shook her head.

"Nairnie, I need you to keep an eye on the children." Vivienne continued to try, but it just wasn't working.

"Hmph! I am sure Cassandra has that handled. She is no' lettin' me do my job. No' to mention Starah seems to like her better. I dinna think the sheriff needs me anymore."

"That is not true," Vivienne told her, as Maleine helped her to pull her soiled gown over her head. "And I am worried about Martin."

"Adrian watches Martin like a hawk." Nairnie seemed to have an answer for everything, and this was making it harder for Vivienne. She'd never get a chance to leave the room if this kept up.

"Really, Nairnie. You should go," Vivienne told her. Maleine tried to help her put her nightshift on, but Vivienne refused. "Maleine, I'd feel more comfortable if I wore a tunic and breeches," she told her handmaid.

"I'll get them right away, my lady." Maleine ran back to the wardrobe.

"Ye're wearin' a tunic and breeches to sleep in? Really?" Nairnie seemed to be able to see right through her, and Vivienne quickly looked the other way.

"I feel as if it is too early in the day to be wearing my night clothes," she told the old woman.

"I see." Nairnie plopped down in a chair and folded her hands over her stomach and closed her eyes.

"Nairnie? What are you doing?" asked Vivienne as she

finished dressing. The woman looked like she was getting comfortable and was never going to leave.

"Ye might think it's too early to sleep, but for an old woman like me, it's always a good time to catch a few winks."

"Maleine, I need you to go tell Cook and Maria that I'm sorry I can't be there to celebrate with them."

"Nay, my lady. I want to stay here with you."

"Please?" she asked, nodding toward Nairnie. "I have the big bad bear watching over me," she whispered.

"I heard that!" came Nairnie's reply, her eyes still closed.

Maleine smiled, almost laughing. "I'll tell them right away, don't worry." She headed for the door.

"Don't hurry back, Maleine. Stay to have a dance with Wymond."

Maleine turned back, her cheeks blushing. "Are you sure?"

"I'm positive," she answered. "Take this time tonight to spend with your man. You don't want to lose him."

"Nay, I don't. Thank you, my lady, I will." Maleine hurried out the door.

Vivienne looked over at Nairnie who still had her eyes closed. She had heard the old woman was a sound sleeper, so mayhap she would still have a chance to sneak out after all. Vivienne bent over to put on her shoes.

"I've never heard of anyone besides a drunken sot well in his cups sleepin' with their shoes on," came Nairnie's voice. Vivienne quickly looked across the room to see Nairnie's eyes still closed. "I can see with my eyes closed, lassie, so dinna even think about tryin' to sneak out of this room."

"Sneak out?" Vivienne forced a laugh and got back in bed without her shoes. "Why on earth would I want to do that?"

"Because ye are a determined, strong woman who doesna like to be told what to do." Nairnie's eyes slowly opened. "A lot like me, I suppose."

That made them both laugh.

"Mayhap you know me just a little too well," said Vivienne. "You can see right through people, and I think you know others better than they know themselves."

"That's no' true," said Nairnie. "If so, I would ken what fills Buzzard's head."

Vivienne realized Nairnie was talking about her husband and the problems they'd been having. She also knew that Nairnie was missing him and might need someone to talk to about it right now.

"I'm sure Bear still loves you," she said in a kind voice.

"I'm no' so certain that he cares about me more than he does his ship."

"He works for the King, Nairnie. That is his job, to go out on his ship to sea. He is protecting King Edward."

"Hmph!" she snorted. "He should be home protectin' me."

"Where is your home? You've never told me."

"Cornwall is where I reside. It is where my granddaughter, Gwen, and most of my great-grandchildren are right now. I really miss the place, and my kin. I especially miss the cute little tykes."

"They mean a lot to you, don't they?"

"Of course, they do. I never had the chance to see my own son grow up, and just recently found my grandchildren, Tristan, Mardon, Aaron, and Gwen. All I want to do at my age is to live the rest of my life being with them. Making memories. That is something I missed out on most of my life."

"Then why are you here in Mablethorpe, Nairnie? You need to get back to Cornwall and be with your family."

"I suppose I came to the East Coast because that is where the King has positioned Bear, and I missed him and wanted to be closer to him. But that doesna matter anymore."

"Of course, it matters. Nairnie, why did you send Bear away?"

"Because he doesna love or want me."

"That's not what he said the last time he was here." Vivienne pulled the blanket up over her.

"What a man says and does are two different things, missy. Someday ye'll figure that out for yerself."

"What if things could be different, regarding Bear's work?" Vivienne knew if she could get them together again, they could work things out. "Would you want him back?"

"What do ye mean?"

"I don't know. What if you could see your husband more often without having to leave the rest of your family behind? Would you want him back then?"

"Of course I would. I miss the old Buzzard. My life is no' the same without him. It took me a lifetime to find true love, and I admit that at my age, I dinna want to lose it. But it would take a blessed miracle for anything to actually change."

Vivienne smiled and lay back with her arms behind her head. "Well, I believe in miracles, Nairnie, and I have the feeling that someday soon, so will you."

Chapter Seventeen

It was already dark outside by the time Zachariah got back home with Cassandra and Starah. Adrian, Martin, Mouse, Isaac, and Grunt were with him, since he had promised to take them in for a while and watch after them. Even with Castor behind bars, Zachariah wasn't assured that Vivienne and her family were safe now. There were still answers he needed before he could rest easily.

Maleine and Wymond, who had spent the entire time together at the wedding, were there to help with the children. Since Zachariah didn't want any of them by Vivienne right now, he'd agreed they could all stay with him for now. He left a message with Lord and Lady Mablethorpe where they'd be. Actually, it was Lord Mablethorpe who insisted Maleine and Wymond stay in town too, so it wouldn't be a burden on him with the younger ones there.

"Maleine, can you get the children ready for bed since Nairnie is staying the night with Lady Vivienne?" he asked.

"Yes, Sheriff Fitch," she answered, taking the young ones upstairs while Wymond and Adrian stoked up a fire and played with Grunt. Thankfully, Midnight was hiding abovestairs.

"I wish you'd let me tend to the children." Cassandra smiled widely. "I like being with them, especially Starah. Zachariah, I am so happy here. This is my home and where I really need to be. I know that now, and wish I had never left in the first place."

Zachariah ran his hands over his weary face before answering his sister. "I told you, it's not going to happen, Cassandra, so stop trying. You can't stay. You made your choice, so now live by it."

Feeling exhausted from such a long day, Zachariah plopped down atop a chair while Isaac raided the kitchen, eating once again, although they all had more food than usual at the wedding. Zachariah had personally brought meals to Vivienne's room where she and Nairnie were chatting like old friends. He hadn't left until he felt Vivienne's life was well protected. He wondered if Nairnie had brought her ladle, in case anyone decided to attack. He was sure she would beat them over the head with the blasted thing.

"Let Cassandra stay in Mablethorpe, Zachariah," said Isaac from the kitchen, chewing on something. "I like having her here."

"So does Magdalena," said Cassandra, brushing off her gown. "If Magdalena is a nun and can forgive me, then why can't you?"

"Cassandra, please. I have a lot on my mind and don't want to do this right now." Zachariah was tired of this same conversation. "I'd like to ask you a few questions."

"About what?" She seemed suddenly guarded.

"Is there anything else at all you can tell me about the man in the cloak who used to visit Fanny?"

"Let me think." She sat down next to him. "Just that he was tall with a deep voice."

"How tall? Like Gandalf?"

"Yes, that's about right. Do you suspect the coroner?"

"I'm not sure. Gandalf is older, but it's possible. Torsten told me that lately he's had a lady friend that he's been visiting, and sometimes they even leave town together."

"Well, good for him," said Cassandra with a nod. "But I don't think the man in the cloak was Gandalf. The man I saw moved with grace. Just by the way he climbed the stairs without holding anything, tells me he was younger than Gandalf and more fit. Plus, Fanny didn't like servicing old men, and always looked for the biggest, richest, most handsome clients."

"You said this man always paid with gold florins?"

"Yes. Fanny told me once when she was a little drunk that it was hush money. That's how I know. He wouldn't tell her where he was from, but she thought he came from Mablethorpe."

"It must be so, since you saw Castor with him at the stew. It would make sense," said Zachariah.

"Hush money? What do you mean by that?" Isaac came to meet them, chomping on a chicken leg now. He held it out to Zachariah, but Zachariah shook his head and held up his hand.

"Fanny knew this man well over the years, and I believe he was paying her to keep his identity a secret."

"So you really think he came from Mablethorpe?" asked Isaac.

"I do. When the man stopped coming, Fanny pushed me to come visit Zachariah here in Mablethorpe. She also told me she was coming with me whether I liked it or not."

There was a knock on the door and Isaac went over to open it. "Constable Dorson," he said in surprise. "You're back."

"Yes, I'm back. Is the sheriff home?" asked the man.

"He is. Come on in." Isaac moved to the side and let the constable enter.

"Emery. How did things go in Norwich?" asked Zachariah,

being the only one who really knew where the constable went and what he was doing there.

"It went great." The man smiled. "I'm happy to say that I've been offered the job as the Sheriff of Norwich, and I have decided to take the position."

"What? You're leaving Mablethorpe?" asked Isaac in shock.

"Yes, Isaac. My wife's family lives there and she wants to be closer to them."

"Well, congratulations," said Zachariah, walking over to shake his hand. "You'll make one hell of a sheriff."

"Thank you, Zachariah. That means a lot to me," the constable answered.

"How soon will you and your family be leaving Mablethorpe?"

"Right away."

"Wait. You're leaving? You're really leaving?" Isaac almost choked on his food he was so excited. "Zachariah, doesn't that mean I'll be your deputy, after all?"

"Yes, Isaac, that's right." Zachariah smiled at his younger brother. "You've proven your worth, so you'll be taking the constable's position."

"Yes!" Isaac exclaimed, hitting the door with his hand in excitement, making Grunt bark.

"It's all right, Grunt. It's just Uncle Isaac acting crazy again," said Adrian from over by the fire, pulling the dog over to him and petting him.

"Sheriff, I've just told my wife and she is anxious to leave. She said there have been two murders since I've been gone and an attempt on Lady Vivienne's life?"

"Yes, that's right," Zachariah acknowledged the facts.

"Then I won't leave yet. I can't. You need me. Even if my wife wants to leave town by tomorrow morning. She's frightened for her own life and the lives of our children."

"We've got the murderer apprehended and in the dungeons of Mablethorpe behind bars," Zachariah told him.

"Oh, then it's over?"

"Not quite, but we have it handled, so go," said Isaac, obviously eager to start his new position.

"Sheriff, I'll explain things to Agatha," said Emery. "I'm sure she'll understand that we cannot leave yet."

"Nay. Go," said Zachariah. "Your most important task is to see to your family and their safety. Plus, I'm sure you'll want to get back to Norwich and start your new position as soon as possible."

"Things are quiet there, Zachariah, and I like the sound of it," said the constable, sounding pleased. "There hasn't been a murder there for years. That is where I want my children to grow up. Not here close to places like Rotten Row."

"And I don't blame you. Leave in the morning as planned." Zachariah felt bad for the constable's family, since his own children had been kidnapped by the Pied Piper at one time, and they had all been through so much. No child needed to live in fear the way his wife and children constantly did now.

"I can't leave before I find someone to rent my house," said Emery. "If I don't find someone to take over the payments, I'll still be responsible, and I can't afford two homes."

"I'll move in," Isaac offered. "I'm looking for a place of my own."

"You?" The constable looked over to Zachariah. "Really?"

"Well, why not?" asked Zachariah. "After all, my home is getting more crowded by the day and I can no longer afford to fill my brother's belly with food, since he eats me out of house and home. With his new position as deputy, he should be more than able to afford it."

"Thank you, Isaac. I appreciate that," said the constable

with a nod. "I'll get right back to my wife and tell her to start packing. We'll leave for Norwich in the morning."

"Goodbye, Emery, and good luck." Zachariah held out his hand and they shook once more. "You've been not only a good friend, but also a wonderful deputy. Also, thank Agatha for me for the times she watched over my daughter."

"I will," said Emery, continuing to go on and shake Isaac's hand next. "I hope I won't be putting you in a bind. You have someone to watch your daughter, don't you, Sheriff?"

"I've got Nairnie," he told him, noticing the pout from Cassandra.

They said their goodbyes and Isaac closed the door.

"I can't wait to get into my new home," said Isaac. "This is great!"

"That will have to wait until we find the man or woman who hired the assassins." Zachariah went to the hook on the wall, donning his weapon belt with all his weapons.

"What are you doing?" asked Isaac with a yawn.

"Get ready, Isaac. We've got work to do."

"Now? Nay, it's time for bed." Isaac yawned again.

"We've got to question the prisoner."

"Tonight?"

"Isaac, do you want the job of deputy or not?"

"Of course I do. I'm going," he mumbled, headed for his cloak and weapons as well.

"I'll watch over the children," Cassandra called out.

"Oh, I forgot," said Zachariah. "I shouldn't leave them unprotected."

"I'll protect them. I brought my sword," said Adrian, having been listening to their conversation.

"And I'll be here too," said Wymond. "Sheriff, we will lock the door and won't let anything happen."

"I should probably stay." Isaac tried once more to stay behind and get some sleep.

"Keep Grunt here with you, and don't let anyone leave the house," instructed Zachariah, heading for the door. "Come on, Isaac, before I change my mind and give the new position to Adrian instead."

"Me?" Adrian excitedly jumped to his feet. "Do you really think I could be a constable someday? I'd love that." He never looked happier.

"Mayhap," said Zachariah. "However, you come from nobility so I think being a knight is more in order for you."

"Sit down, Adrian," grumbled Isaac. "No one is taking my position. Besides, you have more opportunities and live at the castle. I need this more than you do."

"After we question Castor, I'm going to check on Vivienne again," Zachariah told his brother as they left the house.

"Why? Nairnie is with her, Richard is guarding her door, and she'll be sleeping."

That made Zachariah laugh heartily.

"What's so funny?" asked Isaac.

"If you really knew Vivienne as well as I do, then you'd realize none of those things are going to stop her."

"What do you mean?"

"I mean that Vivienne has been searching for her parents' killers for the past seven years. Do you really think she's going to stay locked in her room when the man who can give her the answer she seeks is locked away in the dungeon right in her own castle?"

"I don't know."

"Hell no, she won't. I only hope we can get there before she does, because I have no doubt in my mind that in that pretty little head of hers, she is already devising a plan how to escape both Nairnie and Richard."

VIVIENNE FINALLY GOT the break she needed when she heard Nairnie snoring from the chair. She silently left the bed after pretending to sleep, and quickly donned her shoes. Then she tiptoed over to the hooks on the wall and got her weapon belt and cloak. Next, she went to the door and opened it a crack. Just like she'd hoped, Richard was in a chair and had dozed off.

Sneaking around him, since he sat directly in front of the door, she made her way in the near dark down the corridor. All she wanted to do was to question Castor in the dungeon. When the sheriff had brought her food earlier, he had told her that her uncle forbade anyone besides the guard to go into the dungeon before morning. She had shown the sheriff the bottles of mandrake root oil and told him about their suspicions of her aunt slowly poisoning her uncle. He took the oil and told her that he would handle things and to stay away from her aunt as well.

Vivienne easily sneaked out of the castle and hid behind things on her way to the dungeon that had an outdoor entrance. Once there, she looked around and then entered through the door that led to the guard's post in a small room outside the prisoners' cells.

One lone torch flickered from the guard's room. She stepped inside to see the guard sleeping. On the floor. This was going to be too easy. Then she heard voices from the cells and noticed that the door was open leading to the area where the prisoners were. The key was in the lock.

"What is going on?" she whispered to herself. and hurriedly pulled her sword from her weapon belt and made her way forward. Her heart beat harder and her stomach tightened, doing that churning sensation again like whenever trouble was about to occur. Just when she thought she'd find the mad killer, she heard Zachariah's voice from inside the room with the cells.

"Come on in, Vivienne. I've been expecting you."

"Zachariah?" She lowered her sword and moved forward. "What's going on here?" She looked back at the guard, wondering if the sheriff had hit him over the head and knocked him out.

"We're too late," said Isaac from the sheriff's side. They were standing in front of a cell, looking through the bars.

"Too late for what?" She moved closer, only to see exactly what they meant. There, prone on the floor was Castor, lying on his back in a puddle of blood. His eyes were wide open but he wasn't moving, and looked very pale.

"Nay!" she screamed, hurrying to them as the sheriff opened the cell door wider for her to enter. "He can't be dead. He is the only one who can answer my questions."

"He won't be telling anyone anything anymore," said Isaac.

That's when Vivienne noticed the white goose feather placed directly atop the man's chest. Chills ran through her. "It was the murderer. The man who killed Wallace and Fanny?"

"Mayhap," said Zachariah, hunkering down next to the corpse. "Or perhaps the murderer just wants us to think that, and Castor really did the other killings. I suppose now we'll never know." He opened the man's mouth and held up a gold florin. "Dammit, I'm getting tired of this killer always being one step ahead of us."

"Is the guard dead too?" Vivienne looked back over her shoulder.

"Nay," said Zachariah. "He smelled like that mandrake root oil you gave me, so we think he was just knocked out so the killer could make his mark."

"We're going to try to rouse him and ask him what happened," Isaac added.

"Please tell me that you were able to ask Castor before he died who ordered him to kill my parents."

"Nay. We couldn't." Zachariah stood up and stuck into his pouch the gold florin that he'd taken out of Castor's mouth. "He was already dead when we got here."

"Nay. This can't be happening." Without being able to stop it, tears flowed down Vivienne's cheeks. She felt so helpless. So scared. Why in heaven's name hadn't they come to question Castor earlier?

"What's going on in here?" Lord Mablethorpe entered the guard's room. "Good God!" he exclaimed. Vivienne looked over to see her uncle hunkering down over the guard on the ground.

"He's not dead, just sleeping," Zachariah called out. "However, our prisoner has been murdered."

"Nay." Vivienne's uncle jumped up and ran to them. When he saw the dead body, anger washed over his face and he punched the metal bars of the cell. "Dammit, why did I say to wait to question him? Sheriff, I should have let you talk to Castor right away."

"Why didn't you?" Vivienne asked him.

"Why?" He looked directly at her. "I did it for you and Ellen, Vivienne. You both kept telling me how you didn't want anything to ruin the stupid wedding between two petty servants. Why in the hell did I listen to you?" He let out a bellow and threw his hands in the air.

"There is nothing we can do now, so I suggest we call on the coroner to come collect Castor's body and we continue with the investigation in the morning," suggested Zachariah.

"What about the guard?" asked Isaac.

"Why is he sleeping? I don't understand," said Lord Mablethorpe.

"We believe he was—" The sheriff started to tell him about the poisoning, but Vivienne stopped him by speaking over him.

"We believe he was drunk and passed out," she said. "He probably drank too much whisky from the wedding."

"He'll be reprimanded in the morning," growled her uncle, leaving the room and stepping over the guard. "This is preposterous," he mumbled, leaving them standing there.

"Why didn't you let me tell your uncle about the poison?" asked Zachariah once he left.

"I don't know. My gut told me not to bring it up right now."

"You don't trust him, do you?"

"I don't trust anyone right now," she answered.

"Isaac, I'm going to escort Vivienne back to her room," Zachariah told his brother. "You stay here and I'll send back the coroner for the body. When the guard wakes up, question him about who could have possibly poisoned his drink."

"Is this what being deputy is always going to be like, now that I hold the title? No sleep, no food, no fun?" Isaac stepped over the guard and sat down on the bench.

"Mayhap," said Zachariah. "It's all part of the job."

"He holds the title of deputy now?" Vivienne looked up to Zachariah in question.

"I'll fill you in as we walk. Then I'm going to lock you in your room and place another guard at your door."

"Nay. We need to find the killer."

"He's already struck tonight, and I doubt that he'll do so again before morning. I need to know you're safe so I can do my job. Vivienne, please don't give me trouble."

"Of course, not," she said, feeling as if mayhap he was right in saying she should lie low until morning. "Zachariah, promise me that tomorrow we will find the person who hired that assassin to kill my parents."

"I promise we will," he told her, holding her hand as they walked to her room. "I cannot live like this anymore, fearing that the next corpse I find might be yours, Vivienne. Therefore, I promise you I will find this person if it is the last thing I ever do."

Chapter Eighteen

Vivienne didn't sleep much that night because she couldn't stop reliving the attack on her life by Castor. She'd never been so scared before. Always brave when someone else's life was in danger, she hadn't thought once about her own safety. But this was different. Now the killer was after her, and she didn't know how to stop this madness.

"My lady, wake up." Nairnie stood above her, shaking her by the shoulders. Vivienne hadn't even remembered falling asleep.

"Nairnie? What is it? What's wrong?" She bolted up to a sitting position.

"Ye were cryin' out in yer sleep, lassie, and I couldna stand to watch ye in so much pain so I woke ye."

"Oh. Thank you, Nairnie." Vivienne yawned and stretched. "I just can't get the horrible images of all the slain people out of my head."

"Mayhap a breath of fresh air will help to clear yer muddled mind." Nairnie hobbled over and pulled open the shutter. "That was a stupid thing ye did last night, sneakin' out of here. Ye could have been killed."

"Well, I wasn't. Besides, if I had gone earlier, I might have been able to question Castor before he was murdered."

"I agree."

"You do?"

"Aye. Ye should have told me yer plan and I would have helped ye carry it out."

"Now you tell me." Vivienne let out a deep sigh and fell back on her pillows, staring at the ceiling. The first rays of sun were starting to light up the horizon, and a faint golden hue colored her walls. "I think Fanny, Wallace, and also Castor were all murdered to shut them up."

"What do ye mean?"

"I think they knew who the man in the cloak was. The man who ordered the deaths of my parents. They knew, and that horrible person was afraid they'd talk. That's why their lives were taken."

"Ye could be right about that. Hmmm. That's odd," said Nairnie.

"What's odd?" Vivienne spoke with her eyes closed.

"Lord Mablethorpe is leavin' the castle so early in the mornin'."

"He is?" She jumped up and ran to the window. She saw a man in a hooded cloak atop his horse waiting for the gate to be raised and the drawbridge to lower. "How do you know that's my uncle? It could be anyone."

"Nay. The guards wouldna open the gates for anyone other than the lord or lady of the castle."

"Ah, you are right. I'm going to find out where he goes." Vivienne, having slept in her clothes, pushed her feet into her shoes and donned her weapon belt and cloak in a matter of seconds. This was her big chance and now she'd find some answers. "Nairnie, I need you to help me get past the guards at the door."

"All right, lassie, but ye'd better promise me that ye'll be careful."

"I have my sword and I know how to use it."

"Aye, I suppose ye do. Then get ready because ye'll only have one chance, so pay close attention." Nairnie headed over to the door.

"What are you going to do?"

"Cause a distraction so ye can sneak out. What else?" Nairnie opened the door and Vivienne stood to the side so the two guards wouldn't see her.

"I need to use the garderobe," said Nairnie.

"Go on then," said Richard with a nod of his head.

Nairnie looked back at Vivienne and winked before going out into the corridor. She walked past the guards and then suddenly fell to the ground.

"Och, nay!" she cried.

"What's the matter?" asked Richard.

"Are you hurt?" asked the other guard.

"I've twisted my ankle. Help me," she cried out, and moaned so realistically that Vivienne almost went out there herself to help the poor old woman.

As soon as the two guards' backs were turned as they tried to help Nairnie stand, Vivienne slipped out into the shadows and headed down the corridor, quickly making her way out to the courtyard. Wasting no time, she got to the stables to find Elias, the young stablehand-in-training, there, sleeping in the hay.

"Elias, wake up."

"Huh?" The boy sat up, still half asleep. "My lady?"

"Did Lord Mablethorpe just leave here?" she asked, opening the door to the stall that held her horse.

"Lady Vivienne? What did you say?" The boy rubbed his eyes and yawned.

"Did someone just leave here?" She looked over and saw her

uncle's horse was there, but her aunt's wasn't. That raised suspicion right away.

"I'm not sure, my lady. Since Castor and Wymond were both gone, I had to do all the work by myself. I was so tired that I fell asleep. Were you going somewhere? Did you want me to saddle your horse?"

"Oh, never mind. I don't have time to wait." She jumped atop her horse to ride it bareback, glad she was wearing a tunic and breeches right now instead of a long gown. If she had waited for Elias to saddle her horse, she'd never be able to catch up to her uncle, or whoever it was who just left the stables. Riding at breakneck speed over the drawbridge, she saw the rider a little way up the road, and they seemed to be heading toward the abbey. She made sure to follow. Vivienne was careful to stay far enough behind them so she wouldn't be spotted. Then she saw the rider go toward the catacombs and enter through an old gate that was never used. Of course, she followed.

Dismounting her horse, she hid behind a stone statue, watching as the hooded figure walked up to the catacombs, looked around and then pushed aside a board and entered the crypts.

"I knew it!" She spoke to herself. "I did see a cloaked figure going into the catacombs. I didn't imagine it after all."

The church bells rang, calling the nuns to prayer as Vivienne made her way to the entrance of the crypts. She was about to follow the cloaked figure inside, when someone called out her name.

"Lady Vivienne? Is that you?"

She spun around to see Magdalena standing a way off with several other nuns.

"Yes. It's me, Magdalena." She raised her hand and waved.

The nun told her friends to go, and she made her way over

to Vivienne. "What are you doing here? And so early in the morning? The sun is barely up."

"Magdalena, I just saw a cloaked figure enter the catacombs and I am following them."

"Nay. You couldn't have."

"I did. Now, I need you to do me a favor."

"Certainly. How can I help you?"

"If I don't come back out in five minutes, ten minutes tops, then I need you to find your brothers and tell them where I am."

"What is this all about?"

Vivienne's stomach churned badly and she knew there was trouble waiting ahead. "I can't go into details now, but my life might be in danger."

"Then don't go into the crypts! Please, my lady. Wait for the sheriff."

"I am tired of waiting. I need answers and I need them now. If I wait, my moment of opportunity might pass me by. So remember, if I don't return, take my horse and find the sheriff and send him here."

"But I need to show up for prayers." Magdalena's worried face turned as she looked over to the church where most of the nuns had already entered.

"Please, I beg you. You're my only hope." Vivienne turned and ran to the crypts, hearing Magdalena from behind her.

"Your horse isn't even saddled."

She stopped at the entrance and took a deep breath and released it, holding her sword up in two hands. Vivienne wasn't sure what she would find inside, and honestly, she was scared out of her mind to go in there alone. Mayhap it was because of what she didn't want to find. Or know.

"I'm doing this for my parents. For Fanny and Wallace," she said softly, releasing one more breath and then pushing aside the board and stepping into the dark depths of the catacombs, only hoping to emerge alive.

ZACHARIAH RODE through the gates of Mablethorpe Castle the next morning with Isaac at his side. They'd spent most of the evening at the coroner's office mulling over the events of the murders that had occurred, still feeling not much closer to finding answers than before.

"I'm so tired that I see two of you right now," said Isaac from atop his horse, since they hadn't slept at all.

"Well, wake up and help me solve this mystery and then you can sleep for a week if you'd like."

"Sleep. Yes. Sleep." Isaac's eyes closed and his head nodded to the side.

"Wake up, Isaac!"

Isaac's eyes popped open. "I'm up. I'm up." He looked one way with wide eyes and then turned his head and looked the other.

"It doesn't seem like it to me," mumbled Zachariah.

"Mayhap a little food and drink would help me to stay focused." Once again, his brother was only thinking about his stomach.

"Later," he told him, as the stableboy ran out to collect their horses. They handed him the reins and walked toward the keep. "I'm going to go to Lady Mablethorpe's room to question her about the mandrake oil. You go check on Lady Vivienne to make sure she's all right."

"Got it," said Isaac in a sleepy voice, as they headed in two different directions.

Zachariah would have sent Isaac to question Lady Mablethorpe, but right now he sincerely doubted his brother would remember a word they discussed. Therefore, he decided to do it himself. Plus, it would be faster this way.

"My lady," said Zachariah, knocking on Lady Mablethorpe's door. "I'm sorry to disturb you at this hour. It's Sheriff Fitch. I need to ask you a few questions."

The door swung open and Lady Mablethorpe stood there fully dressed. "Sheriff. To what do I owe this pleasure?"

"Do you have a moment? We need to talk."

"It wouldn't be proper for us to speak in here. Perhaps down in the great hall would be more suitable."

"Nay." He held up his hand. "I'll leave the door open, but I don't want to be around a lot of prying people. This is a private matter."

"This sounds important."

"It is." He reached into his pouch and pulled out the vials. "Can you tell me about these?"

Her gaze settled on his hand and her smile disappeared. "Where did you get those?'"

"From Lady Vivienne who intercepted the apothecary yesterday when he made a trip here to the castle to deliver them to you."

"It's a sedative," she told him, her voice clipped.

"For you? To be able to sleep?"

"Well...nay, not really. It is for my husband."

"Why don't we sit down?" Zachariah escorted her back into the room, being sure to leave the door open. After they sat, he spoke once more. "Do you know what is in these vials?"

"If you mean exactly what makes up the potion, then no."

"It is mandrake root oil."

"What's that?" she asked, sounding believably as if she didn't know what that herb was.

"It's a very dangerous herb, my lady."

"Dangerous? How dangerous? What do you mean by that?"

"If only a little of the potion is taken, then yes, it could be used as a sedative to get to sleep or relax or calm the nerves. But if too much is given, one will start to see hallucinations, have seizures, or they could actually end up going mad."

"Oh my! I had no idea." Her eyes opened wide and she put her hand to her mouth.

"The end result could be death if one is not careful. Didn't the apothecary warn you about this?"

"Nay. Never. But I wish he would have." Tears formed in her eyes but she blinked the away. "I didn't know that, Sheriff, I swear I didn't. You've got to believe me. I only wanted things to go back to being the way they used to be between us."

"You're talking about your husband?"

"Yes." She took out a handcloth and dabbed at her eyes. Either this woman was truly upset or she was a great actor. "Ever since my sister and her husband were murdered, Gilbert has changed drastically and I don't like it."

"How so?"

"He's just not the same loving, fair, kind man that he used to be."

"Yes, I've heard Vivienne say that too."

"He is angry all the time, and on the few times we were intimate over the past seven years, he was very rough with me, and even hurt me. He'd never been that way before. He's even hit me on occasion when he didn't like what I said."

"I'm sorry to hear that, my lady. I wish you would have come to me for help."

"I was embarrassed and thought it was something I did or said that caused him to change. I would have done anything to help make things right between us again."

"Even poison him?"

"Nay! I would never do that."

"Then what do you call this? It is so much mandrake oil, that it could easily kill someone in this amount."

"Oh, Sheriff, I didn't know. I found a vial in my husband's room years ago, and I took it to the apothecary to ask him what it was. He told me it was a sedative to help my uncle calm down and that he'd been taking it to control his anger."

"That explains why you weren't warned of the danger. I'm sure your husband told the apothecary to stay quiet about it. Go on."

"Well, I asked the apothecary if he could make me a bottle of it. I figured if Gilbert just had a little more of it each day, mayhap it would help bring him back to normal."

"And?"

"The apothecary was hesitant to give it to me. I told him it was for me and that I didn't want Gilbert to know about it. So he gave me a vial and I started adding a little in my husband's drink each day. When he started acting as if he were going mad, I added a little more, thinking that he needed it. I promise you I was only trying to help him."

"So Lord Gilbert didn't know you were doing this?"

"Nay. I don't think so. But it didn't work. He just kept getting angrier and meaner. Then he started forgetting things that he's known for years. After so long, I figured I had to give him even more. Actually, I have no idea how it kept disappearing so quickly since I only used a few drops a day, but I always seemed to be out of it. Then, I felt as if I was starting to forget things, because I kept misplacing the bottles."

"And so you ordered more?"

"I had to. I kept moving the bottles to different places, but I couldn't seem to remember where I put them, because when I'd go to get them, they'd be gone. Oh, Sheriff, sometimes I feel like I'm the one going crazy. Losing my mind, that is. But I didn't want anyone to know. I couldn't tell Vivienne. Not after she said Gilbert was losing his mind."

"Lady Vivienne told me that you and she suspect your husband has a mistress. That he goes out riding in the mornings by himself to meet her."

"Yes. I'm sad to say I believe that is true."

"All right, Lady Mablethorpe. Thank you for your time." He put the bottles back in his pouch.

"Sheriff, I'm frightened. I heard that Castor has been murdered now too? And that the killer left a feather on his chest and a gold coin in his mouth just like what happened to the Goose-woman, Fanny, I believe was her name, and poor Wallace?"

"Yes, that's true, my lady. But how do you know about this? Castor was just murdered last night and we've told no one."

"Gilbert told me."

"He did? When?"

"It was early this morning. I heard a noise and saw him out in the corridor, dressed and about to leave. Probably going to see his mistress. He told me about the murder and said I was to stay in my room and lock my door if I didn't want the next victim to be me."

"That's an odd thing for him to say. Why would he feel that your life is in danger?"

"I don't know, but I am sure it is because deep down he still loves me."

"I see. Thank you, my lady." Zachariah got up and headed to the door, but had another thought and turned around. "Did you know the blind man named Wallace from town?"

"No. Not really. Why?"

"How about your husband? How did he know him?"

"I don't believe that he knew him either. We don't really associate with people from town much."

"Did you know that your husband had hired the blind man to make a present for you? To get back in your good graces?"

"He did what?" That seemed to shock her. "What kind of present are you talking about?"

"It is the biggest throne chair I've ever seen. It has gaudy carvings on it and he was going to gild it, too. He paid Wallace well to make it. The man had been making it for years."

"Nay, Gilbert would never do that." She shook her head adamantly.

"Why not?"

"Because, he knows I hate anything gilded or carved. Or overly ornate or big. I like simple things. Plus, I don't even have a throne and neither do I ever want one. I don't like to feel that I am so much better than others. Gilbert used to feel that way too. But he hasn't been the same, like I told you. Not since the death of Vivienne's parents."

"One more thing, if I may. Do you know what your sister and her husband did for a living?"

Lady Mablethorpe was silent and didn't seem to want to answer.

"You do know," he said.

Tears filled her eyes once again. "When my sister married Abiathar, they both worked at the King's palace. It was years before she told me the truth, that they were...spies for the King," she said, whispering the last part. "I told her it was too dangerous and not to do it. I am sure their deaths had something to do with that, even if I don't understand how."

"Why didn't you ever tell Vivienne about it?"

"Nay. She must never know."

"She already does know. King Edward told her when he was here for the joust."

"Oh, no," she moaned, her eyes closing and her body swaying. He ran over to help her sit back down. "I don't want Vivienne to end up like her mother, but she is already following in her footsteps. We never should have given her so much freedom."

"Zachariah, you'd better come quickly."

Zachariah turned around to see Isaac standing at the doorway with Nairnie.

"What is it?" he asked. "And where is Lady Vivienne?"

"She rode out after Lord Mablethorpe earlier, it seems," said Isaac.

"What? Nay! I told her to stay put. Nairnie? Did you know about this?" He ran to the door.

"Of course I did, Sheriff, I am no' blind and deaf."

"Then why didn't you stop her?"

"Stop her?" Nairnie laughed. "We both ken there is no stoppin' Lady Vivienne once she gets a mind to do somethin'. I actually helped her."

"God's eyes, you didn't. I trusted you! I trusted you with her life."

"She is no' a child, Sheriff. She wanted answers and ye were no' gettin' them for her so she saw to do it herself."

"Dammit, Nairnie, I can't trust *you* anymore. Therefore, you are fired!" He burst out of the room in anger and headed down the corridor. "Isaac, are you coming?"

"I guess so." Isaac ran after him, and they didn't stop even when they got to the courtyard. "Where are we going? And should we have left Lady Mablethorpe unguarded? She could try to poison someone else."

"She's not the killer, and didn't even know she was poisoning her husband."

"She's not? She didn't? I don't understand."

"God's eyes, Isaac, keep up."

"I'm trying to but it's a chore just to keep my eyes open right now."

They got to the stables and Zachariah called for their horses, first noticing that Vivienne's horse was gone and so was her aunt's. He knew now, Lord Gilbert probably took his wife's horse to have an alibi for later. "Did Lord Mablethorpe leave here earlier?" he asked the stableboy, Elias.

"I'm not sure," the boy answered. "Lady Vivienne asked me the same thing, but I was sleeping and didn't see him if he did."

"Isaac, help him with the horses. We are wasting too much time." The sheriff turned around and noticed his sister Magdalena riding into the courtyard on Vivienne's horse. It wasn't saddled and Magdalena was slipping off and barely able to hold on. "God's teeth!" He rushed out into the courtyard and helped his sister dismount. "What are you doing here, Magdalena? And why are you on Vivienne's horse without a saddle? You could have broken your neck."

"Oh, Zachariah, I am so worried about Lady Vivienne. She went into the catacombs and told me if she didn't come back out that I should find you and Isaac and send you after her. I was hoping you were here at the castle so I tried coming here first before going to town."

"Why on earth is she in the crypts? What would possess her to do such a stupid and dangerous thing?"

"She was following a man in a cloak."

"Say no more." He turned and sprinted to the stable, grabbing his horse from Elias and jumping atop it. "Isaac, we've got to get to the catacombs at the abbey and we can't waste another minute, so hurry."

"The catacombs? Is that what you just said?" Isaac rode out after him.

"Yes. Lady Vivienne went in following a man in a cloak, and I have a feeling I know exactly who it was. If we don't hurry, she is going to be the next corpse we collect with a feather on her belly and gold florin in her mouth."

Chapter Nineteen

Vivienne heard voices and followed the sound through the dark catacombs, walking slowly and trying not to look around since she'd seen lots of skeletons lying in the walls from the side of her eye. The ceiling was made of dirt and she had to duck to walk through the dark tunnels that were all connected. The farther in she went, the more the air thinned, making her feel as if she couldn't breathe. There were standing stones and coffins covered with stone sarcophaguses all around her. It was dank and dark in the crypts and the smell of death surrounded her. Gooseflesh pricked her skin, making her heart race. Still, she continued. When she felt something run over her foot she jumped back, almost screaming, knowing it was a rat.

She could see a light from up ahead down the passageway, and hurried, trying to hear and see whatever she could.

"Let me in, woman," growled her uncle, and a wooden door opened and she could see more light coming from what looked like a hidden room inside. Her mouth fell open in surprise.

"I wasn't expecting you today," came the woman's soft voice, as she allowed him to enter.

So, he did have a mistress it seemed. And he had her hidden away in here? The poor woman. Straining her eyes, from what Vivienne could tell, it seemed that the woman was much older than her uncle. Old enough to be his mother, actually.

The door remained open and she heard them arguing about something but she couldn't tell what. Then she thought she heard the woman crying.

Wanting to help, Vivienne made her way to the entrance of the hidden room, still gripping her sword. She had started to think that mayhap her uncle was a killer. Or at least he might be the man who hired the assassins to kill her parents. But why? How could he, and why would he, do such a thing? Then she started thinking that mayhap he had nothing to do with the murders at all and just had a woman hidden away. Many nobles had mistresses and even flaunted them in front of their wives. Uncle Gilbert certainly could have brought this woman to the castle if he'd chosen to, so she didn't understand why he kept her hidden in such a horrible place. Or why she was so much older than him.

She bravely moved in closer. But when a couple rats ran over her feet at the same time and one started climbing up her leg, she gave forth a muffled cry and swiped at them with her sword. Losing her balance, she fell backward, dropping her sword, the clanging noise of it hitting against a tombstone ringing out loudly. She ended up on the floor of the caverns sitting on her bottom end.

"What's that? Who goes there?" Her uncle bolted out of the hidden room with his sword at the ready. She figured she needed to tell him it was she, or he might accidentally kill her.

"It's me, Vivienne, Uncle Gilbert," she called out. "Don't hurt me."

"Vivienne?" He looked down at her with angry eyes. His

body was silhouetted since the torch and candlelight came from behind him now. "What the hell are you doing here?"

"I followed you," she admitted.

"I can see that. Foolish move. Get up."

She reached for her sword, but his foot came down over her hand to keep her from picking it up.

"Ow! You're hurting me. Stop that."

"Good," he said, reaching down, but not for her. It was only to retrieve her sword which he pointed right at her.

"What are you doing?" Her stomach twisted so hard now that she thought she would die. "You're g-going to k-kill me because I discovered your hidden mistress?"

"She's not my mistress," he snarled. "What kind of a sick man do you take me for?"

Vivienne was starting to wonder. This was not the uncle she knew and loved. She didn't understand at all why he was acting this way.

"Can we talk?" she asked him.

"I'm tired of talking and I'm tired of you putting your nose where it doesn't belong. Now get on your feet or I'll strike you right on the ground."

"Leave her be," came a man's weak voice from the open door of the hidden room.

Vivienne slowly got up, looking over to the room and her heart almost stopped. Her gaze fastened on the man and she figured her eyes had to be playing tricks on her, because she was seeing double of her uncle. Two men, each of them looking remarkably like Uncle Gilbert.

"Get back inside, Gilbert, or I'll strike her down right here, I swear I will," commanded the man who had his sword aimed at her.

"Nay. Don't hurt her." The man held out his hand. He

looked so skinny and pale and had a scruffy beard and tousled long hair, but she could see his eyes and he truly was her uncle.

"Uncle Gilbert?" she asked in a breathy whisper. "Is that...you?"

"Get inside and shut up!" The man she thought was her uncle, who was holding the sword, pointed at the room and reached out and gave her a shove. She stumbled forward into the room and right into the arms of her real uncle.

"You're not my uncle, are you?" she asked the man who had pushed her.

"What gave it away?" he said with a devious chuckle.

"Vivienne, I am so sorry," said her uncle, crying and still holding her.

"Shut the damned door," commanded the fake uncle, and the older woman in the room did as told, closing them all inside the hidden room together. It was small in there, and smelled like sweat and urine. It was also cold and stuffy. Only stinky tallow candles were burning for light.

"Uncle Gilbert, who is this imposter?" Vivienne glared at the man holding the sword still aimed right at her.

"That, my dear, is my twin brother, Gerard," explained her uncle.

"Twin brother?" Vivienne blinked several times, looking up at her uncle and over to his twin brother and then back at her uncle again. "I didn't know you had a twin."

"No one did," said the real Gilbert. "Except for me. My mother told me about him right before she died, ten years ago. She said she birthed twin boys, but because of all the superstition behind twins, she had to give one of us away or she'd be cursed."

"And she chose me to give away," snarled Gerard. "I was given to a blind man and his wife to raise in Northumbria. She tried to get me as far away from my homeland as she could."

"Blind man?" she asked, looking over at the woman standing quietly at the opposite side of the room. "You're Wallace's wife, aren't you?" Vivienne had never met the woman before, but everything was starting to come together now."

"Yes," the woman softly answered. "I am Brenna, and Wallace is my husband. We raised Gerard together, and were so happy to have him since I couldn't bear children. But before long, Gerard started asking questions, and foolishly, we told him the truth one day."

"That was your first mistake, woman," snarled Gerard.

"He became so angry with us," said Brenna. "He was older, and strong then, and even hurt us."

"That's terrible," Vivienne said, slowly releasing her uncle.

"We were on the run, scared for our lives since he swore he'd kill us. We hid for years, then one day about seven years ago, we decided to come to Mablethorpe to find his twin brother, hoping he would help us. We knew he was the lord of a castle. We told that to Gerard, but we didn't tell him where to find Gilbert."

"It didn't matter," snarled Gerard. "I tracked you and found you, and in doing so found Gilbert."

"He tricked us, since he knew we'd go back to the place where we first got him from a noble, in order to ask for help," cried Brenna.

"They were so stupid that they led me right to my twin," Gerard spoke up, not able to keep quiet. "When I saw him from afar, I realized that he had the good life, while I lived like a pauper."

"That's when he started planning to kidnap me and imper-sonate me," said Gilbert, stepping back and almost falling over since he was so weak that he could barely stand.

"Sit down, Uncle." Vivienne helped him to be seated on a wooden stool.

"Give him the rest of this like I told you to do, woman." Gerard tossed a small bottle to Brenna and she caught it. Vivienne recognized it as the same bottle like the ones that held the mandrake oil.

"Please, Gerard, don't make me do it," cried Brenna. "It's going to kill him, I fear."

"You've been poisoning my Uncle Gilbert with mandrake root oil?" asked Vivienne, finally understanding. "And keeping him imprisoned here for the past seven years, too weak to even try to escape?"

"That's right," said Gerard with a deep, hearty laugh, slightly lowering his sword. He still held on to his sword, but tossed Vivienne's blade atop a torn-up pallet on the floor. "The only reason I haven't killed him off by now and replaced him permanently, was because I was getting all the information I needed to become him. I was pulling it off, too, until you got involved, Vivienne."

Vivienne's anger grew inside her. "You were the one who hired the assassins to kill my parents, weren't you?"

"They were spies for the King! They found out about me and were going to tell him. They met me one day, and said they were going back to report the information to not only my brother, but also the King. You see, I couldn't let them do that, because it would spoil my plan."

"And so you had to kill them for it? And almost got me and my brother and baby killed too?"

"I only hired the assassins to kill the spies," he ground out. "I didn't know you or the boy or the baby were going to be there that night. I didn't tell the assassins to kill you."

"So, when my uncle came down the road on horseback to help me that night...it was really you?"

"Of course it was. I was the ever-loving uncle stepping in to save you, Vivienne." He laughed lowly. "It was a perfect plan, and my secret was safe. I split up Brenna and Wallace, and paid them off not to tell my secret, threatening that if they did, the other would be killed."

"He made me give your uncle this poison and care for him here." Brenna held up the bottle. "He only let me out once or twice a year, bringing me to visit my love, Wallace, so we would know each other was still alive. Is Wallace all right? I am so worried about him. He's blind and shouldn't be alone." Brenna wrung her hands in worry.

"You didn't tell her that...you killed him?" Vivienne asked Gerard.

"Nay!" Brenna screamed and dropped the bottle, the glass shattering on the floor and the scent of mandrake oil filling the air. "Please tell me it isn't true."

"I had no choice," said Gerard with a shrug. "Wallace was demanding gold florins, and was going to reveal my secret since you, Vivienne, just had to befriend him. You, my dear, kept getting in my way. You are too curious for your own good, and you know that now I can't let any of the three of you live, since you all might expose my secret." Gerard took a step toward her with his sword at the ready, and she took a step backward, away from him. Vivienne was finally getting her answers, it seemed, but she never expected this at all!

"Did you kill Fanny and Castor too?" she asked Gerard, stalling for time, trying to come up with a plan.

"I had to kill the Goose since she hunted me down. Fanny had loose lips and I didn't want her here in Mablethorpe. She'd still be alive if she would have stayed in Southwark instead of being greedy and wanting more gold coins and coming to look for me."

"You put that note under the door of our room?" she asked. "The one telling me to meet you in Room 6."

"Yes, but the note wasn't meant for you, Vivienne."

"But it said, *my lady*."

"Fanny often pretended to be a noblewoman for me since she knew how much that got me excited. I'd call her *my lady*, and she'd even dress in the clothes of a noble."

"So that's why she took my cloak," said Vivienne, understanding it now. "Why did you say in the note that you knew the answer? I thought that meant the answer as to who killed my parents."

That made him laugh even harder. "I only meant the answer of where I was since she had been searching for me. But it worked to my advantage since it put fear in you, thinking you were being stalked."

"What about Castor?" she continued, stalling for even more time, slowly making her way closer to the pallet where he'd thrown her sword. "Why did you kill him?"

"I had to kill Castor and also the other assassin I'd hired, who was about to be imprisoned at the joust. They would have sung like birds in order to save their own lives. There is no trust among killers and thieves."

"Dear God, Gerard, how could you have killed Wallace? The only father you ever knew?" Brenna had to hold on to the wall in order not to fall. "He raised you from a baby. He was good to you. We both treated you as our own son. What kind of a beast are you?"

Vivienne realized that Gerard had only hired Wallace to build the throne as a decoy, since Vivienne was starting to ask questions.

"Shut up!" yelled Gerard, taking his fist to the woman's face. She barreled backward hitting the wall. Vivienne started to run to help her, but the tip of Gerard's sword stopped her. "Don't even think about it, wench."

Vivienne understood everything now, although she wasn't sure she'd live long enough to tell Zachariah what she'd learned.

"Uncle Gilbert, you told your brother the wrong answer to that riddle purposely, hoping we'd figure out that he wasn't you, didn't you?"

"I did," admitted Gilbert, struggling just to speak since his energy was dwindling fast. "It was a risk, but I had to take it. I knew how smart you are, Vivienne. So when I heard you'd found Adrian, I had to try to send a message that you'd hopefully understand."

"No wonder Aunt Ellen thought you were going mad. We all knew you could never be so mean or angry. Or forget important things that had to do with family which meant everything to you."

"How is Ellen, Vivienne? Did he...hurt her?"

"Nay. She is fine, Uncle," said Vivienne, not wanting to tell him too much for now.

"I miss Ellen so much. I want nothing more than to see her again and hold her in my arms and kiss her." Gilbert actually started to weep. "It's been so long. And I am...so tired...and...weak."

"Too bad you will never see her again, Gilbert," said his twin brother. "Well, I have no need for you anymore, or any of you, actually. Brother, you will be the first to die. No one will ever know from this day on that I am not you."

"Nay!" screamed Vivienne when he lunged for poor, weak Gilbert.

"I will kill you for killing Wallace, you bastard!" Brenna jumped onto Gerard's back and started to strangle him with her bare hands. Her legs wrapped around him to hang on. That gave Vivienne the opportunity she needed to dive for her sword. When she got up gripping the blade tightly, she realized that Gerard had thrown Brenna to the ground and the woman had hit her head and wasn't moving. Vivienne saw blood and hoped he hadn't killed her.

"Leave us alone," yelled Vivienne with her sword pointing toward Gerard. She was scared and her hands shook, but she needed to protect the others. The scent of the mandrake root oil that had been spilled filled the small room, so strong that it made her head spin. She almost dropped her sword she felt so dizzy.

"Don't make me laugh. No girl is going to take me down," shouted Gerard.

"Then mayhap a man will." Gilbert dove for Gerard, but he was weak and Gerard easily pushed him to the ground as well, stabbing his sword into the man's side.

"Nay! Don't kill my uncle," screamed Vivienne, feeling a slight breeze hitting her face from somewhere. Her sword clashed with Gerard's, but the man was strong and it didn't take much before he unarmed her. With her sword gone, he lunged for her now. She jumped out of the way, almost getting stabbed, but thankfully she was quick enough not to be hurt. He came for her a second time, and now her back was to the wall and there was nowhere to go.

"Nay!" she cried, holding out her hands, knowing this would be her demise. Her body swayed as the scent of the oil started to take over her ability to stand. Slowly, her eyes closed and she felt as if she couldn't move. This was the end of her life, she thought, and she wasn't going to be able to do anything to stop it from happening.

Visions flashed through her mind as she felt Gerard moving his blade closer. She saw her father with his throat slit, and her dead mother giving her the ring of the King and telling her that she was the king's bastard. Then she saw poor Wallace with his open blind eyes, Fanny in her fancy gown with her broken neck, and even Castor with the white goose feather on his chest and the gold florin in his mouth. Martin's smiling face swept through her head next, her beautiful son and her brother Adrian's smile would live in her mind forever. Memories of Aunt Ellen's kindness and Maleine's companionship would stay with her forever, even after her death. But what she'd miss most of all was Zachariah's friendship, his warm touch, and his sweet kisses. She'd never have the chance now to be anything to him...but the next corpse that he buried as he searched for her killer.

The barking of Grunt made her eyes open, and then she heard Zachariah's deep voice as the door to the room was thrown open.

"Don't even think of hurting the woman I love."

As if in a dream and in slow motion, she could do nothing but watch as Gerard turned with his sword drawn and the metal of their blades came crashing together. Then Grunt jumped at Gerard, snapping his jaws and started biting Gerard's leg. When Gerard tried to kick at the dog, Zachariah sunk his blade deeply into Gerard's chest. Gerard fell to the ground, his sword almost hitting Grunt when he dropped it.

Love? That was all she could think of at this minute. Did she just hear Zachariah say he loved her? Her body started to shake in convulsions. It wasn't from almost just being killed, but from inhaling so much of the mandrake oil scent.

"Are you all right, Vivienne?" Zachariah pulled his sword out of the evil man's chest and ran to her side.

"Yes. I am fine, now that you're here," she said softly.

"Good." His gaze settled on Gilbert. "Wait a minute. I just killed your uncle, didn't I?"

"Nay, Zachariah. You killed his evil twin brother, Gerard. This is my uncle, the man wounded and lying on the floor. And over there, is Wallace's wife, Brenna."

"I...think I'll need some explaining."

"You're not the only one," she said, throwing caution to the wind and grabbing him by the shoulders and kissing him hard on the mouth.

Someone cleared their throat, and she looked up to see Isaac and Magdalena standing in the doorway.

"Are we interrupting?" asked Isaac, with a dung-eating grin on his face.

"Deputy, shut up and get in here. We have wounded and a dead man to tend to," instructed Zachariah.

"Deputy," repeated Isaac. "That's me. Yes, I'm here, Sheriff. I'll see to them right away." Isaac ran over to help Gilbert, while Magdalena made her way over to comfort Brenna.

"He was the one who hired the assassins to kill my parents," Vivienne told Zachariah, looking down at Gerard's dead body, so thankful he had been killed by the sheriff. But if she could have done it, she would have killed him herself. "He pretended to be my uncle and we all believed it. I feel so stupid! How could I not have known for seven long years?"

"I've been stupid too, Vivienne." Zachariah stared directly into her eyes. "I should have told you seven years ago that I loved you, instead of waiting till the moment you were almost killed. I don't ever want to lose you, sweetheart."

"And neither do I want to lose you." She stared deeply into his eyes, feeling safe for the first time in a very long time. "Take me home, Zachariah." She glanced over at her uncle who was now sitting up. Isaac held a blanket over his wound to stop the flow of blood. "Take us all home. We have a lot to tell everyone."

"I'm not sure everyone needs to know about this," said Zachariah, looking over at Gilbert as well.

"Mayhap you're right," she said, feeling sorry for her aunt and uncle. "We'll tell Aunt Ellen, and only those whom we trust with our lives, or who we feel really need to know. Otherwise, this might bring too much embarrassment to my family."

"I agree," he said, wrapping her in his arms. "And when this murder investigation is all over, I have something else to talk to you about, Vivienne."

"All right," she said, feeling a fluttering in her belly. She wasn't sure what he meant, but she had a feeling it had something to do with their relationship. Vivienne felt happy and excited and relieved. And also scared out of her mind, wondering what he had to say.

Chapter Twenty

Two days later, things were finally starting to get back to normal. Even though they hadn't wanted to tell anyone about the imposter, her aunt and uncle decided they didn't want to keep secrets from anyone, so now everyone knew the truth.

"I am so happy to have you home, Gilbert." Aunt Ellen sat at her husband's bedside, kissing him and hugging him and never leaving his side. He'd been shaved and bathed and fed, but was still weak and recovering from so much mandrake root oil, not to mention the wound in his side. Thankfully, he would live, but he needed to stay in bed for quite a while until he was healed.

"Excuse me, Lady Mablethorpe, but I need to fluff his pillows." Nairnie had taken over as her uncle's healer, insisting on giving her assistance since she was feeling not needed anymore by the sheriff, since he had fired her. Of course, Zachariah apologized and asked her to come back to work for him, but she'd said no. Nairnie purposely rejected his offer because she was trying to help Vivienne in getting Zachariah and Cassandra to reconcile.

Zachariah had seen how well his daughter accepted Cassandra, and with Vivienne's coaxing, he reconsidered, telling his sister she could stay and take over the job of being Starah's nursemaid, since Nairnie refused to return.

"How are you feeling, Uncle Gilbert?" asked Vivienne. She, Nairnie, and Aunt Ellen were the only ones in the room at the moment.

"I feel loved," he said, staring at his wife and holding her hand.

"Dinna get used to it," Nairnie mumbled under her breath, making Vivienne realize that she was missing her husband Bear. "Here, Lord Mablethorpe. Have some of this." She handed him a goblet.

"Wait. What is it?" Lady Mablethorpe was very cautious now, still not forgiving herself for not realizing that Gerard wasn't Gilbert, even if she knew he was acting different. She felt so bad about poisoning anyone, because she had a kind heart and couldn't even hurt evil people like Gerard. She also said she never wanted to see a bottle of mandrake oil again as long as she lived.

"It's just a little Mountain Magic," said Nairnie. "This is some of the best and strongest whisky ever made. It comes from the MacKeefe clan."

"Oh, I don't know if he should have that." Aunt Ellen frowned, looking at the cup.

"It'll be all right, Aunt Ellen," Vivienne assured her.

"I've been drinking nothing but rancid water and warm bitter ale for years now, Ellen," Gilbert told her. "I'd really like some whisky." He grabbed the cup before his wife could object, and took a swig and made a face. They all laughed. "Mayhap just a little for now until I'm used to it." He handed the cup back to Nairnie.

"Och, ye just need to down it quickly, like this." Nairnie

raised the cup to her lips and drank the rest down without even flinching.

There came a slight knock on the open door and Vivienne turned to see Zachariah standing there with Isaac.

"Come in. Please," said Vivienne, with a wave of her hand.

"Lady Vivienne, Wymond found this missive for you under the hay in the stables." Isaac held up the paper. "It seems one of the horses kicked it under the trough."

"Oh, my missive from the King. Please bring it in. I want to see what it says."

"Ye don't need to read it. I can tell ye what it says." A man stepped out from behind them and Vivienne's jaw dropped to see Bear, Nairnie's ex-pirate husband, standing there.

"Bear?" Nairnie dropped the empty goblet and it clattered to the floor. "What are ye doin' here?"

"Lady Vivienne wrote to her father, the King, and asked that I be given a position closer to home in Cornwall and he agreed."

"What? Is this true, Lady Vivienne?" Nairnie's eyes flashed over to her. "Why didna ye tell me ye wrote to the King?"

"I wanted to tell you, but didn't want to do so until I knew if my father, King Edward, would agree," answered Vivienne with a smile. "Bear, I know that you and Nairnie are still in love, and I wanted to do everything and anything I could to bring you back together."

"I sail for the port of Cornwall in the morning," Bear told them. "Old woman, you're going to be on that ship with me if I have to tie you up and throw you over my shoulder to do it, because I am taking you home to be with your family, where you belong."

"Dinna call me old!" said Nairnie, looking like the Mountain Magic was making her feel relaxed. "And do ye honestly think with yer old body, Buzzard, that ye could really throw me over yer shoulder without breakin' yer damned back?"

"Let's find out, shall we?" Bear stormed into the room and scooped Nairnie up into his arms and then threw her over his shoulder. "Yep, I can still do it."

"Put me down, ye old fool." Nairnie kicked her feet and thumped her fists against his back, making the rest of them laugh.

"I'll put ye down when I darn well feel like it and not before. My lord and ladies," said Bear with a nod to Lord and Lady Mablethorpe and also Vivienne." He turned and carried Nairnie out of the room as she continued to complain and the rest of them remained laughing.

"What just happened?" asked Isaac, watching them go.

"I think Lady Vivienne succeeded once again in bringing two people back together," said Zachariah with a chuckle.

"How is Brenna doing?" Vivienne wanted to know.

"She's in mourning and really missing Wallace," said the sheriff. "But Cassandra has been comforting her, and they are now best friends. Cassandra has also been helping Brenna clean up their house since Wallace was pretty messy."

"Will Brenna be punished for giving mandrake root oil to Uncle Gilbert and keeping him in the crypts?" asked Vivienne.

"Nay," said her uncle. "Brenna was my saving grace for the past seven years, having no one else to talk to. I don't want her punished. I won't press charges. She only did what she was told to do because her husband's life was at stake. If I were in her position, I would have done the same to protect Ellen." He squeezed his wife's hand and Ellen smiled and winked at him.

"But certainly, Brenna can't get away with her part in all this," said Isaac. "As an officer of the law now, I know that it's not right."

"She didn't want to do it, she was forced to do so," Lady

Mablethorpe spoke up. "And even though I don't have any living children, I cannot even imagine how much pain she's been through to know the child she'd loved and raised from a baby as her own son had grown up evil and that he had turned against them."

"That's true," agreed Vivienne. "A mother's love is real and it has to hurt to have a child break her heart that way."

"If anyone should be punished it should be me, for not realizing that evil man wasn't my loving husband." Ellen leaned over and kissed Gilbert on the lips. "I am so sorry, sweetheart. I need to listen to my heart more and not my head. I hope you can forgive me."

"We all need to listen to our heart more," said Gilbert. "But there is nothing to forgive you for, my dear. I have always loved you, and still do. This doesn't change a thing."

Vivienne felt her eyes watering, and had to hold back the tears since this was such a precious, special moment. The aunt and uncle she knew and loved had returned, and it did her heart good to know that their love had never died.

"I suppose there's no need to punish Brenna since no charges will be made," said the sheriff.

"She's been punished enough, losing her husband the way she did," agreed Vivienne.

"What about the throne?" asked Isaac. "What is going to happen to the throne that Wallace made?"

"Well, that all depends. Lady Mablethorpe, did you want it?" asked Zachariah. "It was supposedly being made for you."

"Me?" Lady Mablethorpe scowled. "Nay. Of course not!" Her hand slapped against her chest. "I don't want anything that will remind me of that terrible man. Break it up and burn it for all I care."

"Nay!" cried Isaac. "It's a shame to ruin that good craftsmanship, and Wallace worked so hard on it. If Brenna doesn't want it, I'll take it to put in my new home," said Isaac. "I don't have any furniture, so that chair will come in handy."

"I don't mind," said Brenna. "It's nice to know that Wallace's creation will get a good home."

"Isaac, we'll talk about it later," said Zachariah, not looking pleased by the suggestion at all. "Wallace left behind a lot of gold florins that rightly belong to you, Lord Mablethorpe, since he stole them from you." Zachariah arched a brow. "What do you want to do about that?"

"Gilbert, what do you think?" Lady Mablethorpe asked her husband.

Gilbert thought for a moment and then replied. "Well, my brother did steal from us, but I believe that Brenna deserves a good portion of the money for what she went through for the past seven years. No amount of gold florins will bring back her husband, but mayhap it will help her to rebuild her life."

"I'll help her do that." Cassandra walked in with Magdalena. "Now that our family is back together, I'd like to help others who are living in pain and sorrow. That is my new mission in life."

"Oh, Cassandra, that is wonderful," said Sister Magdalena. "So does that mean you'll be bringing those you want to help, to Mass?"

"Mass?" Cassandra seemed startled with that suggestion. "Mayhap I don't want to be quite that helpful. Yet." Cassandra's answer made them all laugh. "Zachariah and Isaac have offered to take me back to Southwark to collect my things and to contact Fanny's family to let them know what happened. She's actually going to be buried right here in Mablethorpe, thanks to the sheriff."

"That beats having to be buried in the Crossbones Graveyard in Southwark with the rest of the Winchester Geese, I guess," said Isaac with a shrug.

"That's nice," said Vivienne. "Starah will stay here at the castle until you all return."

"Yes, I will help to watch the darling child," added Aunt Ellen. "I've started to consider her my grandchild. The same goes for Martin and Mouse. They are such sweet children and I want to spend as much time with them as possible."

"Can we come in too?" asked Adrian from the door.

Grunt barked and ran into the room and Martin and Mouse and Starah ran in after him, all of them jumping up on the bed with Lord Mablethorpe.

"I guess so," said Vivienne with a giggle. "But be careful, children. Lord Mablethorpe is still healing,"

"My lady, can I be of any assistance?" asked Maleine from the door.

"Or me?" Wymond was with her and holding Maleine's hand.

"I think we all should leave now," said Zachariah. "Lord Mablethorpe needs his rest and this room is getting pretty crowded and noisy."

"Nay, please stay. I like everyone here," protested Lord Mablethorpe. "It's been so long since I've heard the laughter of children or seen anyone at all." Grunt licked his face and he petted the dog with two hands. "I've missed you too, Grunt. The last time I saw you, you were just a puppy. I am so happy to be home and with all of you."

"Vivienne," said Zachariah. "I wanted to talk to you in private, and to you, too, Lord Mablethorpe. However, since that doesn't seem like it's going to happen, I'm going to risk everything and just come out and say it right here in front of everyone."

"Say what?" asked Vivienne, her heart about beating out of her chest with anticipation.

"Lord Mablethorpe, your niece, Lady Vivienne means the world to me."

"You mean the world to me, too, Zachariah," she said out loud.

"It took me some time to get over the death of my wife, but lately I have realized that I need to move on."

"What are you saying?" Vivienne asked him.

"I've had quite a few times lately, Vivienne, when I thought mayhap I'd lost you. It scared me. I realize now that I need to live life for the day. I can't keep mourning what happened in the past, or even fear what might happen in the future."

"Sheriff, I think I know where this is going, and my answer is *yes*," said Lord Mablethorpe.

"Yes? Really?" Zachariah seemed lost for words.

"Yes...what?" asked Vivienne, no longer able to wait for what she thought and hoped was coming.

"I want to ask for Lady Vivienne's hand in marriage," Zachariah blurted out. "If you agree, Lord and Lady Mablethorpe, since you are her guardians." He turned and looked at Vivienne. "And if Vivienne will have me as her husband," he said a bit softer. "I love you, Vivienne."

The room went suddenly silent and Vivienne swore everyone could hear the loud, excited thumping of her heart that was beating just about right out of her chest with love right now.

"I already said *yes*, Sheriff. How many more times do I have to say it?" Uncle Gilbert chuckled lowly, continuing to pet Grunt behind the ears.

"Vivienne?" Zachariah's brown eyes look worried as he waited for her response.

Vivienne was bubbling over with emotion and excitement. But before she answered, she looked over to Starah and Martin who were watching with wide eyes from atop the bed.

"Starah?" said Vivienne. "Before I answer, I'd like to know how you'd feel about having a new mother? And Martin, how do you feel about having the sheriff as your father? Because as much as I want to marry Sheriff Fitch, I want you two to be happy about it also."

"If you marry my father, will Martin be my new brother?" asked Starah.

"Yes, he will," she told the little girl.

"Yay! Then I love it." Starah got up, standing on the bed now.

"Me too! I'm finally going to have a real father. And a sister." Martin jumped up next to her. They giggled and held hands and bounced up and down on the bed. Mouse stood up and joined them. Grunt howled as if giving his permission too.

"Well, Sheriff Fitch...Zachariah...I think you have your answer and it is *yes*, I will marry you and, of course, I want to be your wife." Vivienne kissed him right there in front of everyone. "I love you, too!"

"You have just made me the happiest man alive, Vivienne." Zachariah's eyes seemed to sparkle, no matter how tired he was from everything that had happened lately.

"Zachariah, now when we go on murder investigations together, we'll be able to do so as husband and wife."

"What?" Zachariah seemed a little startled by that. "So...you still want to help me investigate murders, even though you'll be my wife?"

"Do you think you can stop me?" she asked him in challenge and kissed him once again.

"Nay, I know I can't stop you, Vivienne." He kissed her back. "And I don't ever want to even try to keep you from doing the things you love, that make you the woman I love...my future wife, Lady Vivienne Harlowe Fitch."

From the Author:

I hope you have enjoyed **Murder of a Winchester Goose** and will take a moment to leave a review for me on Amazon, Bookbub, or Goodreads.

In medieval times, as you have found out by reading this book, a Winchester Goose was a legalized prostitute who worked in the Liberty of the Clink in Southwark, London. The name, Winchester Goose, originated from the Bishop of Winchester, since this area was under his jurisdiction. He decided to license and tax sex workers and brothels, therefore making money off of them for himself. Of course, those stricken with venereal disease from visiting a brothel were said to have been bitten by the Winchester Goose.

When the whores died, they were not allowed to be buried on consecrated ground, and instead by the late medieval period were buried in the Crossbones Graveyard which was closed in 1853 but today can still be visited and holds the remains of 15,000 Winchester Geese and paupers.

If you haven't already read the previous books in my **Harlowe & Fitch Historical Mystery Series**, (and I hope you have, since you've just read the ending to the ongoing mystery), here is a list of the books that lead up to this one:

Murder at Mablethorpe Castle
Murder on Rotten Row (my favorite)
Murder at Maltby le Marsh
Murder at the Joust
Murder on the High Seas

As always, I incorporate characters from some of my romance novels into other series. One character that my readers love and so do I, is the old boisterous nursemaid, Nairnie. She is first seen in my ***Seasons of Fortitude Series*** as the handmaid to the sisters, Spring, Summer, Autumn, and Winter. (In *Autumn's Touch*, you will discover Nairnie's backstory.) She is also seen in other books, the most popular amongst my readers being my ***Pirate Lords Series*** where Nairnie is aboard a ship with her pirate grandsons, Tristan, Mardon, and Aaron.

I hope you will give some of my romances a try too, since I always have huge plots, lots of action, and also humor added in my writings. My books are medieval, paranormal, fantasy, contemporary and even a few westerns.

To see more of my books (over 100 and counting), please stop by and visit my **Website** at **http://elizabethrosenovels.com.** You can also follow me on **Amazon, Bookbub, Goodreads, Facebook, Bluesky, TikTok, Instagram,** and **Twitter**. I also have a **Private Readers' Group** on Facebook that I invite you to join. Be sure to sign up for my **Newsletter** so you don't miss out on new releases, sales, contests, and free books.

Although the main mystery has been solved for Lady Vivienne Harlowe, she is about to start a new adventure as Sheriff Zachariah Fitch's wife. Of course, she will never stop trying to find justice for those who have had their loved ones murdered. Vivienne and Zachariah will continue to solve murders, along with Grunt. Be sure to read the next book in the series, ***Murder at the Masquerade.***

In the meantime, I'd like to share a short excerpt from my ***Pirate Lords*** book, ***Tristan,*** where the pirate brothers fish poor Nairnie from the sea.

Thank you for your support, and happy reading!

Elizabeth Rose

Excerpt: Tristan

Book 1, Pirate Lords

Tristan glanced over the side of the ship to see what looked like a person clinging to two floating vats of wine that were tied together.

"We've got ourselves a man overboard from their ship," announced Mardon. "Loot him and then kill him quickly. He's of no use to us."

Once the shuttle boat hit the water, Ramble rowed it over toward the survivor. Aaron drew his sword with one hand and pulled the vats of wine closer with the other, reaching over the side of the small boat. "Bid the devil, it's an old crone!" gasped Aaron.

Tristan realized now that an old woman hung on to the rope connecting the barrels, clinging to it for her life. She looked up at them, and her feeble voice cried out. "Help me, please." Long silver, unbound hair floated on the water around her shoulders.

"Well, I'll be. It really is a lass," said Ramble.

"She's old," Aaron remarked, surveying the woman. "What should we do with her?"

"Bring the vats of wine on board and leave the old hag to the sea," commanded Tristan.

"Ye're goin' to leave her to die?" asked Ramble. "Mayhap we should help her."

"Nay. Tristan's right," agreed Mardon. "We have no need for a woman of that age. Besides, it's bad luck to have a wench on board. You know that."

"All right, whatever ye say." Ramble reached out to try to pry the woman's fingers from the rope, but she turned her head and bit his hand, causing him to cry out.

"Ow. She bit me!" he shouted, rubbing his hand. "What am I supposed to do?"

"I don't give a damn, just bring that wine aboard. I'm thirsty," said Mardon, his only interest being in the bounty they'd just procured.

"Aye. Hit her over the head with the hilt of your sword if you need to, but just put her out of her misery," suggested Tristan. "Now get that wine aboard the ship because there is also a trunk I don't want to lose." Tristan and his brothers embraced their pirate ways, having learned from their father to be ruthless, heartless, and cold. Cato Fisher had told them if they started feeling sorry for people, it would be their ticket to doom. He was right. The last thing they needed was on old woman on board. Their ways had worked well for them all this time, so there was no need to change now. They were considered pirate lords of the sea.

"I'm not goin' to touch her again. Ye do it, Aaron," said Ramble, still rubbing his hand, seeming leery of the woman.

"Did ye say *Aaron*?" The old woman's head lifted and she looked first at Aaron and then back up to the others on the ship. She coughed and sputtered, her bony fingers turning white as they clung tightly to the rope while the barrels kept her afloat. "If he's Aaron, are ye two Mardon and Tristan?" she asked, her tired eyes looking up to Tristan and his brother.

Her question surprised Tristan. How did the wench know their names? Mayhap she'd heard them from their father.

"Don't worry who we are, because you're not going to live long enough to remember our names anyway," Tristan assured her.

"Nay, wait a minute," said Mardon with a raised hand. "How do you know who we are?" he asked the old woman.

"Do you know our father?" asked Aaron curiously. "After all, you were on his ship, the *Desperado*, weren't you?"

"Aye, I was, and of course I ken yer faither," she answered, glaring at them now.

"Well, where is he?" asked Tristan. "Why did he sail away when I know he saw us? And why didn't he come after you?"

"Why were you even on the ship to begin with?" asked Mardon. "Who are you to someone like our father? It doesn't seem likely he'd be traveling with an old woman."

"Bring me aboard and I'll tell ye lads everythin' ye want to ken."

Tristan and Mardon exchanged glances, but both of them shook their heads.

"Nay, it's bad luck," said Mardon, crossing his arms over his chest. "No wenches on board."

"Plus, it goes against the code," added Tristan with a shrug.

"I dinna give two hoots about any pirate code! Now bring me aboard," demanded the old woman."

"Why should we?" asked Aaron.

"Because I've got some valuable information for ye," she told them, her fingers starting to slip. "Plus, I can cook and also heal."

"I don't know," said Tristan, not liking this idea at all.

"God's toes, help me already and stop talkin' about killin' me, ye fools," commanded the old woman, not seeming afraid of them at all. Odd, since they were pirates. Most people were frightened out of their minds and rightly so.

"Who are you?" asked Aaron, scrutinizing the woman.

"My name is Nairnie," she spat, looking madder than hell. "Yer sister, Gwen, tells me she sailed with ye lads on yer faither's boat. She said ye were guid fishermen, but she failed to tell me ye were all stupid fools."

"Hush up, old woman." Mardon didn't care about his old life and neither did Tristan.

"Don't call us fishermen because that's an insult," said Tristan, taking more offense at that part then her calling them stupid fools. "We're pirates now if you haven't noticed."

"Oh, I noticed, and it disgusts me," she ground out. "Bring me aboard the ship and I'll make ye a guid meal."

"I could go for something to eat besides hardtack," said Aaron, looking up at his brothers, always hungry.

"You said you know our sister Gwen," said Mardon suspiciously. "So, tell me. How is she?"

"Get me out of this bluidy cold water at once and I'll tell ye everythin' ye want to ken, I swear."

"Let's bring her aboard," suggested Aaron, looking up at his brothers from the shuttle boat, licking his lips. He was obviously thinking about food again. They all were. Another wave slapped over them and the old woman went under and came up sputtering and spitting out water, nearly losing her grip. She wouldn't be able to hold on for long.

"Nay," said Tristan. "And that's final. Now push her off the barrel and get the wine aboard. We need to go. We've already wasted too much time with this."

"I could go for some wine, too," said Aaron, reaching out for her.

"Nay!" cried the old woman. "Ye dinna want to hurt me."

"Really?" Tristan raised a brow. "Why not? You give us a better reason to spare your life than cooking a meal and mayhap we'll consider it."

"If ye leave me to die, ye'll never find out about yer faither."

"Sure we will. We'll track down the ship and find him for ourselves," said Mardon.

"God's eyes, ye mischant lads, ye're twice as troublesome as yer faither was as a lad. Now, get me out of this water before my muscles freeze up."

"You sound like you knew our father when he was young," said Aaron.

"Well, I should hope so," spat the old woman. "After all, Cato was my son."

"Your...son?" asked Mardon, looking over to Tristan once again.

"Then that makes us..." started Aaron, but he was cut off by the boisterous woman.

"Aye, ye lousy scuppers of the sea, that's right. Whether I like it or no', ye're my grandsons! And I can tell ye that ye're already a huge let down from what I hoped ye'd be. Yer faither didna live with me long, but I'm sure he's turnin' over in his grave right now because his sons are plannin' on lettin' their own grandmathair drown!"

Also by Elizabeth Rose

Mystery Series:

Harlowe & Fitch Historical Mystery Series

Murder at Mablethorpe Castle

Murder on Rotten Row

Murder at Maltby le Marsh

Murder at the Joust

Murder on the High Seas

Murder of a Winchester Goose

Medieval Series:

Below the Salt

Legendary Bastards of the Crown Series

Seasons of Fortitude Series

Secrets of the Heart Series

Legacy of the Blade Series

Daughters of the Dagger Series

MadMan MacKeefe Series

Barons of the Cinque Ports Series

Holiday Knights Series

Highland Chronicles Series

Pirate Lords Series

Highland Outcasts

Medieval/Paranormal Series:

Elemental Magick Series

Greek Myth Fantasy Series

Tangled Tales Series

Portals of Destiny

Contemporary Series:

Tarnished Saints Series

Working Man Series

Western Series:

Cowboys of the Old West Series

And More!

Please visit http://elizabethrosenovels.com

About Elizabeth

Elizabeth Rose is an award-winning, bestselling author of over 100 books and counting. She writes medieval, historical, contemporary, paranormal, and western romance. Her books are available as EBooks, paperbacks, and some audiobooks as well.

Her favorite characters in her works include dark, dangerous and tortured heroes, and feisty, independent heroines who know how to wield a sword. She loves writing 14th century medieval novels, and is well-known for her many series.

Elizabeth loves the outdoors. In the summertime, you can find her in her secret garden with her laptop, swinging in her hammock working on her next book. Elizabeth is a born storyteller and passionate about sharing her works with her readers.

Please be sure to visit her website at **Elizabethrosenovels.com** to read excerpts from any of her novels and get sneak peeks at covers of upcoming books. Join Elizabeth's **newsletter** so you don't miss out on new releases or upcoming events. There is also a **Private Readers' Group** on Facebook that she invites you to join.

A small press bound by the belief that every voice matters.

Sign up for our newsletter to learn about new releases and more.
https://oliver-heberbooks.com/subscribe/

Follow us on social media:

facebook.com/oliverheberbooks

instagram.com/oliverheberbooks

amazon.com/oliverheberbooks

youtube.com/@OliverHeberBooksPublisher